THE ECHOING SHORE

J.H.MANN

DARK SPIDER BOOKS

The Echoing Shore by J.H.Mann published by Dark Spider Books of
335 Babbacombe Road, Torquay, Devon TQ1 3TB, UK.

ISBN: 978-1-7392953-2-5

Cover by MiblArt

For all the people who risk their lives rescuing those in peril on the sea.
They are true heroes.

Best Wishes

Josh H. Mann

PROLOGUE

November 1991. Jim Trelawney tilted his head to admire the sweeping lines of the orange and blue lifeboat. There was a purposeful grace to the *Talan Bray*. Out of the water, she appeared immense, her fourteen-metre length filling much of the boathouse. But in the vastness of the North Atlantic on a storm-tossed night, she could feel smaller than the head of a pin. A night such as this, in fact. A shrieking wind was conspiring with falling temperatures and hammering rain in some of the worst weather Trelawney could ever recall.

Heavy boots thudded on the steps at the back of the boathouse, accompanied by raised voices. The Ridley brothers, Bobby and Jed, were exchanging bitter words as they arrived.

'I don't like it. We should get out while we still can,' Bobby Ridley was saying. His anger was edged with a sharp anxiety.

Jed Ridley laid a steadying hand on his younger brother's shoulder. 'Bobby, we need to keep our heads...' The words died on his lips when he saw Trelawney standing nearby. He forced a grin. 'Don't go without us.'

Trelawney slipped on his lifejacket. 'Wouldn't dream of it.' He hesitated as the wild hostility outside rose to a new intensity. 'Is everything okay with you two?'

'Never better. So what have we got tonight?'

'A yacht. In trouble out beyond The Mouls. Taking on water. Two people on board. Sounds bad.'

Jed glanced at the creaking roof before looking around at the ruddy, weather-beaten individuals who'd scrambled to the boathouse on this most godforsaken of nights. The crew were quieter and more sombre than usual. Talk was confined to essentials as each man absorbed himself in checking and rechecking equipment, contemplating the task ahead.

'Where's Harding?' he said at last.

Trelawney climbed aboard. 'John's gone down with the flu.' He nodded at a young man adjusting his lifejacket. 'Seth's stepping up to join us.'

The older Ridley locked eyes with the youngster, a smirk on his fleshy lips. 'So, young Seth, you've been promoted to the A-Team.'

Seth Maltby's broad, open face expressed a steady confidence. 'Looking forward to it, Jed,' he said in his soft Westcountry burr.

Trelawney smiled paternally at the young seaman. 'You'll do fine, lad. I was about your age when I made the first team.'

Thrumming hydraulic machinery raised the *Talan Bray* to the angle of the slipway and the boat's twin Gardner diesel engines were already spewing fumes and starting to turn as the launch team battled with the storm to fold back and secure the boathouse doors.

The lifeboatmen stared down at the heaving black mass of the ocean, their eyes widening when a wave rose almost to the boathouse itself before falling back with a sucking, slurping roar to expose most of the slipway.

'Holy shit.' Jed, in his typical manner, expressed in one

succinct obscenity the feelings of every member of the crew. It was going to be one hell of a night, one hell of a ride.

The *Talan Bray* was lowered outside to be pummelled by wind, sea spray and rain. Her radio and radar masts were erected and then Trelawney, braced with a foot on the wheelhouse, waited for the perfect moment to launch. It was his call and his call alone. If he got it wrong, the rescue could end in disaster before it had begun. Everyone held their breath. They just wanted to be out there now, on their way.

Another surge of water rolled up the slipway, bubbling and frothing, seemingly unstoppable. Its power petered out just short of the bows.

'Now,' Trelawney bellowed above the elemental roar and made a slashing gesture with his right arm.

Jake Bolitho, the head launcher, thwacked the retaining pin with a twenty-one-pound hammer and the lifeboat slid downwards, gathering speed behind the retreating wave.

The *Talan Bray* plunged into the sea, carving a deep, foaming V in its turbulent surface. It was clear of the slipway and under power by the time the next great swell of water loomed out of the darkness. A textbook launch.

In the boathouse, those left behind paused in silence to watch. The masthead light disappeared as the boat charged into a trough, then blinked again as she struggled upwards, shrugging aside the churning water streaming across her decks.

They'd never see the *Talan Bray* again.

CHAPTER ONE

Nearly ten years later

The ancient wooden door, swollen by the damp of autumn, shuddered but stayed firmly shut. Another shove, a stout kick and at last it swung creakily wide. A tousled giant, red in cheek and fleshy of jowl, filled the entrance, dripping with Cornish rain. He unbuttoned his rumpled Burberry coat to reveal a plaid shirt stretched by a paunch.

A drinker, if ever I saw one. But he used the full power of an easy, boyish smile as his gaze settled on me. 'It's raining cats and cows out there. Filthy day for sure,' he said, flinching when a squall rattled the rickety windows of the North Cornwall Gazette.

The north coast was being battered by an Atlantic storm, which drove waves high up beaches, pounded cliffs and headlands and made a stroll down St Branok's winding high street a misery. Spume erupted from the crests of the rollers crashing against Tregloss Point. The seagulls had been silenced for once, their shrieks replaced by the howl of wind and surf.

'Editorial isn't open to the public,' I said with my fingers poised over my computer keyboard.

His smile was unwavering as he strolled into the office.

'Well, I'm actually a journalist myself and there was no one at your reception desk downstairs.'

'Brenda must have popped out to visit a customer,' I said as I wondered about the real cause of her disappearance. In fairness to her, she might have just gone to the loo.

'Brenda?' His dripping face creased in puzzlement.

I stepped out from my desk. 'Our advertising manager. She looks after reception.' Brenda Rosewall did indeed glory in the title of advertising manager, though she was also our receptionist, distribution manager and occasional – very occasional – cleaner.

He held out his hand in the offer of a handshake, which I accepted. His grip was warm and firm. And damp. A minty tang of after-shave lingered. 'The name's Danny…Danny Flanagan.'

'Kate Tregillis. I'm the editor,' I said with a tight smile. I might have added owner, managing director, clearer upper and completer of any task which Brenda didn't get around to. 'And this is Roy Kerslake, our editor-at-large.' I gestured to the only other person in the room – a wizened figure who was far from large, hunched at a nearby desk with an empty Sherlock Holmes-style Calabash pipe in his mouth. Roy's quick, intelligent eyes flicked up from his computer screen. He grinned a greeting.

Danny reached out to shake Roy's hand as well. 'Pleased to meet you, Roy. Sounds like you've got a big job.'

'Roy retired after many distinguished years as our editor-in-chief,' I said. 'But he found retirement a bit too quiet, so came back to us with a roving brief.'

'You name it, I write about it,' said Roy. 'Kate calls me editor-at-large to spare an old editor his blushes, but I'm just a reporter. And I love it; never been happier.'

Danny nodded. 'Oh aye, once journalism is in your blood, it's there for keeps.' There was sincerity in his tone. Clearly, Danny was a journalist through and through. His blue eyes swept around the echoing, empty office. 'So, this is where the magic happens, eh? Where is everybody?'

In truth, there wasn't much magic percolating through our editorial offices at that moment. Roy was finishing a re-write of a report from the local Women's Institute to fill a hole on an inside page of the Gazette. And I was struggling with my scrappy shorthand to turn a dull monthly meeting of the St Branok Chamber of Commerce into an article of remote interest to the local community.

'Everybody?' I coughed. 'What were you expecting?'

A puddle of rainwater was forming on the worn linoleum floor next to Danny's feet. 'I'm used to newspaper offices being a little more…well er…more active. I thought there would be more people.'

'We run a tight operation,' I said. *For tight, read threadbare.* 'These days there's only Roy and me in editorial with a trainee.'

A hot flush crept up my throat. Local newspaper offices aren't noted for their classy decor, but ours had a distinct air of neglect. A line of books, dominated by hardback versions of the Oxford Dictionary and a Roget's Thesaurus, gathered dust on a wonky shelf in one corner. An askew noticeboard covered a large crack and a stain in another. At the far end of the room, a row of grey four-drawer filing cabinets stood like sentinels, empty relics from the days when paper records were king.

The offices were way too big for us these days. They'd existed since the Gazette's halcyon days when circulation was booming – at least by today's standards – and editorial had bustled with a team of senior reporters and sub-editors.

'Looks like I've come along at the right time,' said Danny. 'You could do with an extra pair of hands, and I know my way around. You won't find a better journalist this side of the Tamar.'

There was a crusty coffee stain across a corner of my desk. I made a mental note to give it a good wipe later. 'Sorry, we're not hiring.'

Danny spread his hands, that smile still on his face. 'I'm not looking for a full-time job. I'm down here mainly to do some freelance work for the London press, but I could also knock up a few stories for you and get paid for any published articles. I really need a local base to work from. We'd be helping each other.'

'I don't get it,' I said. 'Why is a London freelancer looking for stories in the wild west? There must be more lucrative pickings to be had from nosing around in Westminster with dodgy politicians.'

'I've been commissioned to write a few Cornwall features. The usual sort of thing: surfing mecca, land of magic and mystery and the delicious Cornish pasty where brave souls pit themselves against the Atlantic. All that baloney.'

'Well, most of it is true. People do risk their lives on this coast every day.' If we were to work together, Danny would learn soon enough that I was fiercely protective of the raw nature of Cornwall. A childhood playing in the dunes and surf had shaped me.

Danny pulled a tatty notebook from an inside pocket. 'The ocean can be a fickle mistress right enough. Anyway, I'll be down here for a while and could help out if you give me a desk and a phone line and pay me whatever your rate is for any articles you publish.'

This was ideal. Too good to be true. I was desperate for

help. Newspaper deadlines were running me ragged as I struggled to run a business and fill a twenty-eight-page weekly newspaper.

'Where did you used to work?' I said.

'In Ireland for many years – for the Telegraph, the Sentinel and the Star before moving to London and freelancing at The Enquirer and a few others. I'm NUJ, of course.' He flourished a National Union of Journalists membership card and then handed me a dog-eared business card with the name *Daniel.J.Flanagan, Investigative Journalist* printed in large letters. 'Give me a chance. You won't regret it.'

'I wrote for The Enquirer,' I said.

'Reporter?'

'Worked my way up to deputy editor.'

His shaggy eyebrows rose. 'And there I was thinking you were a Cornish girl.'

'I am. I was born and raised here in St Branok but moved to London when I was in my early twenties.'

'The lure of the bright lights, eh?'

'I was ambitious back then. Wanted to be at the centre of things.' Enough of me. I needed to do a little more prodding. 'If you were at The Enquirer, you must know the editor.'

'Bob Fletcher? Yes, of course. Great guy. A legend.'

I chewed my lower lip, weighing the pros and cons. The pros won out. 'Okay, let's give it a try. When can you start?' For all his rumpled appearance, maybe Danny was the ray of light we so desperately needed.

His broad smile grew to incandescent proportions, and he held out his hand again. 'Let's shake on it. I can be here first thing tomorrow.' His skin was drier now and his grip even stronger.

He licked cracked lips. 'What time do you guys get off

duty? I spotted a welcoming little watering hole on my way over here. The Mermaid Inn, I think it was called. How about a celebratory drink to mark our new partnership? You can bring me up to speed with the latest in St Branok. I'm sure there's lots to tell.'

I searched his features for a trace of sarcasm but saw only a well-meaning sincerity. Aside from reckless teenagers tombstoning off Tregloss Point and the opening of a new charity shop in the high street, there wasn't much to tell at all. I consulted the clock on the wall. Nearly five o'clock. A bit early for a drinking session, but The Mermaid would be open – it was almost always open. And it was Thursday afternoon, a brief window of time when we could relax because the latest newspaper had been put to bed prior to hitting the streets the following day.

'Why not?' I said. 'It's been a long week. We deserve a break. And I can introduce you to Joe Keast, the landlord at The Mermaid. You'll like him. He knows everybody and everything around here.'

Roy wrapped up his article in record time, I grabbed the jacket I'd bought for a romantic skiing holiday five years earlier, which never happened when Mr Right turned out to be Mr Wrong and we clumped down the narrow stairs to the Gazette's reception, now manned again by Brenda. She was on the phone, cajoling an advertiser into taking a quarter page instead of a single column.

The sales pitch ratcheted up a notch when Brenda noticed her audience. 'If you can make a commitment now, I'll speak to the editor about a free news feature.'

Her round face had turned triumphant by the time she replaced the handset. 'Hodgsons will be taking a two-column ad for the next four weeks.'

'Well done,' I said. I'd speak to her later about offering space reserved for hard news in return for advertising. The Gazette was a newspaper, for goodness' sake, not an advertising leaflet. I gestured to our drying recruit. 'Danny will be working with us for a while.'

With a twinkle in her eye, Brenda eased her ample figure, clad in trackies and a floppy jumper, out from behind the desk. 'Pleased to meet you. It'll be good to have a new face around here.'

Danny's 'one million candles' smile – the one he obviously saved for good news and, I suspected, members of the opposite sex – bathed her in its amiable light. 'Well, well, two beautiful women in one office. We're lucky men, aren't we, Roy?'

Roy harrumphed a vague, indecipherable reply, while Brenda's full features cracked in delight, and she performed a half curtsey.

I suppressed a groan and tugged open the front door to allow the wildness to enter and clear the air of Danny's clumsy compliments. 'Brenda, we're popping over to The Mermaid to see Joe. Are you okay to lock up at five-thirty?'

'No problem at all, Kate,' she said, having settled back behind the reception desk. 'Have a lovely drink in The Mermaid.'

'Thanks,' I said slowly, unused to such helpfulness. It wasn't like Brenda to be all sweetness and light near the end of a tiring week in dreary autumn. 'It'll be a quick one. We probably won't be long.'

Brenda gave Danny a wave. 'See you tomorrow,' she said. Of course, he beamed at her again.

Rain was being driven horizontally up Crantock Street as we strode the short distance to The Mermaid. It had swept shoppers from the streets. On the other side of the road, the ironmongers and a charity shop, which had once been a local bank, were in darkness and locked up tight, having given up on the possibility of snaring any late customers on such a day.

As I pulled up the hood of my ski jacket, I wondered about the wisdom of my flash decision to bring Danny into the fold while knowing almost nothing about him. A charmer, certainly. And experience warned me that that kind of personality often came with deceit. I should have insisted on seeing a CV.

But perhaps I was being too hard on him. Perhaps he would bring a new drive and, God only knew, the Gazette needed something new if it was going to survive.

I glanced over at his flaccid features. His collar-length hair, tinged with grey, was plastered flat on his head and rainwater dripped from his fleshy nose. But he had something: a presence, an easy authority. Saviour or waste of time and space? More likely the latter, but I would give him a try. Anything was worth trying. I had little to lose.

We turned a corner to see welcoming lights streaming from mullioned windows. Above them, swinging in the gale, was the jaunty sign of a smiling mermaid sitting on a rock.

Shelter and alcohol beckoned.

CHAPTER TWO

The Mermaid Inn was hidden in an alleyway off Crantock Street. Think trendy. Think gastropub. And then think the complete opposite. It was a traditional locals' pub – for drink and banter, playing skittles or darts and, on Saturday nights, listening to one of the thrashing local bands.

We trooped in, brushing the rain off our coats, to find the lounge bar empty apart from a few fishermen who had given up hope of venturing out even in coastal waters in this weather. It was a day of lost income for them, and they huddled gloomily together in a corner near one of the flashing one-armed bandits.

'I've caught sweet bugger all this week,' a barrel-chested fisherman was saying. 'If the luck doesn't change, I'll be down the food bank. That's no way for my family to live.'

A warm, homely light suffused the bar, concealing its tacky interior. The golden glow contrasted sharply with the drab daylight of a grey afternoon in a grimy fishing town. The comforting tang of beer inhabited every corner – apart from the ladies' toilet, where it was eclipsed by the kick of a powerful disinfectant.

Angie, a slip of a girl who worked in the pub when she wasn't partying at music festivals or visiting her boyfriend in Plymouth, was behind the bar, cleaning glasses.

Danny rubbed his hands together. 'This one's on me. What can I get you fine people?'

Roy and I opted for pints of Doom Bar and we made small talk about the weather while waiting for our drinks.

Danny fixed Angie with the Flanagan smile. 'What's the local gargle around here?'

Angie beamed right back while pulling Roy's pint. 'If you mean beer, we have our own microbrewery. Try a pint of Wreckers Rebellion. You won't get anything more local.'

'Sounds good. You're a girl after my own heart,' he said, before turning to give Roy and myself a wink.

I edged closer to the bar to get my drink. 'Angie, is Joe around? We were hoping to have a quick chat with him.'

'He's out back. I'll give him a call.'

'We'll be in the snug.'

I led Roy and Danny to a cosy, out of the way spot with soft seating and cushions. We settled at a seat by the window with a view of gritty St Branok Harbour, full of idle fishing boats.

A symbol shaped like a three-cornered knot, pinned to a nearby wall, caught Danny's eye. He pointed to it. 'I've seen similar shapes in Ireland. Didn't think I'd come across them down here.'

'It's a sign used by Pagans and Celtic Christians known as a Triquetra or Trinity Knot,' said Roy, who had an encyclopaedic knowledge of most things. 'The interwoven knot with no beginning and no end stands for a protection that cannot be broken. Cornwall still has strong Pagan and Celtic connections.'

I gazed at it, noticing it for the first time, despite having lingered many an hour in this comfy corner of The Mermaid.

Joe Keast appeared a few minutes later with an oily rag

in hand, his forehead smeared with sweat and grime. 'Kate, Roy – you're drinking early these days. Not that I'm complaining. I could do with the business on a day like this.' He plonked himself down wearily on a stool.

'Problems?' I said.

'The usual. Pump playing up again. Wreckers Rebellion will be in short supply unless I can get it up and running tonight. We're down to our last few barrels of the good stuff.' He rubbed his hands with the oily cloth, which did little to make them cleaner.

'We wanted to introduce you to Danny Flanagan,' I said. 'He's down here from the London press and will be helping at the Gazette for a while.'

'I hear you're the man in the know in these parts,' said Danny. The ready grin was back, as was the handshake. Joe took Danny's proffered hand with a smile of the more cautious, reserved type. The Flanagan smile didn't work half so well with men.

'Any friend of Kate's is a friend of mine. We go back a long way,' he said, nodding affably at me before squinting at Danny. 'What brings a city slicker down to our quiet part of the world?'

My thoughts exactly.

Danny took a long pull from his pint, which drained half the glass and confirmed my early guess that he liked a pint or three. 'Oh, writing a few features about the Cornish way of life, land of mystery and magic on the edge of the great ocean and all that. I'll be looking for somewhere to stay for a few weeks. Any recommendations?'

Joe swept his damp forehead with the sleeve of his grubby sweatshirt. 'We have a spare room above the pub here, which you're welcome to stay in for a while. It doesn't get much use at this time of year, but don't go expecting en-suite bathrooms and all that. It's got a good, comfortable bed and a wardrobe. And if you stand on a chair, you can see Tregloss Point in the distance.'

'I'll take it. When can I move in?' Danny slapped his thighs, which looked thick and muscular.

'Anytime. Tonight, if you like.'

'Great. I'll get my stuff from the car later. Do you want payment in advance?' He pulled out a bulging, battered leather wallet containing any number of plastic cards and a wad of red fifty-pound notes.

Joe flicked a finger. 'Don't worry about that for now. We can settle up in a few days.'

The wallet was gone in a trice, having been returned to the depths of Danny's coat. 'So, who are the movers and shakers here?'

Joe squinted at the oily cloth, which he was still wiping on his grubby hands. 'Mike Pedrick is the local bigwig. He has a finger in just about every pie west of Padstow and lives in a glass and steel palace built a few years ago near the top of the hill. God knows how he got it approved by planning, but then…' He sighed. 'Mike knows a lot of influential people. He owns trawlers, a motor dealership and half a dozen attractions that pull in the emmets by the bucketload during the summer months.'

Danny's forehead creased. 'Emmets?'

'Holidaymakers, tourists, outsiders. Sorry, no offence intended.'

'None taken. So, how did Mike make his money?'

Joe shrugged. 'Who knows? He went from zero to millionaire hero in a few years. Twenty years ago, if somebody had told me that a young oik like Mike Pedrick would become a business tycoon and a local magistrate, I'd have laughed in their face. And now he's Mr Establishment. But he's still not too high and mighty for The Mermaid. He's always in here with his fishing and business buddies.' He paused to wave a friendly hand at two more fishermen who'd walked in, dripping sea and rainwater. He really did know everybody. 'Truth is, he realises we offer a damn sight better pint than his arty farty gastropub and boutique hotel, the Spinnakers Lodge, down by the beach.'

Danny sucked down the rest of his drink until only a few frothy dregs remained. 'Mmmm, this tastes good. Great gravity and texture. It reminds me of a favourite local gargle of mine in Enniskillen.' He tilted the empty glass. 'I'm going to treat myself to another. Anybody else?' We shook our heads.

The conversation paused as another foaming pint of Wreckers Rebellion was pulled. When Danny had settled himself again, he held up his beer. 'Cheers! Or, as I'm told they say in this part of the world, yeghes da!' He looked at Joe over the rim of his glass. 'So what do they serve down at the Spinnakers?'

'Mike's done a deal with one of the big breweries – buys their crap by the tanker load. You won't find many locals in there. It's mainly well-heeled visitors from London who can't tell their barley from their hops.'

I checked my watch as Danny and Joe got stuck into an enthusiastic discussion on the benefits of brewing with wheat and maize rather than barley.

At last, Joe stood up. 'I better get back to sorting the pump. Nice to meet you, Danny. I'll tell Angie you're interested in the room upstairs and she can take you up there when you've got your stuff.'

Roy finished his pint and announced he also needed to leave. 'Dinner will be on the table for me in twenty minutes. It never goes down well if I arrive home late smelling of beer.'

'I need to get back too,' I said. 'Rufus will be wondering where I am. See you in the morning then, Danny. I'll be in the office from eight thirty.'

Danny raised a hand in a cursory goodbye. His eyes were starting to glaze. The alcohol was taking effect. Joe's personal brew was strong stuff. 'I'll grab something to eat and then get my head down for the night. See you tomorrow.'

Rain-splattered locals were filtering in in greater numbers and a hubbub of voices and laughter filled the smoky air.

Outside, dusk was tightening its grip. Roy buttoned his coat to the collar and I zipped up mine as we headed out onto an empty, windswept street. The rain had stopped, but the pavements and roads were slick with the recent downpour.

'If Danny knocks back many more pints tonight, we're unlikely to see him before midday tomorrow,' Roy said as he reached in his pocket for his car keys. 'Joe's brews are lethal.'

'Yes, he likes a drink or two, but so do most journos.'

He hesitated before stepping into his car. 'Kate, it's not for me to tell you how to run the newspaper these days. You're the boss now and I'm a retired hack who helps out when he can, but—'

'But?' I waited for the advice that invariably followed these familiar words.

He took a deep breath. 'Do you think Danny's right for the Gazette? He seems a "don't let the facts spoil the story" sort of chap. Sensational national journalists aren't popular in these here parts after the Talan Bray disaster.'

'I was once one of those national journalists.'

'Yes, but you're a local. You were born and raised here. Besides, you're the most accurate and fair reporter I've worked with.'

His words sparked a twinge of annoyance in the pit of my stomach. They were well-meant, but he didn't understand the depth of my predicament. 'We need help, Roy. I'll always appreciate what you do for me, but I'm trying to juggle everything from filling most of the newspaper every week to keeping the bank manager at bay. Things are…' – I grimaced, weighed down by too many problems – '…difficult. The circulation is falling and even our regular advertisers are beginning to wonder whether there are better ways of spending their cash. More news will make people sit up and take notice. None of us have time for in-depth investigative reporting, but maybe Danny will. And he's costing me nothing if he fails to produce any decent stories worth printing.'

Roy nodded as he pulled his pipe from the top pocket of his tweed jacket, obviously intending to have a puff on the short journey home. Marjorie, his wife, had called a halt to him smoking in their house since the heart attack. 'I'm not trying to question your judgement, Kate. I know things are tough right now. You might be right. Perhaps we do need a fresh face around here. Maybe we're all too set in our ways.'

The patter of rain began again as he drove away, leaving me isolated with a crushing weight on my shoulders. What I'd told Roy about the plight of the Gazette was only the half of it. The fate of the paper was on a knife edge. It could go either way and it was down to me – and me alone – to find a solution. Danny might be part of the answer.

What harm could it do to give him a try?

CHAPTER THREE

I bumped along narrow, high-hedged lanes in my clunky Land Rover, which I'd bought from a retired farmer up on Bodmin Moor. As I pulled and pushed the reluctant gear stick my mood darkened with the growing gloom. I'd told Roy that things were difficult, but 'difficult' scarcely did it justice. Even with a skeleton staff, the Gazette was devouring money. We needed more than a few interesting stories to survive. We needed a bloody miracle.

Roy was invaluable, despite his frailty. He was also an old friend, one of the few people I was able to talk to about most things. But not about the Gazette. Not properly. I didn't have the heart to unload the full drama of our situation on such a fragile person. The Gazette had been his life. He'd been the newspaper's editor in its heyday when it had been the heart of the local community. And he'd taken me on as a trainee reporter and given me a love for words which would remain with me until the day I died.

My home, which looked out over the Atlantic to the grand old lighthouse at Trevose Head, came into view as I descended a steep hill. Gwel Teg, a rambling coastguard cottage at least two hundred years old, was dark and silent, as I knew it would be. I clambered out of the Landy to the percussive boom of waves crashing on the nearby cliffs. Ironically, this kind of bleak and desolate night reminded me of why I'd given up the urban delights of London to return. Here, the elements, red and raw, dominated.

I felt alive.

On the windy doorstep, I fumbled among a bundle of keys for the elusive one to the front door. As ever, it was the last to slip into my cold fingers. It grated in a rusty lock and I stepped inside, followed by a cloud of grit and spray.

A hairy, slobbering monster confronted me as I clicked on the hallway light. Rufus fell on me like I'd been away a fortnight, his tail wagging, his long pink tongue licking. When he at last paused to take a breath, I gave him a hug, stroked his warm head with its grey wiry fur and crooned affectionately.

Rufus was part lurcher and part fifty-seven other varieties, with long legs and a tail that sometimes stood up like a question mark. He was often my only companion. I didn't need anybody else. The lonely years had taught me, or perhaps forced me, to be self-reliant.

I'd spent too long in The Mermaid chatting to Joe, Danny and Roy when I could have been home taking Rufus for his evening walk, stretching his long legs on winding Cornish paths.

A vestige of daylight remained, the dusk not yet replaced by that pure blackness of the countryside which people living in the glaring, traffic-jammed streets of towns and cities never see.

There was enough time.

I grabbed a torch and Rufus's collar and lead and stepped out into one of those nights which are the preserve of dog owners, the insane and heroes. I kept to the inland routes sheltered by hedgerows, well away from the howling cliff precipices.

Rain trickled down my neck and my jeans were soon

soaked. I didn't care. The fresh air cleared my head, clogged by a long day spent indoors and by the pint at The Mermaid. Walking allowed me to think, to step aside from the worries and daily grind of the Gazette. It always worked. Well, almost always.

Rufus was up ahead somewhere, scrabbling out a badger's sett or chasing a rabbit or a fox. I called out to him every so often to make sure he knew I was nearby, but I needn't have bothered. This was Rufus's back yard. He knew every nook, hollow and cranny.

I trudged up a steep, short path through trees, my trainers squelching in the mud and brown leaves, my mind working double time, my thoughts jumping from the emptiness of my bank account to Irishmen turning up in stormy weather to offer the most unexpected of help. The scent of autumn – the tang of decay – was in the air.

When we got back to Gwel Teg in pitch darkness, I was more ready to confront the trials ahead. I sizzled a rump steak, half of which I gave to a salivating Rufus, and sat in front of the telly with a stiff whisky. There was plenty of wood in the store, but I lacked the energy or inclination to start a fire. It was much easier to pull on another jumper and switch on the portable electric heater.

I soon slipped into a doze, only to be jerked awake by the plate slipping from my lap and clattering on the stone floor. I'd barely eaten half my share of the steak. The television was blaring. Rufus was spread out on the worn mat in front of the fireplace, watching me with sleepy, loving eyes. I called him and he padded over to lean against my legs while I stroked his head. The warmth and softness of another living being was so very good.

Time for bed. The wind was still whistling in the eaves

of the cottage as I dragged myself up the narrow stairs with Rufus close on my heels.

Tomorrow would be a big day. There was the arrival of our recruit, assuming he emerged from the haze of a heavy night in The Mermaid to make an entrance. But more importantly – much more importantly – there was my afternoon meeting with George Thompson, the bank manager, who held my future and the future of the Gazette in his grasping hands.

Judgement day loomed.

CHAPTER FOUR

I arrived early at the office the following day, dressed smarter than usual. Much smarter. The black, knee-length dress I'd bought a couple of lifetimes ago from a Mayfair boutique in Albemarle Street had been pressed into service. It was one of the remnants of my London life, before my return to Cornwall; before gumboots, thick woollen socks, fleeces and sensible jeans had taken over.

This was nothing to do with Danny's arrival. Nothing to do with him at all. I needed to pull out all the stops if I was to impress the inscrutable human being who was my bank manager. Behind his round, thin rimmed glasses, George Thompson's grey eyes could be as cold as the North Atlantic. His implacable gaze reminded me of a picture I'd seen of Heinrich Himmler peering into the face of a prisoner in Minsk in 1941. It was said that few people could hold Himmler's chilling stare. Under Thompson's clinical scrutiny, I always felt like an insect ripe for dissection.

But a hint of optimism crept through me as I began a long overdue cleaning up operation in editorial. The whistling gales of the previous day had eased to a strong breeze. The sun was shining, the seagulls were out again – squawking and screeching while riding the sea breezes with barely a flap of their wings – and the heaving ocean had brightened from a dull grey to a jade green flecked with white.

When Danny arrived later – a lot later, I suspected, after Wreckers Rebellion had done its worst – editorial would more closely resemble a working office rather than a neglected repository of wastepaper, grungy coffee stains and dust. I'd cringed when he'd surveyed the room the previous day. The place had reeked of decay and an era long past.

Emily Watson, our trainee reporter, helped with piling old press releases into black sacks and wiping the desks and floors. The weekly cleaner had been one of the early casualties of numerous cutbacks as I'd struggled to balance the books.

The bell on the front door downstairs tinkled as Brenda walked in, clutching any number of carrier bags. I went down to have a chat about giving the reception area a much needed clean as well. She had a more prepared look than usual. A touch more colour on her cheeks and lips. Her hair loose rather than tied up in a severe bun. The trackies swapped for a blue dress last seen at the office Christmas lunch.

Even Roy was smarter when he arrived a few minutes later, empty pipe in hand. A beige jacket matched new trousers, complemented by a fresh shirt and shiny brogues. This was surprising indeed. Nothing short of the arrival of royalty or a senior politician would usually jerk Roy out of his comfortable tweed jacket.

So, before he had even completed a minute's work, the new arrival had caused us all to smarten up our act. Perhaps my misgivings, which had combined with the gales to give me a night of minimal sleep, were unnecessary.

'Had a bit of a tidy up, I see,' was Roy's only comment as he took his usual seat at the desk by the window. Emily was sitting at a desk next to Roy, who was always more than ready to dispense wisdom and guidance. She was working on Fifty Years Ago, a weekly feature showing articles which appeared in the Gazette half a century previously.

Danny arrived shortly before ten o'clock, looking remarkably fresh, clearly a man who could hold his drink. He was carrying a large cardboard Sainsbury's box full of notebooks, pens and papers – and a Cork Constitution rugby mug.

'Take whichever desk you want,' I said, waving at the expanse of empty office space which had once echoed to lively banter and the tapping of Imperial typewriters. 'There's tea and coffee in the cupboard and milk in the fridge. Help yourself. We're having an editorial meeting at noon to discuss next week's paper. Of course, we'd like you to join us. In the meantime, you might want to have a look at back copies of the Gazette. We hold the last year in a file over there. Older editions are kept on microfiche.'

Danny nodded at the box he carried. 'Is there somewhere I can keep my valuables safe?'

'What sort of valuables?'

'Oh, papers from some of my old investigations, that sort of thing. It's important they're kept under lock and key.'

Perhaps Danny was a more thoughtful, careful individual than I'd given him credit for. I gestured to the unused filing cabinets at the back of the office. 'Most of those are empty. Take your pick.'

'Thanks. One of those will be fine.' He paused. 'You're looking very elegant and business-like today, Kate, if you don't mind my saying.'

A warm flush spread into my cheeks, though goodness knew why. 'I've got a meeting with the bank manager this afternoon,' I was quick to point out and then returned to my desk without further explanation. I'd be back to the jeans next week, but perhaps I'd exchange the sloppy trainers for something more stylish. Perhaps.

News was far from my mind as I stared at the computer screen, trying to make sense of the mass of figures I'd need to present confidently at the bank later. Where were the signs of a light at the end of the tunnel, which would take the Gazette into a glorious new world of profit and success? The truth was they didn't exist.

The circulation figures resembled the Alps with peaks during the summer season and whenever a story had captured local attention. Younger people weren't buying newspapers. We were reliant on a dwindling, older readership.

Danny came over with two mugs of tea. 'I made a brew and thought you might like a cup. Do you take sugar?'

'Thanks. No sugar. I'm trying to give up.' I treated him to a compact smile, careful to keep it professional.

He held up two keys on a ring. 'I've put my stuff in the last cabinet on the left. Is it okay if I keep the keys? There's a lot of confidential material in there vital to old investigations.'

I raised a freshly plucked eyebrow. What kind of people did Danny think we were? 'Nobody in these offices would dream of sorting through your papers. We're professionals here.'

Danny's face drooped. 'Sure. I wasn't trying to cast aspersions. It's just that I'd be happier if they were under lock and key.'

Was it worth arguing over? Probably not. I needed to focus on my crunch meeting at the bank, not argue over the keys of a filing cabinet nobody used. 'Okay, so long as you always have the keys available when you're in the office.'

His shoulders eased lower 'Yes, of course.'

I returned to the unhelpful figures on the computer and sipped, leaving a smear of coral pink lipstick on the rim of the mug. It was strong with plenty of flavour. Danny made a good cup of tea.

The mental gymnastics involved in interpreting the parlous situation of the Gazette's finances ate up time, and before I knew it Roy, Emily and Danny were pulling their chairs near my desk for the editorial meeting. Emily turned to an empty page of her notebook, expectant and excited; such meetings were still a novelty to her. Roy sucked on his empty pipe, his usual calm, equable self. Danny emphasised his long length with a stretched out, laid back position.

I scrabbled around my desk for a ballpoint which hadn't run out of ink and found one under a pile of mail. 'What have we got for next week?' I said, determined to sound in control and put right any negative impressions the newcomer might have gained when he'd marched in out of the storm the previous day. We might be a million miles from London, but we weren't hicks.

Roy took his Calabash pipe out of his mouth. 'The town council will next week be debating the proposal to extend double yellow lines in Crantock Street. Naturally, the chamber of commerce will fight it. And a local hotelier is calling for action to be taken on seagulls snatching chips and ice creams from tourists on the sea front.'

I scratched a few words on my notepad in the unique combination of Pitman's shorthand and long hand I'd adopted over the years. 'Thanks, Roy. Yes, they'll both be page leads.' I turned to Emily, who'd been awarded the dubious honour of reading through the upcoming planning applications. 'Anything on planning?'

She flipped a page of her notebook. 'A local developer

wants to build three executive houses on the ground behind the football pitches, and the Porth Manor is proposing a fifteen-bedroom extension.'

'Excellent,' I said, feigning enthusiasm with a smile. They were hardly the explosive stories I needed to boost sales and put the Gazette back on the map.

'Okay, what else?' I asked my audience of three. There was a lull in the conversation while we all consulted our notepads.

Danny pulled up his legs and leaned forward, his eyes bright. 'What are you doing about the tenth anniversary of the loss of the St Branok lifeboat next month?'

'We'll be covering the commemoration ceremony and telling the story of the disaster,' I said. 'And we'll do a feature on the current boat and its crew. The usual stuff. Lives saved, biographies of the crewmen…that kind of thing.'

Danny rubbed a hand across his chin. 'We could do more. A lot of questions never got answered. This is an opportunity to have a fresh look at them.'

Roy glanced at Danny and then at me. 'The marine inquiry looked into the disaster in great detail. I don't see what might be discovered now that wasn't unearthed by the authorities years ago. Frankly, it's a bit of a minefield. A lot of local people were upset by the coverage in the national press at the time. They felt the intrusion into the privacy and grief of the families affected was unfair.'

'But the loss remains a mystery,' said Danny, tapping his pen on his notebook. He was sitting up straight. The easygoing Irishman wasn't always easygoing, then. 'No part of the lifeboat was recovered, and the cause of the sinking wasn't fully explained. She just disappeared. The weather was bad, but the

Talan Bray had been out in bad weather countless times before.'

'Is the tenth anniversary of the loss of the Talan Bray one of the reasons you've come down to Cornwall?' I said. Danny hadn't mentioned it yesterday. He'd been careful to wax lyrical about Cornish pasties, but there'd been no word about the Talan Bray.

Danny wiped his hands on his trousers, his blue eyes squinting shrewdly. 'Yes...yes, actually that is one of the articles requested by the tabloids. It's a fierce good story which remains a mystery, and there's no better time to tell it than on the tenth anniversary.'

I weighed the possible repercussions against the rewards. Danny was right. The loss of the Talan Bray had been the biggest story to hit St Branok in a generation – hit being the operative word. It'd rocked the community to its core. And there remained a bitterness and rawness about it locally which made it dangerous territory. Still, we needed the whole community to be talking about the Gazette. Better to be talked about than ignored.

'If we're going to dig into the cause of the disaster, we need to handle it diplomatically,' I said. 'We aren't going to sell newspapers if we alienate half the local population with guesswork and unfounded accusations.'

'Diplomacy is my middle name,' said Danny, grinning.

'But while you're working here, anything new you turn up needs to be offered to the Gazette first. You can sell the story to whoever you like once we've had a chance to publish.'

A frown creased Danny's broad forehead. 'Okay, I think I can make that work. I'll get on it this afternoon.'

'You must keep me informed,' I insisted. 'The scars from the Talan Bray disaster are still raw in this community.

Wives, sons, daughters, parents, friends…they're all still living here. Everybody knew the eight men who died.'

I glanced over at Roy who was chewing his lower lip. He was too much of a friend to say anything in front of the others, but I knew he was uneasy.

The meeting drifted into less contentious issues. I was only half listening, my imagination already walking through the arguments and strategies I would need to employ at the bank if I was to win a stay of execution. If the meeting went badly, all talk about double yellow line disputes, hotel extensions and tenth anniversaries of the Talan Bray sinking would be pointless. The Gazette would be closed down.

CHAPTER FIVE

I jumped in the Landy's front seat and turned the ignition key to be greeted by silence. Nothing. No whining starter motor, no thundering diesel engine.

Heaving open the aluminium bonnet, I stared down at the unresponsive lump of metal, its wires and pipes going here and there, with absolutely no idea what I was looking for. A loose wire? They all looked loose.

In seconds, I'd given up any absurd illusions of fixing the problem without expert help. My old friend Joe at The Mermaid was a dab hand at patching up most things, but this seemed too big even for him, so I clattered around the corner in my one and only pair of court shoes to Billy Couch. Billy scratched a living at a small back street garage, which serviced and repaired the Landy, miraculously getting it through the annual inspection without too many bills.

Smudged with oil, he emerged from underneath a battered pick-up truck when I called his name.

I got my breath back and brought my voice under control, in keeping with the tone and authority expected of the editor of the august North Cornwall Gazette. 'Billy, the Landy won't start again. I've got an urgent meeting. Can you have a quick look?'

He rubbed grubby hands with an oily rag Joe would have been proud of. 'Looks like it's important.'

'Yes. Very.' I was self-conscious as I performed my sweetest smile.

He grinned back with uneven, yellowed teeth which hadn't seen a dentist for twenty years. 'Let's have a quick look then. I'm always ready to come to the assistance of a helpless maid.' I could've told him where to shove his patronising 'helpless maid' line, but that wouldn't get the Landy fixed so I restricted myself to a grateful 'Thanks'.

I stood to one side wringing my hands while he probed under the bonnet, removing a few caps and plugs and shining a torch into dark, corroded corners. After several minutes, he emitted the doom-laden hiss favoured by mechanics, plumbers, electricians and other tradesmen called to solve a domestic disaster. 'It's an electrical. Most likely the alternator.'

I was none the wiser. 'How long will it take to fix?'

'If it's a new alternator, it'll take a while. I'll have to get the part in and then there's the fitting. We're talking a day at least.'

'That's no good,' I said. 'The meeting's in an hour and I need to get home tonight.'

'Where's the meeting?'

'Truro.'

'You can borrow the courtesy car.' He led me back to his garage and pointed to a brown hatchback skulking in a dim nook.

It was old. It was grubby. It would do. I thanked him profusely and headed off, revving the tiny engine and stirring the rubbery gearstick like a wooden ladle in porridge.

The problems with the Landy took their toll. In the

ladies' of a store near the bank, I washed grubby hands, tore off the remaining shard of a broken pink nail I'd manicured this morning and wiped a smudge of oil from my left cheek. How the hell had that got there? Judging by the mess, you'd have thought I'd changed the Landy's engine. Mercifully, the black dress hid any further oil stains.

A hot and sweaty nervousness swept over me at the bank's anodyne offices. I was ten minutes late. While George Thompson was fetched, I faked interest in leaflets promoting low interest rate mortgages to prevent myself from pacing up and down.

Thompson entered the room Phantom of the Opera-style, slipping out of a shadowy corner. He greeted me with his trademark cold smirk. In return, I forced a slight upturn of my mouth. He was carrying a laptop and a thick file, which presumably covered all the financial twists and turns of the North Cornwall Gazette since I'd taken ownership three years previously. I was surprised it wasn't thicker.

As he approached, I felt like a child confronted by a reprimanding teacher. And, no, I couldn't hold his stare. My feeble attempt at a smile was directed more at the corporate blue carpet than at Thompson. I doubt he noticed it at all.

After a limp handshake, he said, 'Ms Tregillis, thank you so much for popping in. I was beginning to wonder if you were going to turn up. Can I get you a tea or coffee?'

'No, I'm fine thanks.' I shifted from one foot to the other. The court shoes, which I'd only worn twice before, were tight and uncomfortable, but at least they gave me a slight height advantage. Any advantage was welcome.

He turned on his flatter but equally dapper heels. Black leather Oxfords, immaculate and well-polished. 'Please follow me. Interview room number one is free.'

I was led into the inner sanctum to be offered a seat in a small office with two chairs, reminiscent of the austerity of a police interview room. It looked out over a yard and the grey walls of nearby buildings. Peeking out above a slate roof was the central tower of the nearby cathedral. I could pay a visit there later if I needed to pray to some deity above – or more probably below – which looked after desperate journalists.

Thompson thumped the hefty file on the table and we both took our seats. He logged into his laptop, his soft, slim hands sweeping over the keyboard with practised dexterity. At first, I sat ramrod straight, but then eased myself into a more comfortable position, while careful to appear cooperative and responsive.

I flipped open my own file in what I hoped was a confident, nonchalant manner and handed over the spiky alpine graph showing circulation figures for the last twelve months. 'Things have been a little bumpy, but I think we're on the right track.'

He peered at it without comment for a long, silent minute, his pale face unreadable. 'You'll recall that at our last meeting I expressed my concerns at the Chronicle's continuing losses. Has there been any improvement since then?'

'The Gazette,' I corrected. His mistake summed up his interest in my newspaper. To him, the Gazette was one of many struggling local businesses. Whatever happened, the bank wouldn't lose out. Their loans were covered by what they called collateral and I called my home.

A flush of colour tinged his cheeks. 'The Gazette…yes, of course. And what action is being taken to stem the losses?'

Any satisfaction I might have gleaned from embarrassing him was fleeting. 'These are difficult times for any local newspaper,' I said. 'Circulation and advertising have been…er…inconsistent. But we are making progress and have plans for a series of articles and features over the next few months, which should help boost the readership. A freelancer, a top journalist from London, is joining the editorial team for the next few months to root out exciting stories which could attract national attention.'

Thank heavens for Danny Flanagan. His arrival had allowed me to paint a more positive picture than the tale of woe which usually dominated my meetings at the bank.

Thompson continued visually dissecting me. He obviously hadn't been expecting anything new from the meeting – nothing positive, anyway. His thin features expressed a mild surprise, mixed with scepticism. 'A London journalist. Isn't he expensive? As you will be aware, I'm sure, you are close to your overdraft limit.'

I interrupted him. This was one of those rare occasions when I'd got the upper hand. 'He's not costing me anything unless he produces hard results which improve our news coverage.'

Thompson produced a tepid, unconvinced smirk. 'This bank is committed to helping small businesses, which are, after all, the lifeblood of the local economy…'

I waited for the punchline as he spouted the bank's corporate gobbledygook, droning on and on. 'But your business is causing us concerns.' He tapped a few keys on his laptop and I imagined a sea of red on his screen. 'Serious concerns. You breached your overdraft limit last month and you're close to doing so again. When can we expect to see progress on repayment of the loan?'

'I was hoping for an extension,' I said, my mouth dry. Perhaps I should have had that cup of tea or coffee, after all.

Or a slug of whisky. Or a draught of hemlock. 'Just to see us through the next few months until the trading conditions improve. You have the cottage as security. It's worth at least two hundred thousand pounds'

He leafed through the papers in his thick file until he found a photo of Gwel Teg, set high on the cliffs. 'If the cottage had to be sold at short notice it wouldn't fetch anywhere near its normal market value. The bank has already shown considerable goodwill by exposing itself more than usual.'

'Another ten thousand pounds, that's all I need.' I'd gone into the meeting intending to ask for twice that amount, but Thompson's cold presence and my lateness had unnerved me. 'It'll give us enough headroom to get through this patch. I'm sure the bank wouldn't want to cause the death of one of Cornwall's longest established local newspapers.'

Thompson rewarded me with a full blast of his chilling stare. 'You are a valued customer, Ms Tregillis, but however much the bank is committed to your success, it has to operate within the bounds of financial prudence. We have a responsibility to our shareholders and other customers.'

The talk dried up. Thompson did more tapping on his laptop while I waited to find out whether he was granting my request for an extension or calling in the bailiffs to take everything I owned.

CHAPTER SIX

I headed back to St Branok in the wheezing brown hatchback, unsure whether I'd won a great battle which would save the Gazette or condemned it to a protracted, lingering death. I'd got the extra ten thousand pounds – at a higher interest rate, of course – so at least I could be confident of paying the wages and the printing and material costs for the next month or so.

But after that? I should have asked for twenty thousand pounds.

I was on the verge of losing everything I'd worked for over the past God only knew how many years. Thompson had made it clear in his icy, distant way that there would be no more loan extensions, no more reprieves.

The hatchback jiggled round a corner and I got my first glimpse of the Atlantic, glinting in the late afternoon light. It lifted me, as it always did. Further out, away from the crashing shoreline, whitecaps flecked the surface and a sailing boat with its spinnaker out shouldered aside triangular mounds of water.

This was the frontier: the point where raw nature assumed control.

I parked in my familiar spot at the Gazette, intending to talk Brenda through our advertising strategy for the next three months. More income was essential if we were going to survive. We needed to find new clients or encourage existing advertisers to dig deeper into their pockets. Neither of these proposals was realistic in the descent into winter. The Boxing Day and January sales would give us a boost, as always, but the following fallow period from January to March stretched ahead, seemingly unbridgeable.

The Gazette offices were dark and silent. Brenda had taken the opportunity of my absence to slope off early. Our conversation would have to wait until Monday.

I wanted to stroll down to the beach to watch the breakers and gather my thoughts, but the court shoes were rubbing so I headed to The Mermaid in the hope of finding Roy, who would often stop there for a quick drink on a Friday before heading back to his cosy terraced home.

I was in luck. He was sat serenely in the snug with a pint of Guinness and a copy of the Western Morning News, a much bigger rival to the Gazette. The pub was busy for a late afternoon. The end of the week had caused any number of locals to drop in for a drink and a natter. Joe paused from drying glasses and chatting to a couple of regulars to give me a welcoming wave, and I waved back.

A gaggle of harbour labourers were gathered at the bar, dressed in boots and dirty blue overalls. Their rowdy laughter and raised voices carried through The Mermaid, but I didn't mind. I needed humanity and laughter around me as an antidote to Thompson's interrogation. When was the last time I'd laughed like that? Certainly not in the last three years as the Gazette's finances had tightened like a noose around my neck.

Roy smiled at me, and I got a shandy at the bar and joined him.

As I sat down, a strident Irish voice rang out from the direction of the labourers. Danny was among them. He was holding court, telling a story. When he finished, they all roared with laughter.

Roy fixed me with his perceptive deep brown eyes. 'How did it go?'

I did my best to sound upbeat – with indifferent results. 'Yes, pretty good. The bank's agreed to an extension on the loan.' I took a sip of my shandy and flipped over a beermat, the advertising faded and illegible from countless spilled drinks.

'You can't fool an old pro like me, Kate. How bad is the situation really?'

I reached in my bag for a Benson and Hedges and lit it shakily. The mask was slipping, and I couldn't hold it in place anymore – not with Roy, who knew me so well. A long, satisfying drag calmed me. 'I've got enough to tide us through the winter.'

Roy gave me a reproachful look at the sight of the cigarette. 'I thought you'd given up.'

I sucked another mouthful. Bliss. For a few moments. 'I had…I have. It's the odd one or two when I really need it. Anyway, you can talk. You've still got your pipe.'

He smiled. 'Fair point, but I'm a weak old man who can't give up the habit of a lifetime.' He hesitated. 'I've been thinking. I could work for nothing and just get paid expenses until the upturn comes.'

A stream of bubbles rose in the amber liquid inside my glass. If there *is* an upturn. 'You don't need to do that. I already pay you a pittance.' My voice was strained, full of defeat.

'If it means the survival of the Gazette, then I'm happy

to do it. The old lady's been my life for the past fifty years. I'd hate to see her go under. I don't need the money. Marjorie and I can live perfectly well on our pensions. And then, when things improve, you can cough up some back pay.'

I forced myself to meet the empathetic eyes of this caring, elderly man. He had as much invested in the Gazette as I did – not financially but certainly in terms of relentless hard work. He'd been a part of ensuring that the newspaper hit the narrow Cornish streets for longer than most people had lived.

His kindness brought out a vulnerability within me that rarely showed itself. Something hard was rising in my throat. 'If the Gazette goes bust, then I lose everything: the cottage, the newspaper…everything,' I blurted. 'All my life I've worked hard, and what do I have to show for it?'

Roy rested his veiny hand on mine. 'We're going to make it work. You, me, Danny, Emily and Brenda. There's still a place for the Gazette. Once we boost the circulation, the advertising will fall into place. Danny says he has lots of ideas. Well, let him show them to us. Cometh the hour, cometh the Irishman.'

'Yesterday, you weren't sure about him,' I pointed out.

'Maybe I was wrong. Beneath all the blarney, there's a tougher, cannier side. He knows a good story when he sees one. The question is how far he's prepared to go to get it. Perhaps Danny will bring that breath of fresh air we're always talking about.' He gestured towards the bar where Danny, a fresh pint in hand, was still leaning on the counter and laughing with the harbour workers. 'Looks like he's already popular.'

Our conversation petered out for a few seconds while we listened to the raucous conversation at the bar. The Irish equivalent of The Seventh Cavalry, flushed in the face, was holding forth on the difference between an ass and an arse if the snatches of conversation were anything to go by. As if he sensed we were talking about him, Danny glanced over at me and performed that beguiling smile and a sloppy salute. Determined to maintain my editorial authority, I held up my hand in cool acknowledgement.

What was it about Danny that brought out my most serious side? I knew the answer. The arrival of this hard-nosed hack had reawakened my ambition and made me determined to show that, despite my years of willing incarceration in St Branok, I was still capable of cutting it in the tough world of journalism.

There was sudden movement at the bar; somebody had pushed somebody. A voice was raised. The crowd splintered to leave Danny and a tattooed trawlerman facing each other like gunfighters at the OK Corral. The trawlerman's eyes were screwed up and his meaty hands bunched into fists. 'That's none of your damned business, Irishman,' he spat.

Danny held his hands out in a placatory pose. 'Sorry, it was a stupid question. I didn't mean to—'

Two of the trawlerman's buddies intervened to pull their friend away. 'Eddie, it's not worth it. Come on, you could do with some fresh air.'

The tension in the trawlerman's body eased. He took a step backwards. 'You're right. *He's* not worth it,' he muttered as he flashed a final hateful glance at Danny and then allowed himself to be led away.

Danny waited until the men had left the pub before picking up his pint, taking a sip and then meandering over to Roy and me.

'Can I get my colleagues a drink?' He tripped over one

of the pub's uneven flagstones and a small amount of beer slopped out of his glass. He didn't seem to notice.

'Thanks, but I need to get home,' said Roy. 'What was all that about? It looked nasty. I thought you were going to get your block knocked off.'

Danny settled on a stool across the table from us and plonked down his pint a little too hard. The beer swilled in the glass and a few more drops escaped. 'It was nothing. A misunderstanding. He took exception to my asking about his brother who died on the Talan Bray.'

Roy's expression was solemn as he struggled to his feet. 'Be careful, Danny. The Talan Bray is still a mighty source of pain around here. This is a small, tight-knit community with long memories. If you push people too hard, you're likely to get them worked up – furious, even.'

'Sure, I'll be more careful in the future.' Danny turned his glassy eyes on me in a clear signal that the discussion of his handling of the Talan Bray issue was at an end. 'How about you, Kate? Care to join me for a drink? Come on, you can't let a man drink alone.'

'You seem to be doing a good job of not being alone,' I said. 'Sorry, another time. I need to get back as well.'

'And who do you have to get back for?'

A twinge of irritation struck me. Danny's new St Branok contacts had obviously been talking. I could guess the details because I'd overheard them in snatches of conversation in the past: 'Yes, she lives alone with that mangy dog of hers in an old coastguard cottage out on the cliffs. Tough bitch that one. A hard nut. A career woman. God knows why she left London. She's never completely fitted in down here.' Blah blah frigging blah.

'That's none of your business, Danny,' I said after an awkward pause. I tried to soften it with small talk, which I'd never been very good at. 'Looks like you're working hard at getting to know the locals.'

Danny shifted in his seat and scratched his neck. He hadn't been completely unaffected by the fracas at the bar, then. 'Well, as you will know, all good reporters have to spend time on networking.' Now it was his turn to be defensive.

I swigged the remains of my shandy and rose to leave. 'The locals don't really do networking in St Branok, but if you can dig up some new stories in time for next week's edition without upsetting anybody else then I'll be happy.'

Danny chomped on a handful of peanuts, which I suspected might be his dinner. 'I've already got a few ideas. I'll do a bit of digging over the weekend and talk it through with you on Monday morning.'

I made for the door, leaving the lesser-spotted Danny Flanagan in what was undoubtedly his natural habitat – the pub.

CHAPTER SEVEN

On Monday, I made porridge and took Rufus for a long walk along the cliffs as the first fingers of daylight crept across a lightening sky. I couldn't remember the last manic Monday I'd managed anything better than a slurp of instant coffee before a frantic drive to the office.

My mood had been lifted by a late evening call from my friendly car mechanic. Billy had fixed the Landy and it was ready for collection. Miracle upon miracles, the problem had been easier to solve than he'd predicted with the bill just the right side of affordable.

With Rufus sprawled over the back seat, I drove Billy's brown hatchback down bumpy country lanes to reach St Branok as a fleet of small, jaunty day-boats sailed out to sea, a lucrative day's fishing hopefully in prospect. The Atlantic was capable of delivering riches and death in equal measure. Everybody knew the stories of fishermen who'd revelled in big catches only to die in a storm a few months later.

The winding main street was quiet with only the newsagents open when I twisted a key in the lock of the Gazette's front door and led Rufus up to editorial on the first floor, taking the narrow stairs two at a time.

Yes, this was the start of a new era. We were going to turn the corner.

Rufus settled in his familiar spot while I did a ring round of the emergency services to check if anything had happened which might make a story for the Gazette. There had been an accident on the Truro road at a notorious blackspot with two people taken to Treliske Hospital. Police had not yet released the names, but there was still enough to write a few paragraphs. A local councillor had been repeatedly calling for improvements to this section of road. I called her up and got a comment on the need for urgent action.

It was the start of another typical week. Not yet the new dawn the Gazette needed, but the bread and butter of which local newspapers are made.

The familiar tinkle of the front doorbell sounded, heavy footsteps thumped on the stairs and Danny walked in with that tired raincoat of his, but otherwise looking fresh and eager. He was wearing a clean shirt, grey trousers – and that smile. He managed a mock salute a good deal better than the shoddy effort he'd managed in The Mermaid on Friday when he was well on his way to being three sheets to the wind.

'Daniel Flanagan reporting for duty, ma'am,' he said as he headed for the desk he'd chosen.

My acknowledgements remained cool. It was usually the best way to handle effervescent people like Danny. Still, no reason not to be friendly. 'How was your weekend?'

'Productive. I bumped into a marine engineer at The Mermaid and I have an interesting angle on the Talan Bray story.'

I sat up. 'What is it?'

Danny pulled out his laptop, plugged it in and consulted the screen. 'It's a bit too early to say yet. I need to do some checking. But, if my hunch works out, it will make a very nice story indeed. An exclusive.'

I kept my tone firm. 'If you're going to stay working in my offices, you need to be completely up front with me.'

Danny waved dismissively. 'I know, I know, and believe me you'll be the first to be told. I just need to do a bit more research first.'

'Is there anything we can use for this week's newspaper? We could do with something eye-catching for the front page.'

A triumphant grin broke across Danny's face. 'Actually, there is something. The fisherman's cooperative is proposing an extension to the fish quay. It's a multi-million-pound investment.'

This was indeed a great story, and I was secretly affronted that a complete stranger such as Danny could come into a place like St Branok and pick up a story that had escaped the rest of us. There are few more galling experiences for a journalist than to be late to a story or to miss out on it completely. Still, I needed to put my personal pride to one side. 'Sounds interesting,' I said. 'What are your sources for the story?'

There was a gleam in Danny's eye. He'd stirred me up and he knew it. 'A fella you might know called Mike Pedrick. He's got fingers in lots of pies.'

'Of course, I know Mike Pedrick,' I said, unable to hide my exasperation. 'Everybody knows Mike.'

'Well, he was in The Mermaid on Saturday night, and I introduced myself as a friend and colleague of yours. He's helping the fishermen's cooperative put together a financial package. There's a good chance of support from the European Regional Development Fund. He's been getting positive noises from the fund's programme office in Truro.'

Now I was enthusiastic. I couldn't help it, despite Danny's playful baiting. The North Cornwall Gazette would be first with a story which would attract regional television, online and newspaper coverage. It might go even further afield. When was the last time we had led the news? Too long. Far too long. I could beat myself up all I liked that I hadn't picked up the story earlier, but it had been my decision to bring Danny into the fold so at least some of the credit was mine. 'When can I see the story?'

'You'll have it by early tomorrow at the latest,' said Danny as his fingers, surprisingly nimble for such a large man, flew across the keys of his laptop. 'I'm getting quotes from the fish producers association and the European Regional Development Fund.'

The rest of the day passed in the usual Monday blur. I had a difficult meeting with Brenda over the need to attract more advertising. She was defensive, claiming she was doing everything possible, but I persisted, insisting that she call our top advertisers and offer them a special discounted rate if they committed to extra advertising. She disappeared in a huff at lunchtime, but later I overheard her on the phone giving it her best shot, her tone urgent.

Danny beat his own deadline, handing over his story about the fish quay extension at the end of the day. And, I had to admit, it was well written and thoroughly researched. Our best front-page lead story for several months. On an impulse, I contacted the printer and asked for the print run to be increased by a further two thousand copies. Small beer by most newspapers' standards, but a big step forward for the North Cornwall Gazette, which had wasted away on a diet of dwindling revenues in recent years.

Something akin to happiness was rising within me as I drove home in the late afternoon with Rufus panting excitedly on the back seat. This week's newspaper was looking good. There was a new vibrancy to the editorial office. Plus, Billy had performed his usual magic on the Landy and it was running as well as it ever did, which is to say far from smooth but at least starting on the second or third attempt. And producing plenty of murky diesel exhaust smoke in the process.

A reddening sun, hovering just above the horizon, had turned the ocean gold. On an impulse, I dug out my black swimming costume from the cupboard under the stairs and raced down to the cove below my cottage. Rufus dogged my heels, his question mark of a tail high, his nose low. Partly protected from the prevailing south-westerly winds, the waters here tended to be less agitated than those crashing against most of the North Coast. Tregloss Point, a jagged spear of land jutting out into the ocean, tamed the Atlantic's power.

The wind had dropped to a gentle breeze by the time I jumped down onto the pebbles and shingle of the cove. The tide had retreated enough to reveal fine, golden sand, rippled by the swirls and powerful currents of the sea.

I threw a sliver of smooth, pale grey driftwood for Rufus and he chased it into the churning water without a care in the world.

Oh to be a dog.

I plunged through the surf, diving under the thundering rollers to escape the full force of their power. The sea churned around me, expending what remained of its cold fury. Nearby, a cormorant dived to reappear a minute later with a sprat, the stricken fish's silvery scales glinting in the sunlight. Even in death the Atlantic could offer beauty.

For an all too brief spell, I was a willowy girl again, lost in the power of the booming surf, with teenage cares which had seemed huge at the time but turned out to be transient and insignificant. The waves, retaining some of the warmth of summer and early autumn, held me in their bubbling, crashing grip. My body adjusted. Goose bumps subsided.

I was soon out beyond the surf line, riding the surging mounds of green water. This was the embodiment of the dream which had brought me back to Cornwall. The wild nature of the North Atlantic filled me with an elation I had never experienced anywhere else and certainly not in London. How often had I sat in a bland newspaper office, staring out at the city concrete, and dreamt of this? Every morning, every afternoon, every hour.

I trod water and turned to face the ragged land, catching my breath. Rufus was in his element, barking and running at seagulls up and down the shoreline. Beyond the golden sand, the shingle, the pebbles and the cliffs, the slate grey roof of my little cottage was visible. Gwel Teg, a refuge from the everyday shit of life.

Rufus was no longer alone in the cove. Somebody had made his way down the cliff path leading from my cottage and was standing close to the shoreline, looking out to sea with a hand shielding his eyes from the late afternoon sun. The wide stance and stature showed the person to be a man, though it was too far to identify him. Rufus barked and cavorted around him. The intruder was somebody he knew.

I resented their arrival. This was my special place – mine and Rufus's. Especially at this time of year, when visitors were few and far between. The person standing on the shoreline gave a brisk wave. I waved back and swam to shore, making the most of the power of the waves by riding on their crests to reach shallower waters.

At last, my bare feet touched down on hard, rippled sand and I waded over to the stocky, familiar figure of Joe from

The Mermaid. His eyes were in shadow, hidden by the hand he was using to shield them from the glare. 'Kate, you must be crazy swimming out here by yourself. What would happen if you got into trouble?' There was a chiding but friendly tone to his voice.

I held my head at an angle to purge an ear of sea water. 'I know this coast as well as anybody. I know what I'm doing.'

He tsked loudly, but amusement played across his lips. I walked past him to get my towel, aware of his eyes still on me. 'Typical mad Kate Tregillis. Frightened of nobody and no thing. You know there are riptides all the way along this coast? If one of those gets hold of you, then it doesn't matter how strong a swimmer you are. Next stop: New York.'

I rubbed my hair with the towel. 'Rips are rare in the cove and, anyway, they usually run in shallow water, close to the shore. If you keep calm, you can often land a bit further down the coast.' I lowered the towel and lifted my face. 'I doubt you came all the way down here to talk about water safety. Or are you here to welcome me ashore with a pint of the good stuff?'

He laughed his easy laugh, the one he used when he was Mr Affable at The Mermaid. 'Sorry, we don't offer a delivery service even for regulars like yourself. And I'm sure you know more about swimming around here than me. I'm strictly the sailing type.'

'Then, to what do I owe this pleasure?' I stopped drying myself and slipped on a T shirt, which was soon dampened by the bathing costume. Still, it shielded me from the fresh breeze and Joe's glances, benign though both were.

'I happened to be passing and thought I'd pop over for a chat. I knew you must be nearby when I saw Rufus on the beach.'

That was utter bullshit. My cottage wasn't en route to anywhere. It was on a bumpy, pockmarked lane which saw few people out of season apart from the postie and the occasional coastal hiker.

I brushed sand from my forehead. 'And the real reason?'

Rufus trotted over and I threw a pebble for him. He scampered away into the surf with not the slightest chance of being able to recover it from the churning water, but that didn't stop his enthusiasm. Good old Rufus, love of my life.

Joe hesitated, his dark eyes registering something like concern. 'Brenda gave me a call today and spent half an hour trying to persuade me to take extra advertising. She said the situation at the Gazette was, well, pretty bloody desperate. To be honest, it's not the time of year when I'm looking to take more advertising, but I said I'd do as much as I could.' He fixed his eyes on the horizon. 'You and me, we go back decades. I thought I'd pop over and see how I might help.'

I silently cursed Brenda. In her desperation for more advertising, she was spreading the word around St Branok that the Gazette was on the rocks. This was a mistake. The hard-nosed businesspeople in North Cornwall, struggling to make a living from the sea or the tourist industry, didn't do sympathy. They were too busy surviving. Clearly, I'd said too much to her during our heated exchange earlier in the day. If she was going to blab everything I told her around town, I'd need to be more careful. The gossip mill – one of the few things that thrived in St Branok in the colder months – went into overdrive at such tittle-tattle.

I'd hoped that my little newspaper would be creating the news in the future, but not in this way.

I shook my head dismissively. 'You know Brenda,' I said. 'She's a great person but she's prone to exaggeration. We've had a bit of a lean spell but nothing we can't handle. There's a plan to improve the quality of the Gazette over the coming months. Let me tell you all about it. Come up to the cottage and I'll make you a better coffee than you can get at The Mermaid.'

I'd hoped to slip away from the trials and tribulations of the Gazette for the rest of the day, but I might limit the damage if I convinced Joe that the situation wasn't as dire as Brenda had painted. Joe spoke to everybody and would be helpful in passing on a more positive view.

I slipped on my battered trainers and we slogged up the cliff path, the wind at our backs gusting more forcefully now and the sand sucking at our feet. Rufus was somewhere up ahead, as ever, chasing something.

As the sun settled below the horizon and the Atlantic darkened to iodine, Joe sat on a stool in the kitchen while I switched on one of my few luxuries: a serious coffee machine. A good coffee house was one of the few things I missed about London. The Mermaid was an ale and steak sort of place, mainly for the locals, which didn't take coffee seriously. Mike Pedrick's nearby gastropub came the closest to a decent cup of local coffee, no doubt to satisfy the tourists, but it fell well short of the intense bitter sweetness I'd sipped in London.

'All a bit of a storm in a teacup then?' said Joe. 'I'll call Brenda in the morning and tell her I won't be taking that extra advertising after all.' There was a twinkle in his eye.

'You're getting an extra special offer *and* a great coffee thrown into the bargain,' I said.

Joe held up his hands in mock submission. 'Okay, okay, if the coffee is as good as you say it is, I'll keep the advertising.'

I poured the steaming coffee into two large mugs and plonked a carton of milk from the fridge on the table. I knew

Joe well enough not to feel the need to decant the milk into a jug. 'Still a dash of milk and no sugar?'

'Yes, you know me. I never change,' he said. 'So, what are your plans for the Gazette?'

I sipped, running the bitter liquid over my tongue. 'Now that's a real cup of coffee,' I said with undisguised satisfaction. The coffee cleared my mind. 'I've got big plans. I want to strengthen the news content of the Gazette, get people talking about it again, make it the essential part of the local community it always used to be. Once we get the readership up, advertisers like yourself will get more bang for their buck.'

'And then I suppose you'll be expecting us to pay more for advertising?' Joe was smiling, but there was a steely edge to the words. He was only half joking – a businessman first and a friend second.

'Not necessarily; we might increase the pagination. Remember the days when the Gazette used to run to more than fifty pages? We'll probably never reach that again, but we can certainly do better than the current twenty-eight.'

'And this new guy of yours, Danny Flanagan – he's part of all that?'

'Yes, Danny will have the time to find more stories and to dig deeper. He's already come up with a great story which we'll be running on the front page this week.'

'How well do you know him? Is he an old colleague of yours or something?'

I avoided his hard gaze and sidestepped his question. 'He's a freelancer who's helping us out for a while. That's all. We need an extra pair of hands.'

'And what's this exclusive all about?'

I emptied my cup. 'You'll have to buy this week's newspaper to find out. But I can tell you it's a big one.'

'He's certainly wasted no time in getting to know the local community and he's not slow in buying a round of drinks at The Mermaid. He's making a determined effort to singlehandedly boost my bar takings.'

'That's what they call a symbiotic relationship. You take advertising in the Gazette and Danny drinks you dry. You see, we all benefit. Another cup?'

'Go on then. This exclusive…is it anything to do with the loss of the Talan Bray?'

I fiddled with the coffee machine, my back turned to him. 'Why do you ask?'

'Oh, some of my regulars were saying that Danny had been asking questions. They were upset. The poor bastards who were lost…they were all popular guys with families and friends in St Branok. That disaster left five widows and ten children without a father. It will cause a lot of hurt if Danny starts digging it up again without good reason.'

I continued tinkering with the coffee machine, trying to recall the brief conversation I'd had with Danny earlier in the day. He'd said he had a new angle on the Talan Bray disaster but had refused to reveal anything further. Danny was a freelancer and could do what he liked, but locals such as Joe already viewed him as part of the Gazette. Any careless questions wouldn't merely tarnish his reputation; they would also impact my newspaper. We couldn't afford that kind of bad publicity.

'The exclusive I'm talking about is nothing to do with the Talan Bray. But, since you mention it, yes, we'll be producing a commemorative supplement next month to mark the tenth anniversary of the sinking. Naturally, it'll be respectful to those who died and pay tribute to the enormous risks and sacrifices made by them and the current crew. What happened to the Talan Bray was tragic and terrible, but it shouldn't stop the work of the lifeboat being recognised.'

Joe sipped his second coffee. 'Those guys are heroes. Where they find the courage to go out in the Atlantic in the middle of a storm is anybody's guess. I never go out in Albatross in more than a four or five.' Albatross was Joe's sailing boat. One of his few luxuries, he often said. He always talked as if he was a nervous amateur, but I'd heard he was an accomplished sailor.

He looked at his watch. 'Jesus Christ, is that the time? I need to get back to The Mermaid. We've got a skittles night and there's a late delivery coming in from the brewery.'

I showed him to the door. It was now black outside and the wind was whistling. Down in the cove, the waves were smashing on the rocks. The Atlantic was beginning to roar.

Joe thanked me again for the coffee and then was gone in the darkness. Above the wind and the crashing surf, I heard him start his Ford pickup truck. He revved it a couple of times as the pickup's powerful headlights burst into life and illuminated the trees and hedges around my cottage, sculpted by the ocean gales. The tyres crunched on the gravel and he trundled down the gritty lane. I stood outside while his red tail lights became fainter and finally disappeared.

I closed the front door thinking of Danny. I'd been so pleased that he'd uncovered the story about the fish quay that I'd put aside my misgivings. It was a worrying fact that, despite knowing almost nothing about him, I was now implicated in any misdemeanours he might commit. An accessory after the fact, you might say.

Some digging was needed. I still knew many people who worked in the London media. Some of them would have heard of Danny if he'd been freelancing as extensively as he claimed. I'd make discreet enquiries when I got the time.

If I got the time.

CHAPTER EIGHT

The next edition of the North Cornwall Gazette was a great success, thanks in no small part to Danny's front page exclusive about the fish quay. We could have sold far more than the extra two thousand copies I'd ordered. Everyone wanted to read about this spark of optimism. Good news was in short supply. It had been a lean year for the fishing and tourist industries, St Branok's two main sources of revenue. There was less money sloshing around to tide over families and businesses during the bleak, grey winter stretching ahead.

I cursed myself for my timidity. We should have gone for an extra five thousand copies. The fish quay story was picked up by most regional press in the Westcountry and even got a few paragraphs in the nationals. Local people were talking about the Gazette again. For all the right reasons. Now we needed to keep it going.

I made subtle tweaks to the layout and style of the paper to give it a more contemporary look. The front page now carried bolder headlines, and we worked hard to find more dynamic photos and avoid the boring 'suits in a line' type pictures.

Despite my uncertainties about Danny, if there was any magic in the Gazette's editorial office it was coming from him. It was difficult not to fall for his affability and easy humour. With autumn tightening its grip on the Cornish coast and gales becoming colder and more prevalent, he'd turn up in his dripping Burberry coat with a pack of chocolate biscuits and that smile.

I asked him a few times about his Talan Bray story. He continued to assure me that once he had more 'concrete' information I'd be the first to know the details. In the meantime, he provided a steady stream of interesting stories. He'd settled into the room above the pub and, seemingly uncaring of its limitations, showed no sign of trying to find anywhere else. I gathered he spent most of his evenings drinking in The Mermaid, which was doing wonders for the Gazette's coverage of 'off diary' stories, probably at the expense of his liver.

St Branok's annual Shout at the Devil Festival was looming. It was a colourful, though somewhat macabre, event, in which several hundred locals noisily processed through the streets in gaudy costume, following the time-honoured tradition of chasing away the devil while actually being intent on having a booze up. The festival had pagan origins, its long history dating back many hundreds of years. Heavy drinking in the local pubs invariably culminated in minor late-night disturbances, often resolved without the involvement of the local police.

'We should make the most of it this year, get some great pictures and use them for a centre-page splash,' said Danny.

His boyish enthusiasm was infectious and made sense. Locals were more likely to buy the Gazette if their friends and relatives appeared in the coverage. The whole editorial team, even young Emily, agreed to give up their Saturday night to report on the event and get pictures.

The night of the festival was cold and clear with a

glistening three-quarter moon. We gathered early evening at The Mermaid for a warming brandy, provided free by Joe, prior to heading out into the night-time chill. The pub was packed with noisy, animated revellers, but we found a space in a corner. Outside, expectant people lined the streets three or four deep, chewing candy floss or hot dogs. Excited toddlers were perched on the shoulders of mums and dads.

With a toss of his head, Danny knocked back the remains of his brandy and then ordered a second for 'medicinal purposes'. This time, Joe insisted on payment.

Duly refreshed, we quit the pub's warm conviviality. 'Perfect night for pictures,' Danny said. He rubbed his hands together as if relishing the prospect of a freezing night under the stars in his thick jumper, corduroy trousers and shabby chic Burberry coat.

The buzz and banter of the crowd was quietened by the sound of drums, guitars and pipes. The nipping air shivered from the rhythmic reverberation, amplified by the narrow streets. I slipped through a gap between the onlookers to catch my first glimpse of the St Branok raven leading a long line of swaggering, gyrating figures, their masks, horns, wigs and vivid flowing robes enhanced by the flickering light of burning torches. In contrast to its cavorting followers, the raven progressed steadily and regally, its great beak moving from side to side as it regarded the crowd. There was something menacing and ungodly about the display. It was a window on a world long gone when superstition and fear had ruled people's lives.

Danny was suddenly beside me, shouting into my ear above the noise. His hot breath, infused with the sweet and nutty scent of brandy, warmed the side of my face. 'This is fantastic. Who's the raven?'

Our mouths became close as I turned towards him. 'It's a secret. A different person is chosen each year, but their identity is never revealed, though I'm pretty sure it was your friend Mike Pedrick last year. It's an honour to be chosen.'

The procession cavorted its way past, chanting, singing, playing instruments and shaking rattlers. Danny disappeared into the throng as I got a few nice pictures of the bizarre figure of the raven and his or her helpers when they swayed into a side street.

I eased past a group of rowdy trawlermen and left the crowds behind to dash down an empty, gloomy alleyway. It was a short cut to Tregloss Street, where the Tar Barrel Burn would soon be underway.

The alleyway was damp from rain earlier in the day and, as the noise of the crowd faded, I heard steady dripping from a roof a few metres ahead. The cobble stones were slick and slippery. I stepped warily, my freezing hands buried in the pockets of my ski jacket.

A voice behind called out in a Westcountry burr 'Hey Kate'. I turned. A figure I didn't recognise was standing there, his bulky frame silhouetted by the light from the nearby street.

'Yes?'

'I need to talk to you, Kate. It's important.' He came closer, slightly crouched.

'If it's a story for the Gazette, you can contact me in the office on Monday.'

'No, I need to speak to you now.'

He was wearing a dark costume with a gold Venetian mask, which added glitter and menace to his presence. I stepped backwards, but he edged nearer.

There was a blur of movement. I was punched in the

stomach and then gripped by the throat and shoved against a cold, dank wall. Breath was forced from me. I gasped for air but sucked in nothing. Saliva dribbled down my chin. The hold on my throat tightened. I wriggled and twisted to break free, the last of my breath hissing through clenched teeth, my arms and legs turning weak and rubbery and my knees buckling. He held me up with an iron grip.

I was choking. I was dying. This was crazy, absurd. I was being murdered at an innocent festival in my hometown.

I tried to scream. It came out as an agonised groan.

The Venetian mask filled my vision, implacable, the stuff of nightmares. Behind the mask, eyes flickered. Intense. Angry.

'Listen, Kate, and listen good,' he spat out. 'Tell that nosy bastard of yours, Danny Flanagan, to stop digging the dirt on the Talan Bray. He's hurting a lot of people around here. You'll both be sorry if you carry on. Next time, it'll be more than a warning.'

His hand remained on my throat. Vice-like. Sucking the life from me. My lungs and windpipe were on fire. I began to shake. My vision darkened.

The jabber of careless young voices filled the alleyway. A group of rowdy teenagers, fired up by drink and excitement, wandered towards us, absorbed in their own juvenile bubble and unaware of what they were witnessing.

The pressure stifling me, pushing me up against the wall, was gone. I sank to the ground as my attacker hurried away, head down.

Sucking in blessed air, I found I could speak again. 'Stop him,' I gasped to the teenagers and pointed a feeble, floppy arm.

The three teenagers stared down, not understanding.

'Are you okay, lady? Gone a bit long on the shorts tonight, eh?'

I tried to stand but fell back again. The chill wetness of the alleyway seeped into the left side of my jeans. My hands scrabbled around in the alleyway dirt. At last, my fumbling fingers found a downpipe, but it was wet and slimy and of little use in helping me get up. I remained sprawled on the ground. 'That man. He tried to kill me,' I squeaked at last.

'What man?' Their tone was still humorous, unbelieving.

'You must have seen him,' I said as I began to recover my wits. My throat was bruised and sore. A sharp thudding settled behind my eyes.

'She looks hurt,' said one of the teenagers. He was more concerned and helpful – and marginally more sober – than his friends.

'Help me up, please,' I croaked and strong, young arms pulled me to my feet.

My chest heaved. The teenagers studied me in confused silence.

'Do you need a doctor, lady?' the sensible one said at last.

I gulped down phlegm. It hurt like hell. Like I'd swallowed sandpaper. 'I think I'm okay,' I said. 'If you can help me to the end of the alleyway.'

'Yes, of course. No probs. Do you need to go to hospital? My dad's got a car.'

'No, no, it's okay, really, but thank you. You've been wonderful. Saved my life, literally. I need to find a police officer.'

We emerged from shadow into the flaring brightness of the street. The Tar Barrel Burn was under way and caustic, smouldering tar polluted the night air. After asking me again if I was okay, my teenage saviours melted into the throng.

Men and boys dashed past with the tar barrels ablaze on their backs. I looked up and down the street, hoping to see one of the police officers on duty for the festival. Some hope. There was also no sign of the scum in the Venetian mask. He'd slipped away.

A young woman with a toddler was standing on the street corner. She would have had a good view of anybody emerging from the alleyway. Still gulping and coughing, I worked my way over to her. 'Did you see a man in a gold Venetian mask come out of the alleyway a couple of minutes ago?'

'Venetian? No, sorry luv. There are people in masks all over the place.' She chuckled.

'He attacked me in the alleyway. I'm a journalist for the North Cornwall Gazette.'

I reached for my notebook and pen to prove my point, but my pockets were empty. I must have dropped them in the alleyway. They would still be there.

Her hand shot to her mouth and her eyes widened. 'Oh, my God. Did he try to…?'

'I thought he was going to kill me,' I said more forcefully. Shock had been replaced by a determination to see the bastard strung up. If I caught up with him, he could expect a knee in the groin for starters.

The young woman had switched from laughter to sympathy but didn't offer any practical help. I spotted Roy on the other side of the street in typical Kerslake stance – notebook in hand, pipe in mouth. Despite the best efforts of the shifting crowd, I managed to reach him. 'Have you seen Danny?' I croaked.

'Kate, what happened? You look terrible. Did you fall over?'

'Somebody attacked me in an alleyway. If three young lads hadn't come along, I don't know what might have happened.'

Roy's jaw dropped. 'Who? Why?'

'I've no idea. He told me to stop Danny looking into the Talan Bray disaster.'

Roy slipped his notebook into an inside pocket of his coat. 'We need to find Danny and ask what all this is about. I'd heard noises that he'd upset people with intrusive questions.'

'Why didn't you tell me?' I said, the brittle tone reflecting my trauma.

Roy rubbed a hand through his thinning hair. 'I thought you already knew after Danny's stand-off with Eddie Carpenter in The Mermaid. I didn't want to sound negative. You were obviously pleased with the work Danny's been doing. And, anyway, that's what reporting is all about, isn't it – asking difficult questions when necessary?'

I pulled my jacket straight and swept a wayward lock of matted hair from my eyes. My left side was covered in mud and slime from the alleyway. 'You should tell me what you hear. If Danny's upsetting people, I need to know about it.' My conversation with Joe on the beach replayed in my mind. It was all very well having a moan at Roy for not telling me about things he thought I didn't want to hear, but I was the one who'd ignored Joe's comments.

We still knew little about Danny except that he could write a good story, was always ready to stand a round at The Mermaid and made a good cup of tea.

I took a deep, windy breath and tried to subdue my simmering anxiety. 'I'm sorry, Roy. I don't mean to have a go at you. That attack scared me, that's all.'

Roy rested a gentle hand on my arm. This act of empathy was enough to bring me close to tears. I held them in. Just. For a moment, we'd slipped back twenty-five years and he was my editor again and I was a young trainee reporter. 'We need to find Danny, make sure he's okay, and then report all this to the police,' he said.

We walked to the top of Tregloss Street but saw no sign of Danny or any police officers, who, like buses, only arrived together or not at all.

The burning barrel event was coming to an end, the crowd starting to drift away to their homes or the local pubs. The street lighting illuminated countless excited, happy faces. The remains of a discarded hot dog squelched under my foot.

A figure stood at a gloomy corner near a group of men who'd taken part in the Tar Barrel Burn. I couldn't see his face because he was turned away from me, towards an alleyway that led to the harbour, but I recognised the dark clothes and stocky appearance of my attacker.

I jabbed a shaky finger at him as he started to walk away. 'That's him!'

Roy stopped mid stride. 'Where?'

'There. On the corner.' I pushed past a couple of women wearing white masquerade masks and broke into a sprint, my bruises forgotten in the fever of the moment.

Ahead, my attacker slipped into the crowds and disappeared from view.

I nearly collided with an elderly couple holding a decorative lantern, mumbled my apologies and dodged past them to catch sight of him again, still walking.

'Get him!' I shouted to no one in particular.

Revellers paused as if I'd gone insane, and nobody tried to stop the man I was hellbent on catching.

I was getting closer. 'Hey you, stop!'

He slowed, then started to turn. We confronted each other in a small square off Squeeze Belly Lane with an audience of at least twenty baffled people.

'You…' I gasped. My voice trailed away. It wasn't him. This man was wearing a white disguise only covering his eyes, nothing like the full-face Venetian mask which would feature in my nightmares.

'What the…?' His thick lips were contorted, his forehead creased.

'I thought you were somebody else.' I sucked air and my heart thumped.

'Christ, for a horrible moment I thought you were my ex-wife.' He sniggered. There was the smell of beer on his breath.

A gasping Roy caught up with us as I floundered for a half sensible reply. 'It's not him,' I said to Roy. 'I made a mistake.'

I turned back to the man I'd chased through the crowds. 'I'm so sorry.'

Roy stepped forward. 'Kate's had a bit of a shock. It's a simple case of mistaken identity. All done in the heat of the moment.'

'No worries.' The man drifted away, the audience dispersed and we headed towards The Mermaid in the hope that we would find Danny there. On the way, we recovered my notebook, which was still lying open in the alleyway. The pen had been crushed in the scuffle and was useless.

The pub was still busy. Joe, Angie and a young lad called Jack were at full stretch serving thirsty drinkers.

I insinuated myself between a crowd of brawny trawlermen and caught Joe's eye when he finished drawing a pint. 'Have you seen Danny? I need to find him. It's urgent.'

Joe shook his head, his face shiny with perspiration. 'No,

I last saw him when he was with you before the parade. He might have gone up to his room. You're welcome to go and have a look. Second room on the right at the top of the stairs.'

With a breathless Roy following, I headed upstairs to a dimly lit landing. I knew it well because this was also the way to the ladies.

I rapped on the door to Danny's room, then again harder when I got no response. Still nothing. I pulled down on the door handle. It was locked. 'Danny...Danny...are you in there?' Nothing.

'He must still be out on the street somewhere,' I said to Roy. I called Danny's mobile, but it went straight to voicemail so I left him a message asking him to phone me urgently.

We walked back to the lounge bar where the crowd was starting to thin. Roy ushered me to a chair, his movements shaky. 'This needs to be reported as soon as possible. You wait here, Kate. I'm going to find a policeman.'

He slipped out the door and I was left alone, sore and dazed. Joe hurried over, his forehead wrinkled. 'Is everything okay?'

'Not really,' I blurted. 'I was attacked in an alleyway by some murderous bastard.'

Joe joined the growing list of people obviously shocked by the incident. 'My God, that's terrible. You look like you could do with a strong drink. Can I get you anything?'

'Thanks. A small Jameson would be lovely.'

Joe was back in no time with a glass brimming with whisky. 'Have it on us. It's the least we can do after what you've been through. I swear this parade gets wilder every year.'

I took no more than a couple of sips, determined to keep a clear head.

Roy reappeared at last with a uniformed officer in tow. Of all people, it was Police Constable Graham Dobson, known behind his back in St Branok as Dobbie. Dobbie and I eyed each other warily. We had history – in a professional sense.

The relationship between Dobbie and the Gazette was best described as strained. We needed each other, but that didn't mean our aims always coincided. Far from it. Dobbie viewed the Gazette as a necessary evil which could sometimes be of benefit to his enquiries but was far too nosy and asked too many questions. Our uneasy accord had reached a new low when the Gazette ran a campaign calling for more police action against local drug abuse. Dobbie had felt personally criticised.

Oozing weariness, he settled his bulk in a chair next to me and expressed token sympathy. 'Ms Tregillis, sorry to hear that you've been involved in an incident. Please talk me through the details.'

'I was attacked. The attacker— He's still out there somewhere…' My voice faltered at the memory of an encounter so brutal and unexpected I could scarcely believe it. My left knee began to shake. I steadied it with a hand.

Dobbie had his pen and notebook out. 'What did he look like? We can put out an alert.'

My description of a gold Venetian mask, stocky appearance and dark clothing emphasised to me how little I knew about my attacker. The likelihood of finding him was close to zero. Remove his mask and he was no different to dozens of other revellers.

Dobbie was unable to hide his exasperation when I told him about the Talan Bray warning hissed by my attacker. 'Ms Tregillis, my job is to maintain law and order in St Branok. It's not for me to tell you how to run your journalistic operations…' – he enunciated 'journalistic operations' as if they were distasteful – '…but you know as well as I do the strength of feeling in this community about the Talan Bray sinking. There could be a very nasty backlash if you insist on pursuing yet another campaign that needlessly upsets local people.' He added piously, 'We all have a responsibility not to incite violence.'

'Our enquiries aren't needless,' I said. 'They're justified. We're experienced journalists. We understand the risks. But I'm worried that Danny – my colleague, Danny Flanagan – might also have been injured tonight. He was leading our enquiries. I've tried to call his mobile several times since the attack but been unable to get through to him.'

'Yes, I know Mr Flanagan. Our paths have crossed a few times in recent weeks. Rest assured, we'll watch out for him and carry out the necessary checks to ensure he's safe and well.' I wondered about the circumstances of Danny and Dobbie's encounters but said nothing.

Dobbie eyed my glass of whisky. 'Most incidents at the festival are alcohol-related. We're able to resolve most of them without the need for formal complaints. Have you been drinking tonight, Ms Tregillis?'

Under the table, I clenched my hand. 'I had a small brandy here before the start of the procession and now a few sips of this whisky. What happened to me was nothing to do with alcohol. It was a vicious and calculated attack.'

The interview wound up. Having delivered the necessary spiel on the availability of victim support services and that I would be kept informed of developments, Dobbie departed armed with a written statement I'd signed. We'd agreed that the Gazette would publish an article appealing for witnesses to an alleyway incident without naming me as the victim.

Roy gently took my arm. 'Kate, you're very welcome to stay with us tonight if it helps.'

I brushed the drying mud off my jacket and jeans and cleared my sand papered throat, determined to restore some of my usual poise. 'Thanks but I'll be fine. Besides, I've left Rufus at home. I need to get back to him.'

'At least let me walk you to your car.'

'That would be nice.' Roy might be a frail, old man in his seventies, but I didn't want to be out alone.

I drove home slowly, very slowly. The Landy's heavy steering and agricultural suspension highlighted further injuries. The left side of my chest ached when I pulled the steering wheel to the right, and the lane's bumps and potholes sent ripples of pain up my bruised spine.

At the cottage, Rufus gave me the usual waggy, effusive welcome as if I'd been away for a year. I kissed and hugged him, gaining strength from his unrelenting love and muscular solidity.

'You'd have taken a bite out of that horrible man in the alleyway wouldn't you Rufie, eh boy?' I crooned. He licked my cheek.

After taking a shower and then brewing a strong coffee, I slumped into my battered easy chair in the sitting room with Rufus at my feet, trying to make sense of it all. Where was Danny? Was he safe and well?

CHAPTER NINE

A ringing phone woke me. Every fibre of me ached. Sore muscles and strained tendons had seized up during the night. I was fit for little more than a day in bed. But that wouldn't be enough for Rufus. He'd expect a clifftop walk or a stroll down into the cove. I'd have to find strength from somewhere to fulfil my share of the partnership, in which I provided walks and food and Rufus delivered warmth and companionship.

I added a sore left knee to my list of injuries as I limped down the stairs into the hallway. As is the way with ringing phones, it went silent when I reached for the receiver. A check on 1471 revealed that the call had come from Roy's home phone number.

I rang him straight back to prevent him doing anything silly like driving out to the cottage on a Sunday morning to check I was still alive and kicking – with my right leg, at least.

The mental and emotional trauma was hidden deeper, memories of the violence hitting me in flashes. I'd felt more scared and vulnerable than at any other time in my life. And, ironically, it hadn't happened in a dirty suburb of a war-torn city I'd visited in my national newspaper days but in my supposedly quiet, supposedly safe hometown.

'Morning, Roy, you called?'

'Hi, Kate, how are you?'

I stared out of the cottage window at a sunny Sunday without seeing it, imagining a cold, dark, damp alleyway. 'I'm okay; a few aches and pains but I'll survive. It's a pity there weren't any witnesses and that St Branok doesn't have a decent CCTV system like some other coastal towns.'

'I'm so sorry, Kate. All this must have been a terrifying experience.' Roy sounded as perturbed as when both my parents had been killed in a car crash on Bodmin Moor on a brutal, numbing day of disbelief and endless tears, half a lifetime ago.

'The article I told Dobbie I'd put in this week's Gazette about the attack might turn something up,' I said. I was clutching at straws.

'Yes, worth a try at least.' He paused and then said, 'Would you like to pop over for lunch? Marjorie is cooking up a lamb hotpot. There's always plenty spare. We'd welcome the company and the conversation.'

'You're very kind, but I'm going to have a quiet day at home with Rufus. It's a lovely day for a walk.'

'If you change your mind, don't hesitate to give me a call. We can always stretch a meal to three people.'

'Thanks. I don't know where I'd be without you.'

After the phone call, I held my head in my hands, consumed by flaring recollections of last night's horrors: the gold Venetian mask, the hissing threats, the iron grip on my throat, the fall and the numbing collision with the wall and the damp cobbles.

Rufus sloped downstairs on the hunt for his breakfast, the two features at each end of his body – his tail and his tongue – quivering. I got my creaking body moving, let him out by the back door and then bent a stiff and bruised spine to reach down and replenish his water and dog food. I stretched and massaged the parts I could reach. Of course, Rufus did the usual doggy thing of bolting down his food in two seconds then curling up near the warmth of the Aga. I poured a mug of coffee, pulled on a coat over my pyjamas and hobbled outside to a sunny corner in the cottage's small walled back garden. From this quiet, sheltered place, even the rush and crash of the Atlantic breakers was muted.

The caffeine in the hot coffee, laced with two heaped spoonfuls of sugar, overwhelmed the sour taste of old pennies lingering in my mouth as I struggled to get my thoughts in order and come to terms with what had happened. I was angry – at Danny, for stirring things up and leaving me in the firing line, and then, in more considered moments, at my attacker. As far as I could tell, Danny was just doing what investigative reporters do: investigate.

And where had he disappeared to last night? Had he also been attacked? Despite Dobbie's bland assurances, I worried for him.

I fished in my coat pocket and brought out a half full pack of Benson and Hedges. My first cigarette of the day. Today of all days, there'd be more, I had little doubt.

My hands were trembling as I cupped the flame, lit the tobacco and then took a long, satisfying suck of poison. It worked as it always did. The tension simmering in my stomach subsided, and for those few seconds the world seemed easier, more controllable.

I shouldn't be doing this. It was weak. It was destructive. It was killing me. But, heaven help me, it was blissfully good. I needed that soft flush of nicotine.

My gaze swept over my little kitchen garden. At the dilapidated greenhouse. At the corner where wild bluebells flourished in the spring. At the shrivelled remains of the runner bean plants I'd attempted to cultivate in the warmer weather.

When I'd bought the cottage three years ago, I'd had visions of an idyllic rural existence. Of dreamy evenings in front of a roaring fire. Of patiently tending beds of Cornish flowers. Of coming home. Of being close to Mum and Dad or whatever remained of them. They'd loved the Atlantic coast. Their spirits were still out there.

On a pauper's budget but with boundless enthusiasm, I'd whitewashed Gwel Teg's walls, hung cheerful red gingham curtains and placed a few sprays of wildflowers in milk bottles in strategic locations around the hall and kitchen. But rampant weeds had taken over the flower beds and the fire had become an occasional luxury as I spent more and more time at the office, battling to save the sinking ship that was the North Cornwall Gazette. At first, running the paper had been little more than a hobby. Then, as the money drained away, it'd become a fight for survival. A lonely fight for survival.

If only all those who knew me could see me properly – see the caring inner core hidden by the hard outer shell. To some of them, I was a dried-out husk who had long since left any femininity behind in the harsh proving ground of Fleet Street. Good old tough, indestructible Kate Tregillis. Hard as nails. Nobody's fool.

I shuffled inside to call Danny again. The cottage had no mobile signal unless you leant out of the window in one of the back bedrooms, so I always used the landline.

Danny's mobile went to voicemail again. Either it was switched off, out of range, in use or…perhaps it was lying in a gutter somewhere next to an owner who'd been murdered by a thug in a gold Venetian mask? Paranoia was setting in again. I rang several times more. No answer.

The nicotine boost faded.

I needed to do something, anything, to break me out of this grey, dour lethargy. As ever, Rufus got me moving. I changed into jeans, trainers, T shirt and a fleece and took him for a long walk along the cliffs, beyond the cove all the way to Tregloss Point. Slowly, very slowly, I warmed up. The aches and pains subsided. The limp eased.

The easterly breeze, cold but dry, tugged at my clothing as I tramped along the cliff path with my head down, assaulted by flashes of visual memory from the night before. I might have been walking on a grey, busy street in London for all the trouble I took to admire the view. Up ahead, a volley of barking from Rufus dispelled my dark thoughts. He was cavorting in the undergrowth, a picture of simple canine happiness. Behind him, the immensity of Waterlock Bay at low tide stretched down to a rippling blue sea tamed by the offshore wind.

I sank onto a rocky outcrop with a renewed determination to admire it all, to get something from the day. There was no better view in the universe than this. And when Rufus came to join me, I embraced his warmth. He leant against me, loyal and companionable. Out here, in the sun and the wind, my world started to become ordered again.

A mile offshore, a beam trawler surrounded by a cloud of gulls, their excited shrieks muffled by the breeze, returned to port with its 'wings' – long steel beams – held almost vertical.

When I got back to the cottage, tired in body but eased in mind, I cleared out the grate in the sitting room fireplace and brought in ash logs from the outhouse. As the spitting fire took hold, imparting a homely glow, I brewed myself a mug of tea. And made more phone calls. Danny's mobile continued to go unanswered so I tried The Mermaid. Young Angie picked it up, the background hubbub indicating that the typical Sunday lunchtime rush was in full flow. No, they hadn't seen Danny, she said. Despite being rushed off her feet serving a pub full of demanding lunchtime drinkers, she found time to check his room, but reported it locked and apparently empty.

I didn't have the nerve to ask her if she had a spare key.

Was there anything to worry about or was I descending into paranoia? Danny could be anywhere. He might be taking a bracing stroll on the beach (this was admittedly unlikely, knowing Danny) or sampling one of the other local watering holes (much more likely). Despite there being any number of innocent explanations, my fears for his safety grew. My curiosity, too. On an impulse, I dug out my London contacts book and found the name and number of my old editor at The Enquirer, Bob Fletcher. He didn't answer so I left a message, asking him to call me as soon as possible. If anybody would know about Danny Flanagan, it was Bob. He knew anybody who was anybody in London journalism – and quite a few people who weren't anybody.

Having done all I could, I settled down to stare at the fire. Rufus trotted over to stretch out on the hearth next to my feet, and I reached down and stroked his head. His thin tail thumped on the floor.

Finally, I sat back, closed my eyes and drifted into an unsettled doze.

CHAPTER TEN

Danny turned up at the office the following morning bright and breezy, sporting various injuries. A purple swelling and yellow discolouration ran from his eye down to his cheekbone, distorting the left side of his face, and there were scratches and cuts on his chin. He was also limping and, as he eased himself gingerly into his office chair, it was clear his injuries were widespread.

I dragged myself from my desk and hobbled over to where he was firing up his laptop. 'You look like you had an argument with a bus. What happened?'

Danny rubbed his forehead, one of the few parts of his face which remained unblemished. 'You should have seen the other guy,' he joked and then, seeing my serious expression, said, 'Oh, nothing to worry about. I was the victim of high spirits at the festival the other night. I happened across some young local fellas who told me to get my Irish arse back across the water. They'd had a few too many and one thing led to another...' His voice trailed away.

'It looks like a lot more than high spirits. What the hell is going on, Danny? What exactly are you up to? I also was attacked on Saturday night. Some bastard stopped me in an alleyway, strangled me and mentioned you. He said you should stop investigating the Talan Bray, that it was causing a lot of hurt. Anyway, the police have all the details.' I couldn't help sounding accusatory as my anger rose again at the traumatic memory of the alleyway horror.

Danny's eyes flickered. 'Mary mother of God, I'm so sorry to hear that, Kate. What did the police say?'

'The usual. They're putting out an appeal for witnesses, treating it as Actual Bodily Harm.'

Danny's open mouth closed and turned down at the corners. 'I've had enough dealings with bent flatfoots to know not to put much faith in them.'

'I wasn't born yesterday. I worked in London for many years, remember. There's no reason to think that the local police around here are guilty of anything more than a lack of imagination.'

'You'd be surprised what I've dug up since I got here.'

Roy and Emily stared at both of us with worried expressions. Emily's eyes were even wider than usual, and her mouth was a perfect circle. All this was proving quite an education for her. She was learning that local journalism could be more than re-writes and parking disputes.

I was doing a bit of staring myself. At Danny. 'What have you discovered?'

His gaze slipped sideways. 'It's still a theory at the moment – strong, but I don't yet have all the facts. Look, I'm simply doing what I said I'd do: investigating exactly what happened ten years ago.'

'Well, it certainly seems to be upsetting people. If it's creating enough hurt to result in us being attacked, perhaps we should give it a rest.' I was beginning to sound like Dobbie.

Danny clenched his jaw. 'Come on, Kate. Since when does a good reporter stop looking into a story because it's upsetting a few people? It shows that my enquiries are getting close to unearthing something which some people want to keep hidden. That sounds like the basis of a feckin' good story to me. Believe me, I've had worse in Ireland during the Troubles. If they want to start throwing shit around, then I'm ready for it.'

He was right. Of course he was bloody right. Three years buried in St Branok away from the bright lights had left me soft. I'd resigned myself to a life of clifftop walks with Rufus, half-hearted attempts at growing runner beans and feeling sorry for myself while seeking solace from a bottle of whisky in front of a cold, dark fireplace on winter nights.

'At least give us more detail,' I persisted, determined not to be put off so easily this time.

Danny ran a hand through his thick hair. The knuckles of his right hand were cut and bruised. So perhaps he had managed to extract some revenge on his attackers. 'There were lots of questions that never got answered,' he said. 'Why was no part of the Talan Bray ever found? What happened to the yacht the Talan Bray was supposed to be rescuing? It sent out repeated Mayday signals and then disappeared. No boat or people were ever reported missing.'

'We know all that already,' said Roy, who'd sidled over to take part in the conversation. 'It came out at the inquest and the maritime investigation. It was a terrible night. I can still remember it. Sixty-foot waves. The Talan Bray is at the bottom of the Atlantic somewhere. It's as simple as that.'

Danny grimaced as he rolled his shoulders. 'A lot of it is informed guesswork right now. But I know enough to believe that there are secrets about the loss of the Talan Bray that have never been revealed.'

'You need to tell us more, a lot more, if you're going to continue to represent the Gazette,' I said, my tone hardening.

Danny's voice deepened and there was a defiance and toughness in his features I hadn't seen before. 'I'm sorry, Kate. You can't tell me what to do. I'm a freelancer who is doing occasional work for the Gazette. I can go where I like and do what I want.'

My anger flared. I leaned over his desk. 'If you're going to take that attitude, you can do it somewhere other than the Gazette offices. You know as well as I do that you're much more likely to get people to talk to you if they think you're from the Gazette rather than an ambitious hotshot from London.'

He held up his hands in a placatory gesture. The friendly Danny Flanagan had returned. 'Okay, okay. I'll tell you as much as I can. I've mainly been asking around about John Harding.'

I gaped at him. 'You've lost me. Who the hell is John Harding and what's he got to do with the loss of the Talan Bray?' Even as I asked, the name was sounding familiar.

Roy took his empty pipe out of his mouth to cut in. 'John Harding was the luckiest man alive, or that's how the national press described him ten years ago. John was the second mechanic on the Talan Bray. When the shout went up that a yacht was in trouble out beyond The Mouls, he was the only regular crew member who didn't answer the call. He was supposedly suffering from a bout of flu, and his place was taken by one of the runners who'd turned up hoping to fill a vacancy. A nineteen-year-old lad called Seth Maltby went aboard and died as a result.'

'Is it normal procedure to bring in a teenager at short notice in extreme weather conditions?' I said.

'Younger lads than Seth have been to sea with the St Branok lifeboat,' said Roy. 'Most crew members are volunteers. They can't be available one hundred per cent of the time. When the shout goes up, a number of runners also attend, hoping to get aboard. They're usually young men with ambitions to join the regular crew, which is of course a great honour. Seth had been an inshore fisherman for several years. He was well used to the Atlantic, a good seaman.'

I turned back to Danny, who was gazing at his battered hands now spread flat on the table. What was going through his mind? 'So, what interests you about John Harding?'

Danny's bright eyes found mine. 'Harding left St Branok after the disaster and hasn't been heard of since. He told his friends he'd had enough of the lifeboat, St Branok and everything about Cornwall and that he'd be starting a new life elsewhere.'

'Where?'

'Nobody knows. Some say he went to Wales, others say Scotland. I've even been told he emigrated to Canada. I've been making lots of enquiries but can't find any trace of him so far. Basically, he disappeared.'

'It's not surprising that Harding wished to start a new life after the loss of the Talan Bray,' I said. 'The huge amount of speculation into the loss of the lifeboat would have been traumatic for him. And he might well have felt a personal responsibility for the fact that a young man took his place and died as a result. In a close community like St Branok, that would be a terrible cross to bear.'

Danny shook his head. 'That doesn't explain why he severed all his links with St Branok. Harding had lived here most of his life. He had many friends, none of whom have heard from him since he left. But the thing that really got me thinking was when I visited Seth Maltby's mother. She lives on the new housing estate at Trecarne. She's still bitter about the death of her son and hates Harding. She reckons he wasn't ill at all on the night of the disaster, says he'd been seen drinking in The Mermaid earlier in the day.'

'So, Harding had a heavy drinking session in The Mermaid and wasn't in a fit state to answer the shout? He wouldn't have wanted to admit he was half drunk so he claimed he had the flu.'

'Or it might be that Harding had a reason not to be on the Talan Bray that night,' said Danny. The fire in his eyes was brighter and lasted longer.

'What possible reason might he have had? He couldn't have known in advance that the Talan Bray was going to be lost.'

'Couldn't he have?'

I stiffened. 'What the hell do you mean by that?'

He chewed his lower lip. 'I have some theories, but to be honest they're so off the wall it's best I wait until I carry out more investigations.'

'That's not good enough,' I said. 'What you're doing is affecting us all. Come on, Danny, you need to be more open with us.'

He wriggled in his chair. 'If I told you what I'm thinking right now without proper evidence, you'd label me as a crazy man. I should know a lot more in a couple of days. I'll make more enquiries and get back to you with a proper update no later than Thursday.'

I drummed my fingers on the desk, the nails bitten to the quick over the past twenty-four hours. If it was only me at risk, I'd tell Danny to go for it, but there were others to think about. 'If you're going to dig deeper, any of us here might be in danger – not just you and me but even Roy and Emily.'

Roy stepped forward with an eagerness I hadn't seen for a long time. 'Don't stop on my account. I can take care of myself, and I don't think Emily's in any danger. Everybody local knows she's a trainee. If there's any more aggravation, it'll be targeted at Danny and possibly you, Kate, as editor.'

I chewed the remains of a fingernail. Was there a real story here or was it all a figment of Danny's lively imagination? The truth, as Danny had pointed out earlier, was that I couldn't stop him investigating. He was a freelancer, free as a bird: a journalist able to sell his story anywhere he chose. If I told him to get out of our offices, I'd lose any opportunity for the Gazette to be part of the story. The prospect of a major scoop reawakened my reporter instincts.

'Okay, Danny. Keep investigating, but so long as you are using our offices I want to be kept informed with a detailed briefing by end of Wednesday and then daily updates. And remember, the Gazette must have first crack at any story you dig up. I don't mean a story full of speculative crap. I mean a properly researched story with hard facts.'

Danny ran a thoughtful hand across his jaw. 'Sure. You can rely on me.'

Could I rely on him? I wondered. I really wondered.

As our impromptu meeting broke up and I walked back to my desk, I had a queasy feeling that my decision might come back to haunt us all, that we were being led down a tunnel with the promise of light at the end by a person we hardly knew.

Danny remained an enigma.

CHAPTER ELEVEN

My old London boss, Bob Fletcher, rang me back late the next day while I was buried in preparations for that week's edition of the Gazette. He could scarcely have rung at a worse time. We were having tech problems with the layout of some of the inside pages, which were already late being sent to the printers. I recognised his number and picked up immediately, trying to clear my head of all the office nonsense.

'Kate, it's Bob from The Enquirer. Sorry I couldn't get back to you earlier. It's been one of those weeks. Bloody mad house here. How's life in Cornwall?' Same old Bob. Same world-weary London voice, laced with humour and roughened by chain-smoking. He'd been a demanding bastard when I'd worked for him, crushingly condescending when he thought a reporter had failed to make the most of a story, but ready with fulsome praise when he detected something special. We'd had some blazing arguments but also delivered wonderful worldwide exclusives – and enjoyed riotous nights at the Three Abbots, a 'spit and sawdust' pub in a back street around the corner from The Enquirer.

I strolled out of the editorial offices to stand in the corridor, determined that my enquiries into Danny's background should not be overheard by Emily and Roy, who were busy at their desks. Danny himself was out and about – as usual.

We wasted a minute or so commiserating on the state of the newspaper industry and then Bob came to the point. 'What can I do for you, Kate?'

'I've got a guy working with me called Danny Flanagan. He claims to have worked as a top freelancer in London. For The Enquirer among others. I wondered if the name rings any bells.'

'Flanagan…Flanagan…when was he working here? Recently?'

'Yes, very recent. He also claims to have worked as a staffer for some of the big Irish newspapers.'

Bob was silent for a few seconds while he racked his alcohol and nicotine-infused but sharp mind. 'There was an Irish freelancer who helped out on the night desk for a few months. I didn't have much contact with him. Mid-forties, big, sociable guy, very sociable, in fact. A good operator. Worked hard, as far as I know.'

'Sociable' in Bob's world meant drinker. 'That sounds like him. What else do you remember?'

'He wasn't afraid to stick his neck out, had done cutting-edge reporting in the tougher parts of Northern Ireland. Before he came to us, he'd been working for one of those news agencies which are always hiring and firing and aren't too fussy about how they get a good story. He was beginning to make a name for himself when he disappeared off the scene. People thought he'd returned to Ireland, but perhaps he ended up in Cornwall. He was energetic and ambitious, so I guess I'm a little surprised he's in your part of the world.'

'Cornwall isn't a journalists' graveyard,' I said, doing my

best to quell my irritation. Bob was doing me a favour, trying to be helpful. He hadn't needed to return my call at all.

'Sorry, Kate. I'm sure it's a great place to live and work and that you dig out more than your fair share of scoops.'

I hoped he wasn't going to request the details of any scoops I'd written recently. Parking disputes and bring and buy sales didn't cut it in Bob's world of journalism unless they involved a member of the royal family or a disgraced politician.

He painted Danny as a hungry reporter. Hunger was good so long as it was controlled. But the unbridled ambition that often worked in London was likely to be disastrous in St Branok. The last thing I could afford was for the Gazette to be the subject of libel proceedings as a result of a speculative article written by Danny. That would be the iceberg that sank us.

Bob turned jovial. 'So, have you had enough of Cornwall yet? I was hoping you were calling to ask for your old job back.' He added, more seriously, 'You're too good, Kate, not to be at the centre of things in London. You're wasted down there.'

I gripped the phone receiver tightly. Bob had hit a nerve. 'Thanks, but I'm happy here. It's the only place I feel at home.'

He sighed. 'Well, if you change your mind.'

'Sure. You'll be the first to know.'

As I rang off, I was thinking hard – not about Danny but about Kate Tregillis. I'd told Bob I was happy in Cornwall. Was I? Yes, I adored the sun and the sea and the surf and the cottage and the scraggy runner beans – and Rufus. But there was also the debt, the financial battles and the inevitable humdrum nature of running a small weekly newspaper on a shoestring, where pages had to be filled every week with whatever local material you could lay your hands on. The problems loomed like storm clouds gathering on an Atlantic horizon.

And there was the loneliness. I missed the adrenaline-charged nature of London journalism, the camaraderie and the competition, the hustle and bustle. I'd walked away from all that not appreciating how much it had become part of me.

It hurt, really hurt, to think that people like Bob now viewed me as being stuck in a dead-end job in a forgotten rural backwater. And I was only too aware of the disdain with which national journalists viewed local press as dusty country yokels. Bob wouldn't say that to my face – he was a friend, after all – but he'd be thinking it.

The rest of the day passed in a whirl of admin, tense phone calls with the printers, another fiery conversation about advertising with Brenda and any number of other small but essential issues.

Danny appeared eventually with the mellow scent of beer on his breath and a glint in his eye, though he seemed sober. He flipped open his scruffy notebook and began typing on his laptop.

I sidled over to perch on the corner of his desk. 'You look happy. How are the investigations going?'

'Promising. Very promising. That theory I mentioned to you? The more I find out, the more it seems right on the money. It's a massive story.' He glanced up at me, then returned to typing.

I expected him to say more. Some hope. Danny was a man of few words when he wanted to be, and a man of plenty of words when blathering nonsense over a pint at The Mermaid. Bob's description of Danny as a go-getting reporter had strengthened my determination not to be put off by vague assurances.

'You've got until the end of tomorrow to tell me what you know,' I reminded him.

Danny blinked at the hint that my patience was running thin. 'Sure. I just need to check a few more things. Believe me, this story is going to put the Gazette on the map.'

'You've told me that already.' I stomped back to my own desk, wishing I could employ a few techniques beloved by the Gestapo and the KGB to get to the truth. Waterboarding, thumb screws, Chinese water torture…you name it. Danny deserved all those and more. 'This story better be watertight,' I muttered. Now I sounded whingey.

I slumped down in my chair, gave Danny an accusing glare, which he didn't notice because he was still typing, and then with a defeated sigh looked back at my own computer screen. Now, where was I with my own mind-blowing story? Oh yes, the St Branok branch of The Lions Club had raised two hundred and eighty seven pounds at its monthly bring and buy sale.

The autumn days were drawing in relentlessly. Daylight was already beginning to fade and Rufus, curled up in a corner of the office, hadn't had a proper walk all day. There was no way I had time to take him out, so I cajoled the ever-helpful Emily to give him a run on the town beach. I doubted it was the kind of traineeship she'd been expecting when she signed up, but bless her, she didn't complain. She loved Rufus too.

With my mind continually returning to the issue of Danny and his supposed scoop, I took twice as long as usual writing a story about local residents demanding a traffic calming scheme in a nearby village.

I was becoming obsessed. But with what? The prospect of a sensational story which would put the Gazette on the map or Danny himself? He was a character of contradictions: a middle-aged man with a boyish charm, which he exploited to the full, who was naive and yet knowing, warm and yet distant. You bathed in the warmth of those smiling Irish eyes and couldn't help but wonder what was going on behind them.

Something didn't quite fit. Something wasn't quite right. But three weeks of working with him had left me none the wiser.

Or was I just seeing shadows which didn't exist?

CHAPTER TWELVE

Weary and despondent, I drove down the bumpy lane leading to my cottage. It had been dark for at least two hours. The Atlantic wind was whistling and a heavy shower had left the tarmac glistening and slippery. The chunky tyres of the Landy sloshed through murky water collecting in the potholes and ruts.

Outside Gwel Teg, I brought the Landy to a gritty, grinding halt and heaved on the handbrake. Surges of pain jolted through my back, still bruised and weak from the assault in the alleyway, and my stomach was spasming with hunger. So much for Bob Fletcher's vision of me living the carefree, outdoor Cornish life. Rufus shook himself, yawned and stood up on the car's back seat, ready to leap out as soon as I hauled open one of the squeaking rear doors.

I hadn't eaten anything since a slice of toast for breakfast, and there wasn't much in my cottage's kitchen cupboard or fridge for an evening meal. A tin of tuna, boil-in-the-bag rice, an onion and a tomato meant I could concoct a risotto of sorts. It would have to do. I had no time, energy or patience to drive back into town. Not at this time of night.

On the doorstep, I fumbled with my bunch of keys. I needn't have bothered. The door swung inwards before I'd turned the key in the lock.

I halted on the threshold, my stomach tingling. A sudden urge struck me to jump back into the Landy, perform a rapid U-turn and go in search of a safe haven for the night – the Gazette offices, if necessary. I could return to Gwel Teg in daylight when everything would be lighter and less sinister. But something else stopped me beating a panicky retreat. My pride perhaps. And Rufus, who was as formidable a friend as anybody could wish for. It was hard to imagine anybody wanting to take on his razor-sharp teeth.

So, I stayed on the doorstep breathing deeply, quelling my nerves and gathering my wits. I was being paranoid, surely. Had I forgotten to lock up this morning in my rush to get to the office? It was a possibility after everything that had happened.

This was silly. This was stupid. This was my home. Nobody and nothing would ever stop me coming here.

I reached inside and switched on a light. The hallway was its usual minimalist self: a slate floor, a small table with a telephone, a wooden chair and a rug, ruckled and curling at the corners.

Nose glued to the ground, Rufus slipped past me and headed into the kitchen. I followed, reassured by his insouciance. He finished off the remains of a half-eaten bowl of dog food while I looked around.

I moved into the sitting room, hypervigilant. The battered easy chair, my favourite spot on winter evenings when it was too dark or cold to spend time in the garden or out on the cliffs, was pulled up close to the fireplace. Exactly where I'd left it the night before.

All normal. All undisturbed.

Still…

I walked back into the hallway and switched on the upstairs light.

'Rufus, Rufus, come here, boy.'

His feet pattered on the kitchen floor and he appeared, his head cocked to one side. I stroked his wiry fur and led my four-legged bodyguard upstairs to complete the search.

On the landing, I stopped again, straining my ears. The wind, rising and falling, was louder up here. Surf crashing in the cove below was also more intrusive.

The landing light was a naked bulb, desperately in need of the lamp shade I'd been planning to buy for the past three years. Its harsh brightness illuminated the landing and most of the three bedrooms and bathroom leading from it.

One day I'd spend serious money and get the whole of the inside of the cottage sorted: new furniture, warm carpets and thick rugs. One day. But not now.

A window in my bedroom, held on a latch, rattled. I strode over to close it without bothering to turn on the room's overhead light. The wooden window frame was bloated from the recent rains and shutting it took a few tugs. Rain pattered on the glass and I shivered at the cold air that had crept inside.

Rufus was sniffing in the corners. He gave a little growl, and the hairs on the back of my neck sprung to attention. 'What's up, Rufie?'

I stroked his head and got a wet lick in return. His firm, hairy body pressed against my left leg in a doggy hug.

And then I saw it. A brown business envelope lay on the bed. On the pillow. My pillow. I picked it up with tingling fingers. It was sealed. KATE was written in block capitals with a blue pen.

I inserted my index finger behind the flap and ripped it

open. The corner of a sheet of white paper peeked out. I snatched it out of the envelope and moved closer to the doorway to examine it in a better light. One edge was rough and uneven, as if somebody had folded a sheet of A4 paper and used the crease to tear it in two.

Somebody who'd broken into my cottage, invaded my privacy.

The writing was in capital letters, as if scrawled by a child. But the meaning was anything but childish.

STOP YOUR FUCKING LOVER BOY FROM HURTING PEOPLE WITH HIS STUPID QUESTIONS ABOUT THE TALAN BRAY

My hands shook. I dropped the sinister message on the bed as if it was too hot to hold, but I was unable to look away, mesmerised.

One simple letter with a simple message – and so much more implied. It said: *I can come to your home. I can walk into your bedroom. You're not safe here if I don't want you to be. Nowhere is safe for you.*

Gwel Teg, my home, had been violated.

Could they still be hiding here? I swung round and listened, but there was only the wind in the nearby trees and the surf in the distant cove, muffled since I'd closed the window.

Rufus jumped onto the bed and stretched himself out with his nose resting on his front paws. My fear subsided. If anybody was here, he'd bark the house down. But I still carried out a search of the whole cottage, every nook and cranny, every closet, even the cupboard under the stairs. Twice. Of course, I found nothing. If not for that message, that short terrifying message, it would be another quiet evening at the cottage with Rufus and a hastily concocted meal for company. Everything was normal and ordinary and yet somehow changed.

I reinforced the front door by propping a chair against it and then snatched up the phone to dial Dobbie. It went to answering machine. I left a message asking him to phone me as soon as possible. It was all I could do to avoid sounding panicky.

I stared at the handset for a few seconds and then called Roy. I didn't know why. There was little a frail septuagenarian several miles away could do to make me any safer or more secure, but his mellow, authoritative voice was comforting. On the phone, it was possible to believe that Roy was still the robust editor of decades ago.

'Sorry to bother you, Roy…' My voice faded as the appropriate words deserted me.

'No problem at all, Kate. Marjorie and I were just finishing dinner. What's up?'

'Oh, I'm sorry. Have I interrupted your meal? I can call back later.'

'No, no, we're finished. You sound upset.' So much for my pathetic attempt at hiding my emotions.

The knuckles of my hand holding the handset were white. 'Somebody's broken into the cottage. They left a threatening note demanding that Danny stop his investigations into the Talan Bray.'

'Have you called the police?'

'Yes, yes, I left a message on Dobbie's phone.'

'If he's not available, you could try the police control.'

'There's no point. They're unlikely to investigate at this time of night.'

Roy was silent for long seconds. At last, he said, 'Come and stay with us until all this is sorted out. The spare room barely gets used these days and Marjorie would welcome the chance to chat to somebody other than me in the evenings.'

The thought of staying at Roy's cosy terraced house near the seafront in St Branok was enticing. But if I succumbed to its temptations, the cottage would become even more cold and hostile. I wanted to confront this threat head on. 'Thanks, but I'm fine. I've got Rufus. He'd tackle an army of intruders.'

'Well, the offer's always open. Is there anything else I can do to help?' Roy was struggling to understand my reason for calling him. In truth, so was I. I'd again turned down his offer of accommodation so there was no practical way he could help other than as a shoulder to cry on. And I didn't do crying.

I sighed. 'No, but thanks for the offer. It was just such a bloody shock finding that note. I needed to talk to somebody.'

In the background, Marjorie was asking who was on the phone.

'It's Kate, luv. A threatening message has been left at her cottage.'

Marjorie said, 'Oh my goodness,' and I imagined her standing in their tidy hallway, her rounded, motherly features pale and slack.

Roy said to me, 'Let's talk it over with Danny in the morning. Things will seem brighter and we'll all feel a lot better for a good night's sleep. Danny's hitting lots of raw nerves with his investigations.' His unflappable tone was reassuring.

'Yes, you're right. It was such a shock, though…in my home of all places. See you…see you in the morning.'

I put down the handset, trying to get past the simmering

panic and to think logically. Somebody was hellbent on bringing a halt to Danny's enquiries – determined enough to break the law, to break into my cottage, to beat me up. Was it simply a case of Danny raking over old hurts and causing distress or was he uncovering something more significant? The nagging uncertainty about Danny returned with a vengeance.

If only I knew him better.

Hunger gnawed at me. I still hadn't eaten.

The need for a weapon occurred to me as I chopped the tomato and onion for the 'risotto'. Yes, I had Rufus and he would never let anything happen to me, but something to hand would be comforting. There were the shears in the garden shed, but they were unwieldy and, as I'd discovered when I tried to cut back the rampant rhododendrons in the summer, as blunt as my brain cells after a few drinks at The Mermaid.

My best kitchen knife was blunt and worn – and had a four-inch blade. That would have to do, at least for tonight. Tomorrow, I would stop off at the Dreckly Harbour Store and buy a wickedly sharp fish filleting knife stretching to seven inches. Short of a baseball bat or a Kalashnikov, it was the best I could think of.

I wolfed down my evening meal almost as quickly as Rufus devoured his, and then I settled myself in my familiar seat by a cold, dark fireplace in the sitting room with a stiff whisky and only Rufus for company. No warming fire tonight. I couldn't be bothered. But a whisky involved nothing more than twisting a screw cap and sloshing liquid into a glass.

I tried to limit myself to no more than two fingers of whisky, but old London habits die hard and too often during long evenings I resorted to three or even four fingers. Tonight it was four bordering on five. That glorious smoky tang hit the back of my throat as I glugged down the first mouthful. My body thawed. Rufus settled next to my feet, his black eyes fixed on me, unblinking. He sensed my anxiety. We were kindred spirits, as Anne of Green Gables might say.

I reached down to rub his coarse fur, and his scraggy tail thumped a few times on the rug. Another slug of whisky slipped down my throat, more measured this time, and I slumped back in the chair reflecting on the latest twist of the knife by my mystery enemy.

The threats against me were growing by the day.

CHAPTER THIRTEEN

I slept somewhere between badly and not at all, tossing and turning, half expecting a shadowy figure to appear in the doorway of my bedroom.

In the early hours, a drumming on the windows marked the arrival of heavy rain. I tiptoed downstairs to make myself a mug of tea and, with my hands wrapped around its heat, spent several minutes standing in the dark, beside the kitchen window. I tried to be rational. A security light at the front of the cottage and better locks would help. I would get them fitted as soon as possible. Having a plan eased my angst a tad. Reassured, I went back upstairs and lay down again.

At last, that endless night came to an end and I rose tetchy and tired from a rumpled, sweaty bed to drive into the office with Rufus curled up in the back of the Landy and that brutal message taking pride of place on the front seat next to me.

A bright Cornish morning of shining wet roads and vibrant seas helped to lower my bubbling anxiety. Shafts of sunlight broke through towering clouds to create pools of brightness in the grey of the ocean as I reached the high ground before descending into town. A snatching breeze ruffled the tops of the hedgerows.

When I turned onto the seafront road, a man and a woman clad in wetsuits and carrying surfboards were heading down to the beach with nothing more important on their minds than catching a big wave. Their faces expressed a simple, heartfelt joy. Oh, to be them. Surfers by day, lovers by night, spending long, cold nights intertwined in each other's pulsing warmth and deep, steady breathing, savouring the taste of the other's salty skin. One of them would be gently woken by the other. Softly, very softly. Wet, needy mouths would come together, tongues would explore and bodies would press against each other.

A sigh escaped me. I'd never known a proper, long-lasting love of the intensity I imagined for those two surfers. I was a newspaper woman through and through, and for that I'd paid a price. Too thick skinned and independent for many men. Always a colleague, rarely a partner. There'd been a few flings, one more special than the others. For a few heady months, I'd hoped…only for us to eventually go our separate ways, intent on furthering our careers.

The daydream dissipated and my usual matter-of-fact self was back in charge by the time I strode into an empty office with Rufus at my heels. Ready to take on whatever might be coming my way. Head-on, if necessary. I'd find out who left that awful message and I'd confront Danny yet again and demand to know what he was up to. No half answers this time.

I kept myself busy until the others arrived, making the usual calls to the emergency services to check if there'd been any incidents overnight and polishing off a few re-writes of reports sent in by local clubs and organisations.

Emily arrived not much later. She was using a different desk, nearer to Danny. Was a young crush developing? She laughed readily at all of Danny's jokes, of which there was no shortage, and was regularly at his desk asking for advice. Oh dear, that could make office life complicated.

Danny appeared next with a cheery, 'Morning to yer all.' He was as buoyant as always, the opposite of how I was feeling. His injuries were healing well, and the autumn wind and sun had given his skin a golden glow. The breezy Cornwall air was doing him a power of good.

Roy arrived last and immediately made his way over to me, the lines on his face deepening. 'Are you okay, Kate?'

I dredged up a rueful, forced smile. 'I'm fine. The whole thing seems a bit bizarre now.'

Roy sat in a chair next to me. He was breathing quite hard. Even the flight of stairs up to the editorial offices left him breathless these days. 'I'd describe it as more dangerous than bizarre. Do you have the note with you?'

I nodded, removed the envelope from under an old notebook on my desk, pulled out the message and placed it in front of Roy, who studied it in silence.

Danny walked over to stand behind Roy. 'What is all this?' he said as two deep creases formed on his broad forehead.

'A note left at my cottage last night.' I avoided saying I'd found it on my bed. It was too intimate a detail to share with Danny.

Danny's eyes were wide. 'What's all this lover boy crap?'

My weariness got the better of me. 'You tell me. What have you been saying to your drinking pals at The Mermaid?'

Danny stepped back, those affable features of his stretched with surprise. 'Nothing. I wouldn't ever discuss anything about you and me with those guys.'

A hot flush rose up my neck and settled in my cheeks. Both Roy and Emily were looking at me. 'There's nothing to discuss,' I blurted. 'There's no "you and me".' I stopped talking, aware I was digging a massive hole.

Roy stepped in, saving me from further torture. 'Have you managed to speak to Dobbie yet?'

'I'm still waiting to hear from him. I tried again early this morning, but he didn't pick up.'

'If he hasn't got back to you within a couple of hours, I can call a senior police contact of mine in Truro,' said Roy. 'I expect Dobbie will respond quickly enough then.'

A deep breath helped me to recover my equilibrium. The flush subsided.

'What's the latest on your investigations?' I asked Danny, putting on my best 'don't muck me about' expression.

Danny went back to his desk and picked up his tatty notebook. 'Well, as it so happens, I have at last tracked down the luckiest man alive.' His pause for effect was almost smug.

I froze. 'Harding?'

'The very same. He hadn't gone as far afield as people thought. He's living in Plymouth, of all places. I've got an address but no phone number, so I'm thinking of having a day out in Plymouth on Saturday to chat with him face to face.'

'Who told you?'

'An old girlfriend of Harding's.'

'I might come along,' I said, aware that Roy and Emily were gazing at me again. A cosy trip together to Plymouth would fit the ridiculous suggestion in the note, but I needed to better understand what Danny was up to. His continual assurances that he was dealing with the whole issue diplomatically were ringing hollow.

Danny grinned. 'Great idea. Shall I drive, or will you?'

'I'm not sure the Landy will make it all the way to Plymouth,' I said. 'Probably best to go in your car.'

The impromptu meeting was broken up by two phones

ringing at once – the one on my desk and the one on Danny's. As I reached mine, Danny was already talking animatedly. 'Thanks for ringing back. Yes, I just wanted to ask you about…really…really.' He scribbled in his notebook, holding the handset between shoulder and ear.

Then my attention was taken by my own caller. Dobbie. At last.

'Ms Tregillis, I got your messages. More threats, I understand?'

'Yes, my cottage was broken into yesterday and a note was left with another warning about our investigations into the Talan Bray.'

Dobbie sighed. Reckless journalists were taking up too much of his time these days. 'I could call in at your office before lunchtime. I'd also like to speak to Mr Flanagan.'

'Okay, I'll let him know.'

I replaced the receiver and looked for Danny.

No sign.

Footsteps rapped on the stairs down to reception.

'Where's he gone?' I said to Roy.

He shrugged. 'No idea. He said it was urgent. Asked me to tell you he'd be gone for the rest of the day.'

I went to the window and glimpsed the broad figure of our Irish recruit heading purposefully down the main street, his destination another mystery.

CHAPTER FOURTEEN

Fingerprints were taken from Gwel Teg and the hateful note, but only mine were found. Dobbie made a flippant comment about my needing to be more careful with evidence in the future. He tracked down Danny and conducted the sort of laboured, heavy interview which sounded a repeat of the one he'd carried out with me. The importance of not 'needlessly' provoking violence was again emphasised.

'A sorry looking article. I don't think he'll be finding out anything worthwhile any time soon,' said Danny of Dobbie as we drove through the tired outskirts of Plymouth heading for John Harding's home.

Harding lived in a terraced house in the Devonport area, a seedy neighbourhood dripping deprivation.

Drizzle was falling from a dismal sky as we turned into a shabby street hemmed in by grey walls. We cruised in Danny's battered Volkswagen Golf past lines of equally shabby saloons and trucks to pull in behind a four-wheel drive so scratched and muddy it might have been used for extreme off-roading. With its faded green paint and missing hubcap, Danny's car looked right at home in deprivation street. Adding to the car's misery was a black round hole in the front grill where the VW logo should be, reminiscent of a person missing a front tooth.

Number forty-seven had been painted custard yellow but the city grime had taken its toll, dulling the brightness. Streaks of black trailed from the windows like tears tinged with mascara.

There was no sign of life in the neglected yellow house and no lights on despite the greyness of the day.

'The luckiest man alive,' Danny muttered with irony. Harding didn't look very lucky from here.

We climbed the steps and pressed the buzzer. It wasn't working, so we rapped on the cheap PVC front door. No answer.

'Are you sure this is the place?'

Danny shuffled on the doorstep, his hands in the pockets of his Burberry coat. 'This is the address I was given.'

'By the ex-girlfriend you mentioned?'

'Yes, she happened to come across Harding a few years ago in Plymouth city centre and he invited her back here. She still sends him a Christmas card.'

It sounded less than solid. I cursed myself for not asking more detailed questions before heading out on what might turn out to be a wild good chase. I could have been out and about walking the cliffs and beaches of the Atlantic coast with Rufus rather than standing here on a grubby Devonport doorstep. Still, we were here now. Might as well make the most of it.

There was a light on in the front room of the house next door. 'Let's try one of the neighbours,' I said.

The buzzer on the door of forty-nine also didn't work, but this time a sharp knock on the door got a reply. A woman in her thirties in trainers, trackies and sweatshirt, with a baby on her hip, opened the door. Warm air, tainted with the tang of cooking fat, washing and babies, filtered out onto the street. Could I have ever lived a life like this? As a mum, looking after a screaming toddler and endlessly changing dirty nappies and washing, washing, washing? Probably not.

'I'm looking for your neighbour, John Harding,' I said. 'Do you know if he's around?'

She nodded, friendlier than I'd expected. 'If he's not at home, he might be down the pub.' She added with a knowing look, 'He likes a drink or two, does our John.'

So, Danny's intelligence was correct. This really was Harding's bolthole. The trip wasn't a waste of time after all.

'Which pub?' I said.

The first glimmers of suspicion sparked in her eyes. 'The Albion. It's around the corner. Are you friends?'

'Yes,' I lied. 'We knew him when he lived in Cornwall and thought we'd look him up as we were in the area. How is he?'

Her expression eased. 'Okay, I think. To be honest, I don't see much of him from one week to the next.'

'Well, thanks. We'll pop in at The Albion. We won't keep you hanging around on the doorstep in this weather.'

The Albion was one of those pubs which hadn't changed in thirty years. It was in a steady state of decline, catering for a diminishing clientele, navy types many of them, interested in little more than hard drinking. The outside was painted light blue – a less garish colour than the yellow of Harding's home, but it still made The Albion stand out from the grey buildings nearby. It did nothing to add sophistication, however.

We stopped outside the tired blue edifice for Danny to pull out a picture of the St Branok lifeboat crew of 1990. 'Harding's the third person on the left,' he said. I squinted to remind myself of his appearance. Stocky, average height, close cropped brown hair, unremarkable in most respects. His smile was measured, not whole-hearted like most of the crew's. A shadowy reserve lingered in his eyes. But, of course, it's easy to jump to all sorts of ridiculous conclusions from a single photograph. Mother Teresa would have looked suspicious if pictured at an unfortunate moment.

Inside, cheap chairs and tables stood on bare, stained floorboards. Most were empty. The place reeked of stale beer. Saturday lunchtime wasn't a busy time for The Albion, if ever there was a busy time. Perhaps it got livelier when the navy was in town.

A barman, middle-aged with long sideburns and a substantial paunch which made Danny's torso look positively sylphlike, was cleaning glasses behind the bar. He made no attempt to acknowledge our arrival.

'I'll get these,' said Danny, as usual. 'What would you like?'

'A small dry white wine please,' I said. 'Put the drinks on your expenses. We're here on newspaper business, after all.'

Danny ordered a pint of 'the black stuff' for himself from the unsmiling barman and, drinks in hand, we scanned the room. The white wine was vinegary. Cheap Spanish plonk. A young couple sat holding hands at a table near the window and four scruffy middle-aged men, none of them Harding, were nursing pints on a table near the cold, empty fireplace. And that was it, at least from this vantage point.

We sauntered through the lounge bar into a smaller room. Two men sat at a table, heads down, talking. One of them was John Harding. He was a greyer, heavier incarnation of the person in the photo, but it was him. He had the same nose and the same hard eyes set more deeply in folds of skin.

There was something about the two men's posture and the way they sat together, hunched forward, talking in low voices, which discouraged an approach.

Danny and I chose a table in a discreet corner – just another couple, silent most of the time, able to hear the odd word uttered by Harding but not sentences. Occasionally, our eyes flicked over to the two men, who remained in a huddle. Harding seemed disgruntled, emphasising the points he was making with chopping gestures of his right hand.

Time passed. Danny glugged down his pint and I braved the vinegary wine. Our glasses were soon empty and still Harding and his friend, colleague or whoever it was remained in deep conversation. Harding became more frustrated. The other man whispered something which calmed him a little.

Danny got in another round. 'Our expenses claims are going through the roof this month,' he said.

I sampled the latest glass of caustic plonk, acting unconcerned although any additional expense, no matter how small, worried me.

At last, the discussion at the nearby table ended. Harding and his companion made for the door, and Danny and I followed at a respectable distance, leaving our latest drinks half full. The two men went their separate ways as soon as they reached the street with barely a parting word. No cheery goodbyes. They were not friends or, if they were, something had soured their relationship. Stony-faced, Harding zipped up his coat, pulled up his collar and, with hands in pockets, trudged off in the direction of his home.

'Let's wait until we get to his house,' I murmured. The encounter wouldn't get off to a good start if Harding thought we'd been following him.

Harding was slotting a key into his front door when I

went forward, leaving Danny at the bottom of the steps. An approach from a woman, rather than a big bluff Irishman, was more likely to get a favourable response.

'Mr Harding?' I gave him my friendliest look.

He paused, eyes wary. 'Who wants to know?'

'I'm Kate Tregillis from the North Cornwall Gazette. Can we have a quick chat?'

'What about?'

'We're doing a feature on the tenth anniversary of the Talan Bray, which includes an update on some of the people who were involved. We were hoping you had a few minutes.'

Danny joined us. The top step was getting crowded.

'How did you get my address?' After noting Danny's sizeable frame, Harding's tone had turned aggressive.

Danny edged closer. 'A friend in St Branok gave us your details.'

Harding turned the key. He seemed keen to be off the doorstep. 'Well, they had no fucking right. I've got nothing to say beyond what was reported in detail ten years ago. It's long in the past now and I certainly don't want to talk about it with the Gazette or anybody else for that matter. It was a terrible, terrible time.' He slipped inside and started to close the door in our faces. One of Danny's hefty brogues brought the door to a juddering halt.

Harding shoved harder. 'Get your bloody foot out of my house.'

Danny kept his foot where it was and leant in closer, pushing on the door. 'Mr Harding, all we're asking for is a brief chat. A few minutes, that's all.'

'Are you deaf? I told you I'm not reliving what happened for you or anybody else.'

Danny's face turned uncharacteristically cold. 'Do you

feel any guilt that you survived and a nineteen-year-old boy took your place and died?'

Harding heaved on the door, snarling at Danny's foot. 'You're talking bollocks. We all knew the risks. I'd have been on the Talan Bray that night if I hadn't been ill. Now get out the fucking way.'

Danny stayed right where he was, solid and immoveable, clearly no novice of doorstep journalism. It was further evidence that the friendly Irishman had his tougher side. 'But you weren't ill, were you? You were sinking pints in The Mermaid earlier in the day.'

'That's bullshit. I called in there for a few minutes to see a friend. I wasn't drinking pints of anything.'

Danny was relentless. 'Why did you leave St Branok? Why haven't you contacted Seth Maltby's family since the disaster?'

Harding stamped on Danny's brogue and, while the Irishman hopped around in pain on one foot, slammed the door shut. There was a muffled 'Piss off and don't ever bother me again' from behind the door.

We trotted down the steps and stood in the street. 'That went well,' I said.

'It might have been worse,' said Danny, ever the optimist. He twisted his battered foot. 'Wow, that hurt.'

'You should have told me you were going to go in hard on the illness angle.'

Danny was careful not to put too much weight on his battered foot as we headed back to the car. 'It was obvious he wasn't going to talk to us so I thought I might as well hit him with the key questions. See his reaction.'

I sighed. 'You're probably right. We did learn a few important things.'

'Such as?'

'That even after ten years the issue is still sensitive and raw. His comments fit with his having disappeared to escape the aftermath of the Talan Bray. He was determined to put it all behind him.'

The corners of Danny's mouth turned upwards. 'It must have been a mighty shock for him when we turned up on his doorstep. I bet he's wondering right now how many other people know where he's living.'

'We also learnt something else,' I said. 'If he's telling the truth, he didn't drink enough at The Mermaid to stop him answering the shout that night. He was sober and not too ill to meet somebody at the pub.'

We reached the Volkswagen and Danny jumped in to lean across and open the front passenger door from the inside. 'To my mind, it's mighty suspicious,' he said. 'By all accounts, Harding was a reliable lifeboat crewman. He always responded to an emergency.'

'What are you trying to say?'

'I'm saying that Harding knew the Talan Bray was doomed that night and he was determined not to be aboard.'

CHAPTER FIFTEEN

We headed back to St Branok, talking animatedly about Harding's disappearance and hostility.

'Why would anybody want to harm a lifeboat, of all things?' I said. 'It doesn't make any sense. The lifeboat is there for one reason – to save lives.'

'I have a theory,' said Danny as he shoved the Volkswagen's reluctant gear stick into fifth gear. 'But it's so fecking mad you'd think I was an eejit suggesting it. I need more proof.'

'Try me.'

'Monday,' he said. 'Wait until Monday. There are still a few things I need to check up on and then I'll give you the full griff.'

As the grey sprawl of Plymouth flashed by in a blur, a surge of optimism exhilarated me; we were on the verge of something huge. 'Okay, you've got until Monday, but then no more secrets. The Gazette is a small local newspaper. Any story we publish needs to be rock solid.'

'Sure, but this story will put the Gazette on the map. Sometimes, as journalists, we need to push the boundaries. You feel the same, I know.'

'You know hardly anything about me.'

'I know that you don't get to be a deputy editor on a

major London newspaper without being a damned good journalist.'

Memories of those heady days surfaced, but I pushed them away. 'All that was a long time ago.'

'You've still got that spirit in you, I can tell.'

'It's much easier being gung-ho when you have the backing of a multi-million-pound newspaper group,' I said. 'Now I run a small Cornish newspaper with limited resources.'

Danny chuckled. 'Much safer to stick with flower shows, long council meetings and re-writes of reports by the Women's Institute, eh? Is that it?'

'It's not as simple as that. We can't afford to get into any serious legal disputes. We're on the limit—' I stopped talking. Enough said.

As Danny's Volkswagen trundled with an uneven beat across the Tamar Bridge and then through villages and down country lanes, I wrestled with the caution, which had sapped me in recent times. Meanwhile, a steady whine from somewhere at the back of the car grew in intensity. I commented on it.

'It's nothing. It comes and goes,' Danny assured me with the blustering confidence of a man who knows nothing about a subject, and we drove on in the fading autumn light. As we left the main road, I directed Danny down a narrow lane much favoured by locals as a short cut. It would take a couple of miles off our journey and was wonderfully scenic.

The lights of St Branok were already twinkling as we crested the final rise. The ragged coast and a sombre Atlantic greeted us. I loved that view. It always brightened my mood. Nearly home.

Danny shifted down a gear. 'What do you say to a drink

at The Mermaid before I drop you home? We could grab something to eat as well. My treat.'

I hesitated. But Rufus was being looked after by my occasional dog minder, Suzie, and the thought of spending the rest of the evening alone in a cold, dark clifftop cottage was less than enticing. The warm, convivial atmosphere of The Mermaid on a Saturday night beckoned.

'Great. Thanks,' I said. 'A quick drink and a steak and then I'll need to get back home.'

'Sure,' said Danny, his cheeks flushing.

The Mermaid was packed with a local band, the Boomtown Besties, making a din, but we managed to ease our way through the crowds to the bar. Joe waved when he saw us. 'I see you two are socialising at weekends now,' he said.

My laugh was a little forced. 'Danny and I have just got back from a job in Plymouth and we decided to have a quick drink and something to eat before heading home.'

Joe pulled a pint of the local brew for Danny without asking, sure of his customer's preferences. 'Plymouth. That's a long way out of the Gazette's area, isn't it?'

'We went to see somebody you might remember from a long time ago,' I said.

Joe sloshed ice and lemon in my gin and tonic. 'Don't keep me in suspense, Kate. Who?'

'John Harding.' I paused for effect.

Joe handed over the gin and tonic. 'John Hard…John Harding, I know the name. Oh, you don't mean THE John Harding, the guy who survived the Talan Bray?'

'The very same. We wanted to run an article about what he's been doing since the sinking.'

'And what did he say?'

'He wasn't happy to see us. Said he'd put all that behind him.'

'Well, well, I wondered what'd happened to him. I heard he'd gone to Canada. How the heck did you find him?'

Danny tapped his nose. 'I have my sources.' In the background, the Boomtown Besties were killing a version of 'Fast Car'.

'Joe, can you rustle us up a couple of steak and chips,' I said. 'We'll try to find a table out of the way.'

'No problem. Let me know where you're sitting.'

Danny and I found a table for two in the snug, where the raucous mayhem from the band was less than deafening and we were able to talk.

He held up his pint. 'Here's to the dream team of Flanagan and Tregillis. I think we worked together brilliantly today.'

I clinked my glass against his. 'It's great to get away from the humdrum local reporting.'

Danny tilted his head. 'Sorry, I don't get it. What's an experienced journalist like you doing in a backwater like this?'

I took a sip of my gin and tonic. 'This is my home. I was born and raised here. I heard that the Gazette was going to be closed and so I stepped in to keep it going. I thought I'd get it back to its glory days.' I hesitated, trying to find the words to do justice to the unending struggle of the past three years without resorting to melodrama. 'But it's proved a lot harder than I thought.'

The steaks arrived and we ate them hungrily. They were thick and juicy and cooked just right. The Mermaid did a top-notch steak. Joe had a deal running with a local farmer noted for his grass-fed organic beef.

We lingered, chatting longer than I'd intended. As we finished, Danny raised his empty glass. 'Another gin and tonic?'

I sat back, fuller and happier than I had been in a long time. But enough was enough. 'No, I really should be getting home. I need to pick up Rufus from Suzie's early in the morning.'

The Flanagan smile bathed me in its warm and affable light. 'But the night is yet young. Come on, Kate, live a little.'

'The night might be young, but I'm not and I need my beauty sleep. And, besides, if you're driving me home, you need to stay sober.'

He shrugged. 'Okay, but one night I'm going to take you out for a serious drinking session, the Enniskillen way.'

We were both laughing as we strolled towards the door, and this time my laughter was easy. I went to wave goodbye to Joe, but he was nowhere to be seen.

The old Volkswagen huffed and puffed as we climbed out of St Branok before taking the minor road leading to Gwel Teg and a few other coastal properties and hamlets. I wondered if Danny harboured any thoughts of spending the night at the cottage. Well, he'd be disappointed. I'd had enough spur-of-the-moment relationships with colleagues to know they rarely worked out well, usually ending in embarrassed looks and stilted office conversations.

Blinding headlights broke my reverie. A car was coming up behind us fast – very fast – with its lights on full beam.

Danny squinted into his rear-view mirror. 'Who's this eejit? He's driving like a maniac.'

We reached a short section of straight road with the car behind sitting on our rear bumper. The high-pitched squeal of thrashing metal and tortured tyres rent the night air as the driver of the car behind changed down a couple of gears and red-lined his engine. He swerved into the oncoming lane to thunder past in a swirl of dirt and spray.

'Jesus, crazy driving,' said Danny. He was gripping the steering wheel with white knuckles.

'We should report that idiot to the police,' I said.

'I didn't get a registration number. Did you?'

The red tail-lights retreated rapidly into the distance until they disappeared around a corner. 'No, I'm not sure he had a number.'

Our pulses slowed. Danny's irrepressible humour returned. 'I've seen racers going slower at the Ulster Grand Prix. I thought Cornwall was supposed to be a quiet place of cream teas and lumbering tractors.'

We carried on, Danny driving steadily, perhaps more shocked than his humour suggested. 'We're nearly there,' I said. 'I'll be glad to get home—'

A piercing bang stopped me mid-sentence. The Volkswagen slewed sideways, rubber screeched and we careered towards a large oak tree on a corner while Danny wrestled to keep control. We missed it by a fraction, but then plunged through a hedge into a field. Twigs and branches slapped against the windscreen, the Volkswagen went up on two wheels and nearly overturned, then crashed down again. It slewed to a halt in thick mud with my side lower than Danny's.

I stared open mouthed at Danny, who was unpeeling his fingers from the steering wheel. 'Mother of Mary, that was a close one,' he said.

I tried to gather my wayward wits. 'What happened?'

'There was something in the lane, a block of some kind. It was right on the bend. I didn't see it until the last second.'

I gulped down a sob. 'That was bloody terrifying.' There was the tang of burning rubber from somewhere. I needed to get out, get clear. I unclipped my seatbelt and pushed hard against the door, my movements snatching and rapid. It wouldn't budge. I heaved again. It moved an inch but no more. 'I'm stuck. Help me!'

Danny got his door open and wriggled clear. 'Climb out my door.'

'I can't...the angle.'

Danny waded through glutinous mud to my side. 'It's okay. I'll pull your door open. Don't worry. I'll have you out in a second.'

I sensed his extreme exertion as he applied all his strength and bulk to the task. He grunted and groaned, and at last the door grudgingly opened. Something squealed as iron twisted and bent. I squeezed through the gap, full of frenzy, and crawled to safety on my hands and knees. My breathing was ragged. 'I thought I was going to get fried in there,' I gasped.

'We're out now. We're safe,' said Danny. He crouched by the side of his car, using his mobile as a torch. 'What a frigging mess. I'll have to get it towed out.'

He tapped buttons on his mobile and then sighed in frustration. 'Shit. I can't get a signal.'

I reached into my handbag, which I'd dragged from the car, and was unsurprised that my mobile was no better. 'Nothing,' I said. 'We're going to have to walk down to the cottage. It's not far. It shouldn't take long.'

Covered in slimy Cornish mud, we clambered through a prickly hedge to stand on the blessedly hard surface of the lane. The offending block was easy enough to find despite the darkness. A hefty slab of oblong concrete. Right on the bend. How it had got there was anybody's guess.

'Fallen off the back of a lorry, perhaps. Like most things in Cornwall,' Danny said, valiantly attempting the weakest of jokes. 'Seriously though, how the hell did that thing end up in the middle of the road?'

Straining every sinew, he pushed it to the side to prevent it being a hazard to anybody else who might come along.

I led the way towards the cottage.

Danny caught me up and we walked side by side. 'I'm so sorry, Kate.'

I forced a shaky laugh. 'I've heard of boyfriends pretending their car's broken down, but you didn't need to go to the trouble of a full-blown crash.'

'I only go to the trouble of a crash for the good-looking ones.'

I self-consciously brushed my hair behind my left ear. A jokey compliment, but still a compliment. There hadn't been many of those in recent years.

The lane was completely black where it was hemmed in by high hedges and trees. Our shoes crunched on leaves and gravel and mud washed into the lane from the nearby fields. 'Perhaps a kindly soul will come along and give us a lift,' said Danny.

'Out here at this time of year? Unlikely.'

'Ah well, two people shorten the road, so they say.'

The rumbling of a distant car coming towards us grabbed our attention.

'Maybe we'll get that lift after all,' said Danny. He stepped out in the road, waving energetically to flag it down.

The car slowed as it came near. We blinked in its headlights, which were still on full beam. The engine revved hard, and then the car shot straight at Danny, who, for all his size, was suddenly vulnerable and exposed.

I stood transfixed, dazzled, unable to be anything other than an onlooker. The car was going to smash into him. He was going to die or be seriously injured.

At the last moment, he dived out of the way into a hedge in a feat of athleticism which belied his heavy body.

He'd escaped. By inches.

CHAPTER SIXTEEN

In the darkness, I found Danny half sitting, half lying in the hedge, shaking his head, stunned. I reached for his outstretched hand and did my best to pull him up, almost falling into the hedge myself as I did so. He was even heavier than I'd expected.

Meanwhile, the car had raced on and disappeared down the lane at warp speed.

'Shite in a bucket,' Danny said as he stood in the lane. The departing car was now nothing more than an angry whine in the distance. 'This is turning out to be one helluva night.'

I brushed some of the mud off my jacket and jeans. It was hopeless. I was covered. 'Who…who the hell was that maniac?'

'I'm pretty sure it was the same idiot who overtook us earlier.' Danny's voice was hoarse. 'Are you okay, Kate? That was a right shocker.'

'I'm fine. Don't worry about me. You're the one who almost got run down.' I gulped down bile, determined to be the supporter rather than the victim, despite being battered and fragile. 'We can tidy ourselves up once we get to the cottage.'

I started walking again, desperate to get off this bloody lane – almost literally bloody. My right thigh was bruised, but the pain eased as I got it moving.

Danny drew alongside me, groaning. 'Have you got any booze at your fine place? I could do with a stiff one to calm my nerves.'

'I've got half a bottle of Jameson,' I said. 'You're welcome to most of that. Just leave a little for me.'

'Ah, Irish whisky. The best. You're a woman after my own heart so you are, Kate.'

'I seem to recall you saying something similar to Angie at The Mermaid when you first arrived in St Branok,' I pointed out.

'Yes, but I really mean it this time.'

When Gwel Teg hove into view, a half-moon had appeared between clouds, silvering the landscape and the wet road. In every sense, we'd emerged from the darkness. I rummaged in my handbag for keys, had a moment of thinking I'd dropped them in the confusion and then found them in an inner pocket. Thank heavens.

I unlocked the door and stepped inside. This was the first time Danny had visited Gwel Teg. 'It isn't what you might call plush, but it's home.' I caught my apologetic tone and added, 'And it's got the best views of any house on this coast.'

Surf was crashing below, the boom of each wave echoing off the cliffs. 'Sounds like the sea is damned close,' said Danny.

'It is. It's a fantastic place for clifftop walks. Rufus loves it. Each part of the coastline has its own unique sound. Hundreds of years ago, when visibility was bad, Cornish sailors would use the waves breaking on the shore to work out their position. Surf against a cliff sounds different from surf on a reef or a beach.'

The promised whisky bottle turned out to be well under half full, more like a quarter. My lonely evenings with only

Rufus for company had drained it more than I'd thought. I sloshed the remainder into two glasses, one full and one half full. Danny got the full glass.

He raised a quizzical eye. 'Wow, that's a hefty load. You don't do anything by halves, Kate. I'll give you that.'

'We deserve it,' I said.

My hands were shaking again as I raised the glass to my lips. Danny noticed. 'You sure you're okay? Maybe we should see a doctor.'

I gulped and clutched the glass harder. It stopped the shaking. 'No, no, I'll be fine. Really. That incident in the lane scared me.'

A frown swept across Danny's broad features. 'Me too. If I get my hands on the driver, I'll wring their fecking neck.'

His hands didn't look like they'd be good at wringing anything. For such a large man, they were surprisingly slim with long fingers – the sensitive hands of a pianist. But the nails were jagged and filled with dark mud from our adventures in the field.

'We need to report this to the police,' I said. 'I'll call Dobbie in the morning.'

Danny took a slug of his whisky. 'It needs to be investigated, sure, but don't expect too much from that work shy jobsworth. Pity we didn't get a registration number. We could have nailed the bastard. I'm pretty sure it was an old Ford Fiesta in a dark colour, like black or blue.'

'That reduces the list of suspects to about half the people who live around here,' I said. 'The town is full of clapped-out Fords.'

We sat at the kitchen table, drinking our whisky more slowly. A warm, fuzzy softness eased through my body. The alcohol was doing its work, taking me to a friendlier place for a little while.

My glass was empty already. 'I'm going upstairs to change. There's a spare room at the back of the cottage you can use. It's not the warmest, but the duvet is good.'

Danny leant forward. 'Much appreciated. By the way, you've got mud on your forehead.' He pulled out a polka dot handkerchief from a pocket of his Burberry and wiped it gently against my forehead. 'That's better.'

The caring touch of another human being silenced me. I stayed sitting. Frozen. Uncertain.

Danny was smiling gently, warm and understanding.

I got out of my chair and found my voice again. 'I need a shower. I'm absolutely filthy.'

Danny stood as well and stepped closer. There was a twinkle in his eye. 'I've been looking for a filthy woman for years.'

I ducked under his arm and headed into the hallway, light-headed – and not only from the alcohol. 'I'll let you know when the shower's free,' I called.

'Okay. Thanks.' He sounded disappointed but resigned.

I surfaced the following day to a tapping on my bedroom door. The door swung open to reveal a smiling, unshaven face. Danny was holding a mug of tea, which he placed on the small table next to my bed. I muttered a thank you while holding the duvet firmly beneath my chin. Underneath the duvet, I was naked.

'A cup of something to start the day,' he said, retreating to the door. 'I've finished the last of the milk. Sorry.' Outside, car tyres crunched on gravel. Danny looked out the window. 'Ah, it's here,' he said. 'I used your phone to order a taxi. I hope you don't mind. I need to get off to sort out my car before some farmer ploughs it into his field.'

I blinked in a ray of sunlight, which fell on my face through a gap in the curtains. 'I would've driven you into town. You didn't need to order a taxi.'

Danny turned at the doorway, his bulky body framed by the morning light. His coat was stained with Cornish mud on one side. 'You looked exhausted last night. You deserve a lie in. It is Sunday, after all. See you tomorrow.' And then he was gone. As the throaty sounds of the taxi died away, I lay in bed, sipping my tea, replaying the night before. What might have happened if I hadn't run from that awkward moment in the kitchen?

CHAPTER SEVENTEEN

The next day, among the mound of Monday morning mail waiting for me as I pushed open the Gazette's creaky front door was an innocuous brown business envelope with 'KATE TREGILLIS, EDITOR' written in block capitals in blue ink. It was little different to the plethora of other letters delivered by hand over the weekend.

Dumping the hefty pile on my desk, I went to brew myself the essential morning mug of tea to kickstart my office day. The kettle boiled. The milk was poured. My thoughts gathered. On my mind was the road accident and the maniac in the dark Ford Fiesta, if it had been a dark Ford Fiesta. I'd phoned Dobbie the previous day and left him a message. Unfortunately, he'd called me back when I was out walking Rufus, so I called him again, only to get his answerphone.

The Monday chores began with the familiar ring round of the emergency services to check on any overnight incidents, and then I opened the first letters. Roy's slow steps up the stairs were followed by Emily's lighter, quicker footsteps. Then Danny arrived, as quick up the stairs as Emily but heavier. The towering Irishman delivered his familiar incandescent smile as he walked into editorial looking a million times cleaner than the last time I'd seen him.

'That was a massive weekend,' he said.

Emily was smiling equally widely. At Danny.

With Danny's arrival everything was brighter. 'I heard Joe Keast used his pick-up to get your car out of the field,' I said.

Danny opened his laptop. 'Sure did. He's a top man. I changed the wheel and managed to drive it back into St Branok. The left wing's a bit of a mess, but she's driveable. Did you speak to Dobbie?'

'Not yet. We kept missing each other yesterday. We'll sort it out today.'

'Well, I wouldn't hold your breath.'

While Danny recounted the terrors of Saturday night to Roy and Emily, I ripped open more morning letters – mainly bills and reports from local organisations, such as the Rotarians or the Lions. Still, these local reports were the essential bread and butter of a diminutive newspaper like the North Cornwall Gazette.

Finally, I got to the brown business envelope with my name in blue ink. A single piece of lined white paper was inside. The same writing on the envelope was on the white paper. A few words. More blue ink. More capitals. They sent a bolt of electricity through my stomach.

SATURDAY NIGHT WAS A FINAL WARNING. STOP YOUR TALAN BRAY INVESTIGATIONS.

My hands shot to my mouth as I stifled a gasp, but not completely. Danny and Emily looked up from their computer screens. Roy's elderly ears had missed the sound and he continued tapping away on his keyboard. I scanned the message again to make sure I hadn't gone insane.

In a moment, Danny was up and walking over to me, his face twisted. 'Is everything okay, Kate? You look as if you've seen a ghost.'

'This note,' I said. I spread the malicious message on the desk, and Danny snatched up the paper.

'Jesus, where in God's name did this come from?'

The abrupt action had now attracted Roy's attention.

'It was at the office front door this morning with all the other mail,' I gushed. 'Hand delivered.' I stood up and tottered forward, my stomach queasy and my heart hammering as if I'd sprinted the length of Waterlock Beach. The incident at the festival, the message left on my bed in the cottage, the terrors of Saturday night...and now this.

Danny's heavy brow was creased. He put a hand on my shoulder and guided me back to my chair. 'I'll get you a glass of water.'

I subsided into the chair, sucking air. Danny disappeared into the small room which passed as a kitchen. Cheap china clinked and then he reappeared holding a large mug with a pink heart and 'I Love Cornwall' emblazoned on the side. It was placed under my nose. 'Here, drink this. You'll feel better.'

I swallowed a mouthful. It didn't help. 'Thank you, I'm fine. It was a shock, that's all, a bloody shock after everything.'

'What does it mean?' said Emily. She placed a sympathetic hand on mine.

'It means,' I said, 'that the incident in Tregenna Lane near my cottage on Saturday night was part of something much bigger. Somebody is desperate to scare us away from the Talan Bray.'

Roy took off his glasses and wiped the lenses with a cloth, a gesture he often did when thinking. 'But nobody could know that you'd be coming down Tregenna Lane at a specific time.'

'Well, it's a warning for sure,' said Danny. 'Perhaps they

want us to think it was planned. Word got round quickly yesterday that my car had ended up in a field. Half a dozen people turned up to watch Joe hauling it out. Whoever is trying to put the frighteners on us might have decided to take advantage of that.' He threw his hands up in a gesture of frustration. 'I asked around about a dark Ford Fiesta but didn't come up with anything worthwhile.'

I rubbed my forehead, thinking the unthinkable. 'It was planned. I'm sure of it.'

Roy slipped his glasses back on the end of his nose and pursed his lips. 'How?'

'Think about it. Say John Harding was sufficiently rattled by our visit on Saturday that he called somebody in St Branok. That somebody then arranges for us to have a nasty little road accident on our way back to the cottage. He follows us from St Branok, overtakes and then leaves a massive great block on a blind spot, knowing we'll be along shortly. At the very least it would give us a shock and probably cause an accident.'

Danny interrupted, his eyes ablaze. 'Well, damn him. He doesn't know who he's dealing with.'

Roy rattled the end of his empty pipe against his teeth. 'I think we might be jumping to conclusions. There's no shortage of local youngsters who hurtle around country lanes on a Saturday night at breakneck speeds, and the fact that you had visited Harding could be a coincidence.'

'If it was planned, it shows they're prepared to kill,' I said.

We stared at each other.

CHAPTER EIGHTEEN

Fear had taken a foothold in my little newsroom. We got on with our jobs – of course we got on with our jobs – but we were wary. Of dark corners. Of solitary footsteps in an alleyway. Of a ringing phone which went silent when answered.

Our usual frantic Monday work rate was interrupted by Dobbie, who turned up to take details of the latest encounter. Both Danny and I signed statements, and the most recent threatening note was placed in a sealed bag. The usual assurances of thorough investigations were made, though Dobbie left us in little doubt that the chances of tracking down the car and the culprit were minimal without a registration number and a better description. We agreed to run a short article in the Gazette appealing for anybody to come forward who might be able to identify a car, possibly a dark Ford Fiesta, involved in an alleged careless driving incident on Saturday night.

But the Gazette was becoming stronger. Our news coverage was better and circulation was going up – the first sustained rise since I'd taken over as editor and owner. Danny's slim hands were tapping out stories the rest of us didn't have time for. They were good local stories, too, which were getting people talking about the Gazette again. And Brenda was finding it slightly easier to sell advertising.

I sent an e-mail to George Thompson at the bank, telling him about the improvements. I was rewarded with a deadpan response, thanking me for the information and reminding me that the next payment on the loan was due in three weeks.

We would use that week's edition to trail our coverage of the tenth anniversary of the loss of the Talan Bray, letting readers know that there would be a major pull-out feature the following week. It should boost circulation again and, on this basis, I instructed the printers to increase the print run by five thousand copies. A hefty financial burden, bearing in mind the parlous state of our finances. But worth it, definitely worth it, I assured myself over and over again.

How much could we say in the trailer? If Danny did have a scoop, backed up by hard facts, then we could run a tantalising teaser about a dramatic new twist in the Talan Bray disaster. Even five thousand extra copies wouldn't be enough, and the bank might at last be satisfied.

At two o'clock, after I'd bolted down a cheese and chive sandwich from St Branok's only delicatessen and indulged in a quick walk with Rufus on the town beach, Danny pulled up his chair at my desk and said, 'Right, we were going to talk about my theory on the Talan Bray.'

'I hope it's more than a theory,' I said. This wasn't a good start. 'We need solid facts if we're going to claim that the loss of the Talan Bray was more than a tragic accident.'

Danny ran a hand over his chin, which didn't look like it'd seen a shaver for a few days. 'Absolutely. Yes, of course.'

I pushed the myriad of papers on my desk to one side and smiled at him, not quite reaching the dazzling level achieved by one of his grins but warm and friendly by my tight standards. Time to get down to business. 'So, what do you know?'

Danny flipped a couple of pages of his notebook. 'The loss of the Talan Bray was a deliberate act, sparked by a dispute between the crew. John Harding was at loggerheads with two brothers who worked as trawlermen and were lifeboat crewmen, Bobby and Jed Ridley. I've interviewed several people who recall them arguing in the weeks running up to the disaster. Two days before the Talan Bray was lost, Jed Ridley was involved in a fight with Harding outside The Mermaid. It was pretty vicious, by all accounts. Harding ended up with a black eye.'

I shifted on my seat, uneasy. And sceptical. A rift between the lifeboat crew which had become so bad that it played a part in the loss of the lifeboat would be hugely controversial. And hard to believe. Any attempt to besmirch the names of the heroes of the Talan Bray would make the Gazette extremely unpopular. 'What are you saying? That the safety of the Talan Bray was compromised by a stupid disagreement between Harding and the Ridleys? It doesn't make sense.'

Danny's chin jutted forward. 'Look, it all adds up. The escalating arguments between the crew in the weeks running up to the disaster, the fact that John Harding found a reason not to be on the Talan Bray…and his disappearance after the disaster.'

'It's all circumstantial. We need a much clearer picture if we're going to make these kinds of allegations. What was the reason for the feud?'

There was a flicker of weakness in Danny's eyes. 'Well, that's the bit I'm still working on. I have a theory but need to confirm it.'

There it was, that word 'theory' again. It wasn't encouraging. It wasn't enough.

'What is your theory?' This time I wasn't going to be put off by vague promises.

Danny took a deep breath and looked at his hands spread on the desk. 'I think it might be linked to paganism.'

'Paganism?' I almost screeched the word. *Tell me you've got more than this, Danny. Please. For God's sake.*

Danny held up his hands as if fending off imaginary punches. 'It sounds mad, I know. There were lots of rumours in St Branok at the time of a secret organisation. The Ridley brothers and John Harding were involved. And Harding was well known to be a pagan. Here, look.' He pushed over a black and white picture of a person elaborately dressed as the raven at the annual Shout at the Devil Festival. 'That's him.'

It might have been Harding. It might not have been. It was somebody about his height and shape but it was impossible to be sure. I held my head in my hands. I'd expected more than this from Danny. I'd counted on it. The last few weeks I'd wafted along on his charm, believing we would be able to publish a scoop which would turn around the Gazette's fortunes once and for all.

Now I knew it was Flanagan flannel. Bullshit.

'This is cloud cuckoo-land stuff,' I said. I was bitter. He'd let me down. Roy and Emily were being careful to keep their gazes on the computer screens in front of them. 'What possible argument on paganism or anything else could have ended in the loss of the lifeboat?'

Danny gulped hard, sending his adam's apple bobbing up and down. 'There was something going on, something big. I'm sure of it. Lots of people, even those in influential positions, were careful not to ask too many questions.' His voice faltered.

I groaned. 'The Gazette can't run this story. There'd be an outcry from the local community.'

Danny stood up. 'But there's a great story here, a story which has never been told.'

'Harding's lawyers would have us on toast if we tried to imply that he was, in any way, responsible for the loss of the Talan Bray.' A sharp headache was building. Deep down, I'd feared Danny's investigations into the Talan Bray might result in something like this.

Danny was unrepentant. 'I'm not saying he was directly responsible for the sinking. It might have been that he knew something which caused him to stay away. Anyway, we wouldn't name Harding. But if we got the disaster inquiry reopened—'

I tried to massage away the throbbing in my forehead. 'They'd need a lot more than guesswork to reopen an inquiry of an incident ten years ago.' I was unmoving. I'd made my decision.

Danny grabbed his coat, impatient. 'There's a story here and I'm going to tell it.'

I pointed angrily at him. 'It's easy for you. You can write a story and then head back to London. You can walk away and never have to face the friends and family of the men who died. It's not so easy for us. St Branok is our home.'

'You're not listening to me.' He stormed out, banging the door behind him. Out of the window, I saw him stomping down the street, head tucked low, hands in pockets. I'd half expected him to head to The Mermaid since it seemed the solution to most of his problems, but he marched straight past, heading for God only knew where.

An awkward silence fell over the office. I was sorry that Emily and Roy had witnessed it all. It was more than a disagreement between colleagues – much more. I'd lost my cool completely. If it'd been a simple case of telling a reporter his story didn't hold water, I could have managed that calmly and professionally. I'd done that many times in the past during my city days in London. No, it was because Danny and his Talan Bray story had begun to mean much more to me.

It wasn't just any story. It was the lifeline on which the Gazette depended. And Danny had become more than just any colleague.

CHAPTER NINETEEN

Danny didn't appear for the rest of the day. Or the next. Or the next. The office seemed echoingly empty. Roy was his usual self, ploughing through the re-writes, writing up local council meetings, reporting on plans for St Branok's Christmas lights and so on and so on. He was an anchoring rock in my swirling world.

But Emily was quieter. She missed Danny.

And so did I.

The deadline loomed for that week's newspaper and I was forced to make a final decision on how to word the upcoming Talan Bray commemoration supplement. There would be no new angles to the story, I decided. We'd simply recount the details of the disaster ten years ago, pay tribute to the men who died and run a feature on the current crew. All very predictable. All very safe.

With aching embarrassment, I recalled again and again that final scene with Danny as I walked Rufus along the cliff path near Gwel Teg. The wind had died, leaving a stillness. The Atlantic was a brooding dark mass, edged with thin lines of small surf. Gentle waves tickled the shoreline. Far out, it was hard to tell where the ocean gave way to the sky. Everything was grey. The sea. The sky. My life.

On the Thursday evening, Roy and I visited The

Mermaid for our usual drink to celebrate having put the Gazette to bed for another week. Another edition completed. How many more would there be? In every sense, we were drinking in the last chance saloon.

I ordered a pint for Roy and a gin and tonic for myself and asked Angie whether she'd seen Danny.

She glanced at me – a knowing glance, I thought – while pulling the pint. 'No, he's been a bit scarce the last few days.'

'Is he still renting the room upstairs?' It occurred to me in a fearful moment that he might have given up on St Branok and scuttled back to London.

She finished pulling the pint. The dark liquid swirled and then settled in the glass. 'Oh yes, he's still around, but he's out a lot. I thought he must be at the Gazette. Do you want a single or a double gin?'

I put on my unreadable face. 'Single, please. No, we haven't seen him for a few days. He's been working on a project of his own. I was hoping to catch up with him.'

'He's usually available on his mobile.'

Why had Angie been ringing Danny? And, more importantly, why did I care? Danny and I were colleagues, nothing more.

'Sure.' I turned away from the bar and, glasses in hand, made my way back to Roy for a safer, easier conversation.

He'd settled in the snug with his pipe stuck between his lips, puffing gently, the vision of a modern-day Sherlock Holmes. The smoke was warming and comforting. Pipe smoke always reminded me of solid, knowledgeable Roy.

He looked at me over the rim of his upraised beer glass. 'Any sign of Danny?'

'No, he's been out and about a lot. How did you know I was asking about him?'

'I guessed you might be.' He sipped his beer. 'That tastes good. I've been dying for a pint all afternoon.' He put down his glass neatly on the beer mat. 'Is Danny planning to come back, do you know?'

I swirled my gin and tonic, the liquid dipping in the centre. 'I don't know. I haven't heard from him since the…' I searched for the word to diplomatically describe the difficult scene in the office and settled on 'argument'. There was no point in describing it as anything else. Not to Roy. Twinges of angst and regret shivered through the pit of my stomach every time I thought about it. 'He hasn't said he's not coming back,' I added, lamely.

'We could do with the extra pair of hands,' said Roy. 'Danny's made a real difference over the past few weeks. At first, I was sceptical. But you were right to bring him on board, Kate. He's picked up some very nice stories.'

I nodded. Forced a smile. I didn't need reminding. The conversation lapsed into silence. Somebody played Scott McKenzie's 'San Francisco' on the jukebox, a record Danny had sometimes chosen. But it was a thin man standing there – certainly not Danny. My morale slipped back to zero.

Roy and I usually had no difficulty chatting, and when there was silence between us it was easy and relaxed. But the abrupt departure of Danny – and Roy's obvious understanding that Danny and I had become more than colleagues – added an edge to any discussion about him. We filled the void by sipping our drinks. Eventually, the conversation started flowing again about something innocuous like the weather. Anything but Danny.

The tall, commanding figure of Mike Pedrick strode into the bar with a couple of his trawler skippers – stocky young men in their early thirties, wearing the thick woollen sweaters, yellow oilskins and boots typical of trawlermen fresh from the boats. They were guffawing at a wisecrack Pedrick had muttered out of the side of his mouth. Even in The Mermaid, he acted as if he owned the place. Everybody always laughed at his jokes. Everybody except Joe.

The crowd parted like the Red Sea and Pedrick was soon leaning against the bar, attracting Angie's attention with an upheld, authoritative hand. She hastened over – Pedrick had that effect on people – and, as she was pulling the pints, he treated me to the royal wave. I smiled back faintly, wondering why I'd been honoured by the Pedrick spotlight.

Roy and I talked for a little longer and then he said, 'Marjorie's expecting me home for dinner. I really must be off. Can I walk you to your car?' Wonderful, thoughtful Roy, doubly caring and gallant after the alleyway attack.

'Yes, please. Thanks.' I swigged the remains of my drink.

Before we could stand, Pedrick strolled over and sat on a stool across the table from us, confident he was welcome everywhere. 'Kate. As it was Thursday, I was hoping I might find you here for a chat.' He glanced at Roy. 'Alone.'

My cheeks warmed. Was he really sufficiently interested in my whereabouts to know that I had a celebratory early evening drink at The Mermaid when the latest edition of the Gazette had been sorted? Then again, Pedrick kept tabs on everything in St Branok. And everybody.

Roy hesitated meaningfully. 'I can wait at the bar if you like.'

I beamed an assured expression. I was more than capable of handling the mighty Mike Pedrick by myself. 'No need to wait, Roy. I'll be fine. It's only a short walk to the Landy.'

Roy rose to go. 'Well, I'll be off. Night then, Kate. See

you in the morning. Night, Mike.' He disappeared into the crowd, a small, slightly bowed figure.

I focused on Pedrick. 'How can I help, Mike?'

'Your advertising girlie has been pushing my businesses to take extra advertising. She's been saying that the Gazette needs the extra revenue. Is everything okay?'

So, this was more fallout from Brenda shooting her mouth off. I could tell him to mind his own goddamned business, but that wouldn't help me get more advertising.

I was careful to exude a positive air. 'It's tough but we get by. In fact, things are looking up. More people are reading the Gazette and we're getting more advertising. I've been thinking of increasing to thirty-six pages.'

There was a flash of scepticism in Pedrick's eyes. 'Look, Kate, I know how tough running a small local business can be. I've been through challenging times myself. Thank God, that was a long time ago. The Gazette is part of the local community. It'd be a disaster if it had to close down.'

Clearly, the rumour mill in St Branok was running at breakneck speed. I sucked the dregs of my gin and tonic, now little more than melted ice with a tang of lemon. Still, it gave me something to do. And time to think. 'Who's saying the Gazette is closing down?'

I'd talked to Brenda about times being hard, not possible closure. Perhaps it was merely a case of an astute individual like Pedrick putting two and two together. The miserable state of local newspapers everywhere was hardly a secret.

He leaned forward. 'All I'm saying is, if things are getting desperate, I can help.'

'Help? How?'

He locked gazes with me, suddenly intense. 'Have you ever thought of a partnership? I'd consider making a sizeable investment in return for a majority share. It would wipe out any debts you might have in a stroke. And you'd still be the editor and run the business day to day.'

His dark eyes and the tempting offer on the table gripped me. The constant worry of mounting debt would be gone, leaving the bank to devote its time to torturing other cash-strapped customers. And Gwel Teg – my remote, ramshackle, beautiful cottage – would be safe. I would be able to enjoy my Cornish life, swim happily in the surf, take Rufus for long walks and do some serious veg-growing in my kitchen garden without the nagging fear that the bank was about to pull the rug out from under my feet.

But – and this was a massive but – it wouldn't be *my* newspaper anymore. I'd become little more than an employee with a minority stake in the business I'd given up London for.

'Thanks, Mike,' I said. 'I appreciate the offer, really I do, but we're fine. As I say, things are looking up for us right now.'

Pedrick leaned back, still scrutinising me. 'If you ever need any help, you know where to come.'

'Sure, and thanks.'

One of the trawler skippers still hanging around the bar, now on his third pint judging by the empty glasses, called over, 'Mike, we've got something for you to see.'

Pedrick held up a silencing hand. 'I'm busy.' He turned back to me. 'How's that new star reporter of yours, what's his name, Lonnie Donegan, getting on? Everybody's talking about him. He's asking a lot of questions.'

'Yes, that's what good reporters do,' I said. 'Actually, it's Danny Flanagan. And he's fine, as far as I know.' I was tired of Pedrick's forced bon homie and overbearing presence and it was beginning to show. I wanted him to clear off and get back to his laughing, raucous trawler mates and whatever else he did in his spare time. Pedrick might own most of St Branok, but he didn't own the Gazette. Yet.

He persisted, oblivious, used to deference not resistance. 'When I say questions, I mean deep, prying questions which are hurting local people and making them angry. He should be careful.'

I bristled. 'Prying questions about what exactly?'

'About the Talan Bray, of course. The press coverage of ten years ago caused a lot of pain. All that speculation about what happened was irresponsible. Now your Danny is wanting to open it all up again.'

'He's not *my* Danny. He's his own boss. He's a freelancer who is helping us out. Nothing more. I can't tell him what to do.'

Pedrick sighed as he struggled to contain his natural impatience. 'Yes, but he's working in your offices and you have more contact with him than anyone. I'm asking nothing more than for you to bring your influence to bear. It's in your interests, Kate. Hopefully, the Gazette will be here long after some ambitious Irish freelancer has hightailed it back to London.'

I'd heard enough. I reached for my handbag and rose to go. 'I've got to dash. I'll see you around, Mike.'

He finished his pint and also stood, towering above my five feet eight inches. He was a formidable figure in every respect. 'Another deadline to meet, eh? Have a think about what I said about investing in the Gazette. I'm serious. With the extra backing, you could make real improvements. More staff. New equipment. Refurbished offices. It could be the start of a new golden era for the—'

'Thanks. I've thought about it and we're doing fine as we are.'

I hastened outside, wishing I didn't have to walk back to the Landy alone despite my assurances to Roy. It was raining lightly. Wet pavements shone in the orange streetlighting. Cars – most of them old, none of them dark Ford Fiestas – rumbled past, their tyres hissing in the surface water. I was tired, grubby and desolate. Roy had gone back to Marjorie and his cosy, comfortable home. Pedrick had returned to his guffawing trawler skippers. Danny was probably practising his Irish charms on somebody he'd met, male or female. And I had a cliffside cottage waiting for me with cold, dark, empty rooms and an even emptier fridge.

It had been a grim day near the end of a grim week, during which the fantasy I'd created had been blown apart.

Footsteps thudded behind me.

Fast. Heavy. Close. Too close. A man's footsteps.

Over my shoulder a bulky, solitary figure, silhouetted by the street lighting, was walking straight towards me.

I upped my pace, staring ahead but alert to what was happening behind, all of my senses in overdrive.

My shoulders tensed. Ready for whatever might come.

The footsteps faded. He'd turned down an alleyway. Just another person on their way home.

I strode on, keen to get off the darkened street. The shadows in my life were becoming deeper and darker.

CHAPTER TWENTY

The storm hit on Sunday morning. Not from the wilds of the Atlantic, this time. No, this was worse.

The first indication of the incoming malevolence was a phone call. I was still in bed, staring at the ceiling, with little to get up for. Faithful Rufus was stretched out at the bottom of the bed, warm, watchful and patient as ever.

I allowed the phone to ring. And ring. And ring.

The weather was worsening, growing colder. Hauling myself out of bed was becoming harder. I tugged on a thick jumper over my pyjamas, then staggered downstairs, half expecting the phone to go silent as I reached for the handset. But no, it kept ringing.

A simmering sense of unease washed through me, reminiscent of that moment in the alleyway before I'd been attacked. The caller was determined. And persistent. Something important had happened. It might be anything, from Roy having had another heart attack to half of St Branok burning down.

At last, I picked up the receiver. 'Hello?'

'You lousy bitch.' It was a woman's voice I didn't recognise, with a Cornish twang. Local. She was shrieking.

My mouth was dry. 'What? Who is this?'

'You and your kind are scum, filthy scum. You just had

to rake up everything about the Talan Bray again, didn't you?'

I stood in the hallway of the cottage, confused, the cold of the flagstones seeping into my bare feet. 'I don't know what you're talking about. Who are you? How did you get my number?'

'You'll be sorry you did this. Bitch…lousy bitch.' The ranting continued, spiteful but unspecific. I remained none the wiser.

'You're making no sense, no sense at all. Tell me what's happened.'

'Your lies are plastered all over the Sunday newspapers. My sons died on the Talan Bray trying to save other people's lives and all shits like you want to do is drag their names through the gutter.'

Now I was getting somewhere. There had only been two brothers on board the Talan Bray: the Ridleys. I'd never spoken to their mother, though I'd seen her in town at the supermarket checkout. A middle-aged woman in the queue in front of me had given her name as Ridley and I'd noted her features. Drawn. Pinched. Sour. From a life of barely making ends meet. She'd paid for her groceries with a collection of notes and lots of coins, as if she'd been saving up. This was the indigent background from which the Ridley brothers had emerged to become lifeboat heroes.

'Mrs Ridley, I haven't been writing any articles for the Sunday newspapers. What exactly has appeared and in which newspapers?'

A dark suspicion was worming its way into my mind.

Danny? Surely not. But, oh yes. It had to be him.

'You'll pay for this. You'll pay—' There was a click and then I was holding a silent handset.

My mind gyrated. My stomach performed somersaults. What to do? I did what I'd done when I was a wet-behind-the-ears fledgling reporter: I called Roy. Roy was in town, near a newsagents, and he always got a selection of newspapers delivered on a Sunday morning.

The phone rang once, twice, three times and then Marjorie's soft tones wafted down the line. 'Hello?'

'Marjorie, I'm so sorry to bother you on a Sunday morning. It's Kate. Is Roy about?'

'Morning, Kate. Yes, we're having breakfast. I'll get him.'

The line went dead for a few seconds and then Roy's steady voice said, 'Kate? What's up?'

I resisted the urge to gush. Barely. 'Is there anything in the Sunday newspapers today about the Talan Bray?'

'I'll go and have a look. Shall I call you back?

'No, I'll hang on, thanks. It sounds like the sort of story which would upset a lot of people. I've just had the very angry mother of the Ridley brothers on the phone.'

'Give me a few minutes.' There was the sound of the phone being put down on the small cream-coloured table in Roy's hallway. I paced impatiently while Roy flipped through his Sunday papers, often vast tomes covering everything from news, economic and political analysis and sport to how to lose a stone in weight in three weeks and what to do on a short break in Iceland.

Marjorie was admonishing Roy for letting the remains of his breakfast get cold, warning that gulping down half eaten meals wasn't good for his heart. Roy assured her that yes, yes, he'd be 'back in a mo'.

At last, he said, 'I've found it. There's a feature about the loss of the Talan Bray in The News. It's a big piece. A page lead. And it's bylined Danny Flanagan.'

I flopped into Gwel Teg's hallway chair. My feet were freezing, but I didn't care. 'What does it say? No, don't bother to tell me. I'll come over and see for myself.'

It occurred to me as I slammed down the handset that I hadn't asked Roy whether it was okay to go over and disturb his Sunday morning. We'd known each other for so long that I'd presumed. He was the closest thing I had to a father after the death of my parents.

I opened a tin of dog food for Rufus. I could manage without breakfast – and without lunch or dinner, if necessary – but I didn't want to inflict the same on him. He wolfed it down and within two minutes was ready to do my bidding, whether it be a clifftop walk, a leap about in the waves or a day in the Gazette office.

We dashed outside. A lull in the blustery weather had been replaced by a brisk south-westerly. The grey Atlantic was now flecked with whitecaps. The waves were building, the surf beginning to bellow and clouds scudded across the sky.

The Landy miraculously started on a single turn of the key and, with Rufus curled up in the back, I made jolting, rapid progress down narrow country lanes, uncaring of the potholes, the mud and the surface water. We bounced along, every dent and imperfection in the road's surface communicated by the Landy's unforgiving suspension.

As we crested a rise, St Branok lay before us, peaceful on a cold autumn day. The Atlantic coast was losing its colour in the descent to winter. Dull skies, grey seas, bare trees and empty fields, broken only by the few remaining yellow flowers of gorse bushes. The St Branok locals would describe the day as 'wisht' – pale and ill. Wisps of smoke rose from some of the houses and were swept away by the gathering wind. Far out, a trawler was headed for the sanctuary of the harbour. It might have been one of Pedrick's boats, which were bigger and more modern than most of the rest of the fleet.

Marjorie greeted me at the door and gave me the warmest of hugs. 'Kate, you look shattered. Can I get you a cup of tea, dear?'

I managed a smile, I think. It might have been a grimace. I was a complete mess. I'd hauled on a pair of jeans muddied from a walk with Rufus the previous evening, a T-shirt I'd picked up at the Zelah Folk Festival and my old ski jacket. Anybody who saw me in this get-up couldn't accuse me of not immersing myself in rural Cornish life. 'That would be lovely. Thank you.'

'Roy's in the front room. Please go through.' She disappeared to the kitchen with Rufus at her heels; Marjorie was always good for a doggy treat.

Roy was in his familiar high-backed chair with sections of the Sunday newspapers spread out on the floor in front of him. Since our phone call, he'd popped down to the local newsagent and bought every newspaper on sale. He stopped reading as I entered. 'The story's only been featured in The News, as far as I can tell.' My heart sank as he pointed out the article. It stretched across a tabloid page with grainy pictures of the Talan Bray and its crew. The big and bold headline left little to the imagination.

SECRET FEUD OF DOOMED LIFEBOAT CREW

I skim read it and then studied it more closely. The article was a mixture of fact, supposition and implication. It reiterated the story of the loss of the Talan Bray, which had been probed in so much detail ten years ago, and then talked about arguments between some of the crew. An unnamed source described the atmosphere between the crew before the disaster as 'toxic', and there were references to paganism being popular in Cornwall.

Danny had been careful to avoid naming the individuals involved in the feud. But Harding was identified as the only member of the regular lifeboat crew to have survived the disaster. And there was that bizarre picture of the raven at the festival, which Danny had shown me.

As I read, Marjorie reappeared and placed not only a steaming mug of tea but also a sandwich full of thick slices of bacon beside me. The sandwich must have had half a pound of pig in it. Motherly Marjorie never missed an opportunity to feed me. She was careful with her words, but I'd always be a gangly teenager to her, thin and scrawny.

Roy reached for his pipe and slipped it empty between his lips. 'That story's going to upset an awful lot of people in St Branok. It's raking over all the old hurt of ten years ago. Danny's going to be very unpopular around here.'

'And judging from the phone call from Mrs Ridley today, some of the flak will be heading in our direction,' I said as I sipped the hot tea. It was extra sweet. Marjorie had slipped in at least three sugars.

Roy pointed the mouthpiece of his pipe in the direction of the offending article. 'We need to be clear that this is nothing to do with us.'

'But everybody knows that Danny has been working for the Gazette. His byline's been on any number of our stories.' Having bolted down the bacon sandwich, I chewed the jagged remains of a nail. What a fool I'd been, introducing a freelancer I knew nothing about to all and sundry as the Gazette's new recruit. I'd been desperate, looking to Danny to help haul us out of the mire. Now we were paying the price.

I was angry with Danny and even angrier with myself. How could I have seen him as anything more than a freeloading freelancer with no loyalty to the Gazette and St Branok? He'd be gone soon, gone forever, leaving the rest of us to pick up the pieces.

Marjorie reappeared in the doorway as I held my head in my hands, staring at their green carpet. 'You and Rufus are welcome to stay for lunch, dear. We could find a nice juicy bone for Rufus.'

I rose on unsteady feet. 'You're so kind, Marjorie. I'd love to stay, but I've got so much to do today. Rufus and I'll be fine.'

A gust of cold air hit me as I left the warm, welcoming embrace of Roy and Marjorie's home, the offending article in my inside jacket pocket. The sharp wind was a slap in the face – a slap which I probably deserved. I put my head down and sunk my chin into the collar of my jacket as I marched away with Rufus trotting beside me. Thank goodness he didn't know I'd turned down the opportunity of a juicy bone on his behalf.

The Mermaid was starting to get busy with customers when I got there. I found Joe in the cobbled yard at the back of the pub, moving empty beer barrels. He shifted them with ease. Joe wasn't tall, but he was strong and retained the muscular energy of his youth.

'Is Danny around? I need to see him urgently.' I was brusque, terse. I couldn't help it. My anger was growing to include almost everybody and everything. The wind. The rain. The Atlantic. The cliffs. Pedrick and his overbearing antics. And Danny. Most of all, Danny.

Joe was amiable. He obviously hadn't yet heard about the monstrosity in the newspaper. 'Kate, is everything okay? Yes, I think he's still upstairs in his room. Follow me. You can come in through the back door.'

As ever, the malty tang of beer struck me as we walked down a corridor behind the public bar to the stairs. Joe stopped at the bottom. 'I think you know the way well enough.'

'Thanks, Joe.' I jogged up to the first floor. What had Joe meant? I'd visited Danny's room once. I was hardly a regular visitor. But rumours spread like wildfire in a town like St Branok, and no doubt there were already murmurs of a torrid affair between Danny and myself.

I rapped on his door. Silence. I rapped again, harder this time. 'Danny, are you there? We need to talk. Now.'

There was the squeak of bed springs and a scuffling movement. 'Kate? Is that you?' A bleary voice.

'Of course it's bloody me. Open the door.'

'Wait a minute. I'm not dressed.'

I waited with Rufus. And waited. A tap ran for a minute, followed by an Irish curse and then more scuffling before the door eased open to reveal a drowsy and dishevelled Danny, his hairy belly protruding from the gap between a Motorhead T shirt and jeans. He stretched and yawned. 'What's up, Kate?'

I pushed past him into the room, which was small with antiquated furniture, probably acquired by Joe at a secondhand market. It was also surprisingly orderly, with Danny's items neatly stowed. Rufus wagged his tail at Danny and gave him a lick, unaware of his misdemeanours.

'I've seen the Sunday newspapers. You bastard. It's irresponsible, bloody irresponsible. I've already had the Ridley brothers' mother on the phone, cursing you, me and every newspaper hack between here and Wapping.'

Danny's face was a mixture of defiance and satisfaction. 'Ah, so they ran the story then?'

By way of answer, I tugged out the article, opened it up to its full size and pushed it in his face. 'This is going to cause a lot of trouble. For you, me and everybody else.'

Danny spread the article on the table near the room's one window, sat down and started reading. 'They used my story almost word for word.' There was an infuriating smugness in his voice. He seemed oblivious to my anger. Rufus was similarly uncaring, having curled himself up on Danny's bed.

I wanted to scream. 'Can't you see what you've done? You can walk away from all this and head back to London, Belfast or wherever. I can't. All this is going to cause a lot of damage to the Gazette.'

Danny shrugged his shoulders. 'How can this damage the Gazette?' In an accusatory tone, he added, 'You refused to run the story.'

I could have kicked him in the shins. Jesus Christ, was there no limit to the stupidity of this man? 'Everybody knows you were working at the Gazette. We're sucked into whatever you do.'

He was momentarily slack-jawed. Then he pushed his chair back and said thickly, '*Were* working at the Gazette?'

'You can't come back after this. It's over. Finished. If you're going to stay in St Branok, you'll be doing it without the help of the Gazette. I want you to collect your stuff from my office as soon as possible and not come back. Not ever.'

I grabbed Rufus's lead and headed for the door. 'And don't forget to return the office keys,' I shouted as I stomped down the hallway.

At the bottom of the stairs, I stumbled into Joe, who was

hanging around there, doing nothing in particular. Had he been listening? He must have heard the raised voices.

'Everything okay?'

'No.' My voice was full of tension.

'What's happened? Have you two fallen out?'

I strode past, on course for the exit. My ability for small talk, limited at the best of times, was non-existent. 'Sorry, Joe. I can't talk right now.'

I needed a consoling hug, a rarity for a tough-as-old-boots hack like me. Roy and Marjorie's offer of warm companionship and a hot lunch was enticing, but I had no appetite and was worried I might spend most of the time in gloomy silence, unable to indulge in meaningless Sunday chit chat. Marjorie and Roy's caring, gentle personalities brought out a vulnerability in me I wasn't prepared to show even to them.

The drive back to the cottage was pedestrian compared to the earlier blast into town. The Landy meandered along, bumping into the potholes and hissing through the puddles. The brown and yellow autumn leaves had become sodden in the rain and were now well on their way to being roadside mush. Rufus sat in the back, as quiet, trusting and loyal as ever.

He leapt out, intent on a walk the moment the Landy had ground to a halt and I'd opened a back door. I couldn't deny him. We headed down the clifftop path from the cottage to the cove below. The tide was out, exposing its full width and depth. There was nobody in sight, the summer visitors having long since returned to their desks and their concrete suburbs. It was one of the saving graces of late autumn and winter.

The waves crashed and the wind strength was still

growing. Typical Cornwall. The Cornwall I loved and always would love as long as a breath remained in me.

The clouds parted to allow a shaft of sunlight on a bleak sea and golden sands, fashioned into runnels and rivulets by the tides and the currents. My mood eased.

Rufus had long since left me far behind on the trail of something. He was already on the beach chasing seagulls, who rose languidly into the air, shrieking.

Danny was clumsy, infuriating and obstinate. Yet there was something about him which had caused me to hope. He'd be gone soon. He'd got his scoop and there was surely nothing to keep him here. And to shove him on his way, I'd kicked him out of the office.

The irony struck me: on a blustery autumn day, when I had the beauty and splendour of the cove all to myself, I was desperate to share it with somebody.

CHAPTER TWENTY-ONE

The media storm gathered momentum.

By mid-morning Monday, the first press arrived in St Branok to report on the tenth anniversary of the lifeboat disaster, their appetites whetted by Danny's Sunday newspaper story. Many of them didn't have a clue where to start in such a small, tight-lipped community. Camera crews were seen filming at the lifeboat station. Some had the nerve to turn up on the doorstep of the Gazette, asking where they might find John Harding and even Danny Flanagan. I sent them on their way with a strained smile but no useful information.

Pressure was mounting. Deadlines were looming. They were always bloody looming, but without Danny, the old problem of trying to produce a newspaper worth reading on absurdly small resources had returned to haunt me. We were back to square zero. All my boasting about a new start for the Gazette had become as empty as the Atlantic on a still winter's day.

I was the centre of attention when I escaped from the office for a few minutes, ostensibly to buy groceries but mainly to get a couple of bottles of whisky. In Crantock Street, glances in my direction flicked away when confronted with my own gaze. Mothers with pushchairs, delivery men in white vans, an elderly woman crossing the street…I could guess what they were thinking. Or perhaps I was seeing a meaning where there wasn't any. Paranoia has its own momentum.

I arrived back at the office as breathless as Roy usually was after climbing the stairs. The whisky bottles were concealed in a carrier bag beneath my token attempt at a healthier lifestyle – a loaf of bread, tomatoes and half a dozen eggs – and a beautiful spray of roses that would take pride of place in my kitchen. Roy and Emily were tapping away at their keyboards, but, in the absence of Danny's larger than life presence, the office was unwelcoming. It was the last place I wanted to be. I wanted to walk straight out again and take Rufus for a walk on the town beach or wrap myself in a duvet at the cottage. But no; I had a responsibility to the Gazette which would remain with me to my dying day. Or, more likely, to the Gazette's dying day – probably not so far away.

The phone rang and Emily picked it up. Part of her job was to screen the incoming calls to editorial, to rebuff the cranks and the time wasters. 'It's Danny. He's asking to speak to you,' she said, her eyebrows raised while holding a hand over the mouthpiece.

I clenched my fists. Did I ever want to speak to Danny again? Yes, yes I did. 'Put him through,' I said at last, trying to sound as if I was accepting the call grudgingly.

'Kate, is that you?' Danny was unusually quiet. Reserved. Resigned, even.

'What do you want?' I sounded offhand, as if Danny could take a running jump off Trevose Head for all I cared.

'When can I come to the Gazette to pick up the rest of my things? I've got various confidential items—'

'Yes, I know,' I interrupted him. 'The sooner you get

your kit out of here the better. And don't forget the keys to the office and to *my* filing cabinet.'

'Thanks. Tomorrow okay? Will there be an opportunity for us to have a chat?'

I twisted the knife. With some satisfaction. 'We've nothing to talk about.'

'Oh, come on, Kate, be reasonable.'

'I'm not the one being unreasonable.'

'Tomorrow then?'

'I'll be in the office all day,' I eventually conceded.

The call ended. I didn't say goodbye. I rammed down the phone. The noise reached even Roy's septuagenarian ears, and he paused his typing but said nothing. Emily was wide-eyed. She'd never seen me apoplectic before.

'Danny will be calling in tomorrow to pick up the rest of his stuff,' I said, immersing myself in the paperwork on my desk. The pile was steadily building into a mountain.

Brenda's familiar steps on the stairway were quicker than usual.

She popped her head round the door, blinking and flushed. 'Melkshams have pulled their advertising for next week.'

Melkshams was a local estate agent. One of our staples. They advertised week in and week out. Every week, in fact, apart from Christmas, when the life of estate agents and prospective home buyers took a festive turn and moving house was the last thing on everybody's minds.

'Why? What's the problem?' Regulars like Melkshams were essential to our survival.

'They didn't say.'

'Did you ask?' I pushed the mass of papers accumulating

on my desk to one side, hard enough that a few at the top fluttered to the floor.

'Of course.' Her voice faltered, though. She hadn't asked, I concluded.

I sucked my lower lip. 'I'll give Robert Melksham a call later and find out what's going on.' If Brenda wasn't going to find out, then I would.

'I can call him back. Talk it through with him in more detail.' Brenda remained in the editorial office doorway, her stance defensive.

'No, it's okay. I want to have a chat with him about other stuff as well.' It was feasible, though it wasn't true. Robert Melksham was one of those pillars of the local community with affluent fingers in lots of St Branok pies: Chairman of the Lions Club, local magistrate, past president of the chamber of commerce…you name it, Robert Melksham had done it. And, as editor, I had a better chance than Brenda of getting him to perform a U-turn.

'Who else might want to take the Melkshams' slot at short notice?' I asked.

'Wyndhams?' suggested Brenda, obviously dredging up the first name which came to mind. Wyndhams was a local furniture store. They advertised on an ad hoc basis, mainly during the New Year and spring sales and rarely in the autumn.

I feigned enthusiasm. We both knew it was a long shot. 'Yes, give them a try and call the other estate agents. They might be interested in taking extra space at a discount. Offer them twenty-five per cent off.'

Brenda's face brightened. 'Fine. I'll let you know how I get on.'

I called Robert Melksham immediately, even though I had a million and one other issues demanding my attention.

All were urgent, but the loss of any advertising – our lifeblood – made other urgencies pale into insignificance.

The phone rang twice and then a woman answered. Young. Professional.

'Melkshams Estate Agents.'

'Hello, is Robert Melksham about? It's Kate Tregillis from the Gazette.'

'Sorry, he's out with a client. Shall I ask him to call you?'

'Thanks, but I can try again later. What time is he expected back?'

There was silence for a few moments while I was put on hold and then she said, 'About four o'clock.'

The conversation ended. I replaced the handset, more gently this time, and gazed sightlessly at the desktop. Four o'clock was several hours away, but I had no shortage of problems and issues to take up my time, and I was soon lost in the familiar editorial nightmare. The fact that it was the Talan Bray commemoration issue and we had another five thousand copies to shift added extra urgency to everything.

Time passed. Articles were edited, headlines created, pages filled and contacts contacted. I dithered over having the word 'crisis' in the headline of three separate stories in the same newspaper. It was a short word that neatly fitted a headline, but were there really that many crises in North Cornwall? Probably not. More a slow, grinding decline. I changed one 'crisis' for 'row'. Two crises in one week were enough.

At four o'clock precisely, I punched out the Melkshams phone number again. The same young woman answered the phone as before, in such a similar, monotone manner that she might have been an automated answering service.

'It's Kate Tregillis, of the Gazette. I called earlier. Is Robert Melksham back?'

'I'll check. Can I ask what it's about?'

'Advertising.'

Silence again. And then, 'I've spoken to Mr Melksham and he says we're not taking any further advertising at present.'

The brush-off sent a hot flush spreading under my skin. 'I know Robert very well,' I said. 'Can I speak to him?'

'Sorry, he's not available right now.'

'When will he be available?'

'I'm not sure. He's busy.' The young professional faltered, not used to dealing with persistent callers. Well, Kate Tregillis could be bloody persistent. And bloody minded.

'I need to speak to him as soon as possible. Please ask him to call me before he leaves the office tonight. I'll be here until late.'

I slammed down the phone for the second time that day. Robert Melksham was always ultra-available when he wanted to speak to me about the Lions or a new fund-raising project. Well, if he didn't get back to me by close of play today, he'd find I wasn't so available anymore either. The Lions would need to find another way of promoting their worthy causes.

He must have come to the same conclusion because he phoned as I was shutting down my computer and reaching for Rufus's lead for an evening walk. I was alone. Roy and Emily had long since departed for their centrally-heated homes and were no doubt eating tea cooked by somebody else. No empty, chilly dark cottages for them.

'Kate.' He was distant, cold.

'Robert. I was wondering when you might ring.' My tone was tinged with irritation.

'It's been a busy day. Anyway, I'm here now and you said you wanted to talk urgently?'

'You've pulled your advertising for next week. Is there any particular reason, anything I can help with?'

'We've been reviewing our budgets.' A standard line, a non-answer.

'You've been reviewing your budgets and...?' I prompted.

There was a pause. He was obviously searching for the right words. 'We've decided, after due consideration, to take a rest from advertising in the Gazette.'

'For how long?' My stomach tingled. The conversation was taking an even darker turn.

'For the time being.' More evasion. Why couldn't he say what he meant? When he wanted something, he was precise.

'Are we talking weeks? Months?'

'I'm not exactly sure yet.'

'Is this anything to do with recent press coverage of the Talan Bray?' I blurted.

There was a long pause and then he said in a deadpan voice, 'As I say, we've been reviewing our budgets, taking into account a range of factors.'

'It's not fair to blame us for what has appeared in other newspapers. The Gazette has acted responsibly—'

'Rest assured, we'll get in touch with you again when we're in a position to proceed.'

The call ended. I was now more worried than annoyed. A brief suspension of advertising, which was difficult enough, had become an indefinite halt. It sounded terminal.

And, despite my best efforts, I didn't have an explanation. Not a proper one, anyway. A 'budget review' was a neat line I'd heard many times in my life as a journalist. It was often PR speak for swingeing cuts or mass redundancies. An explanation which wasn't an explanation.

The situation at the Gazette was going from bad to worse.

CHAPTER TWENTY-TWO

The strange, stilted conversation with Robert Melksham lurked in my head long after I'd slammed the phone down. I mulled it over in the darkness as I took Rufus for a walk down the narrow St Branok streets to the town beach, where the surf was churning and there was a strong but not cold breeze. The tide was out, the wrinkled sands exposed.

The street lighting on St Branok's sea front provided enough light for me to wander down to the water's edge. My trainers splashed in the puddles. The sea boiled and churned, expending its force until it came ashore as gentle, frothy ripples.

Hands in pockets, I sauntered by the water's edge, taking stock. Perhaps Melkshams was going through a bad patch and having to rein in its spending. But if Robert Melksham was having a bad time, then the other estate agents who advertised in the Gazette would also be suffering. The property section was one of the few remaining strong sources of revenue for the Gazette. The well-heeled visitors from London and the Southeast, looking for a holiday home so they could indulge themselves in the Cornish dream, would often pick up the local newspaper to see what was available. Without the property section, the Gazette was finished.

My thoughts meandered back to Pedrick's offer. It

would remove my money worries in a stroke, but also end my control of the Gazette. It was a tempting deal with the Devil I wasn't prepared to make.

A security light I'd had fitted flicked on as I pulled up outside my home, its white glare vanquishing the blackness of the night and easing my fears. But I couldn't casually stroll inside any more. Now I paused before stepping through the front door. Sounds which once had added to my enjoyment of the cottage had taken on a sinister tone. The whistling cry of the wind gusting over the cliffs into the nooks and crannies of my cottage had become a mournful warning of hidden threats.

The cottage was exactly as I'd known it would be. As it always was. Empty. Unheated. It was a place you fell in love with on a hot summer's day or when there was a good fire burning in the grate. On an autumn night, with my spirits at rock bottom, it was plain unfriendly. And, after the message left on my bed, it no longer felt safe. My old apartment in London, which had looked out over Putney Heath, was an oasis of warmth and homeliness by comparison.

I should have been hungry after the walk with Rufus on the beach and a frantic day sustained by a breakfast slice of toast, a prawn sandwich from the local delicatessen and numerous anaemic cups of tea, usually brewed by Emily, which weren't a patch on Danny's strong cuppas. Instead of crying out for food, though, my stomach was twisted and full of bile, anger and depression. I imagined Marjorie's perceptive, motherly expression; she was always telling me I was too thin.

I opted for the quick and easy approach, stuffing a potato in the microwave, heating up baked beans and grating a hard, cracked slab of cheddar cheese. Dinner was accompanied by a slug of whisky and a few guilt-ridden sucks on a cigarette. It would do. I was capable of surviving on microwaved potatoes indefinitely.

I sloshed another finger of whisky into the glass – a finger if you stood the finger upright – and then, after double checking the front door was locked, headed for the bedroom with Rufus and a book about Cornish flowers. I had no energy or inclination to do anything other than lie down and read in a dozy, alcohol-induced stupor.

The duvet was cold and heavy, pinning me down. What would it be like to have another body to warm the sheets? For us to lie skin to skin? For a brief while, I'd hoped. At least Rufus, stretched out at the bottom of my bed, provided a blissful spot of heat for my feet.

The whisky did its work. My chin was soon drooping onto my chest as I tried to absorb anything worthwhile about Bulbous Buttercups, Cats-ears and Sea Campions. Heavy rain began to hammer on the roof. I sleepily got out of bed and secured the window. A half-moon disappeared behind thick cloud and I shivered at the sound of the surf down in the cove.

I pulled the duvet up around my ears and finally drifted away.

Rufus barking dragged me out of deep sleep. The barking was strident, sustained. He was standing facing the door, his tail up and his powerful, wiry body rigid. Rufus rarely barked at night. A fox would occasionally set him off, though. A vixen had a night-time trail that brought her close to the cottage.

I put my arms around his neck and tried to quieten him with soft words. At last, he stopped. The bellow of wind and surf took over. I'd convinced myself that the disturbance had been caused by the fox, a badger or some other furry denizen which inhabited the lanes and the cliffs at night – that, in short, my fear was paranoia – when Rufus cocked his head and launched into another volley of barking.

A rash of goose bumps crawled across my arms. I reached out to pacify Rufus again, patting his warm head and shushing him, keeping a smooth, easy tone even though I was anything but calm.

What to do? Stay cringing in the bedroom while Rufus howled his head off? Why hadn't I kept something sharp or heavy by the bedside? Things were getting that serious.

I eased myself out of bed, as silently as an ancient bed with creaky springs allowed, slipped my warmest cardigan over my nightie and then tiptoed barefoot down the narrow stairs with Rufus close behind. He was no longer barking but remained alert and taut.

The rain grew in intensity and then stopped. The moon flitted out from behind clouds and a pool of cold light illuminated the Cornish slate flagstones in the hallway. I halted at the bottom of the stairs, holding my breath. Rufus's damp nose nudged the back of my legs and I reached down and stroked his neck.

Outside, autumn leaves swirled and rustled in the breeze. Then the moonlight was lost and I was in blackness once more.

The security light hadn't been activated, but I still felt bound to check the doors and windows again. I'd been careful to lock up before going to bed – careful in a way which wouldn't have occurred to me three months ago. That had been a London precaution, not one for my little cottage on the cliffs on the edge of the Atlantic. Slipping from room to room, I tested everything. Every latch. Every lock. The front door and then the back door, which led into the kitchen garden.

It was all fine, all safe and secure.

At the kitchen window, I strained my eyes and ears. There was movement, but it was only the swing of branches and the ripple of hedges as they shifted in the Atlantic breeze. I crept back into the hallway.

Rufus trotted to the front door and sniffed at the whistling gap between the bottom of the door and the flagstones.

I wished he could talk.

The vixen. It had to be.

He scrabbled at the door and whined to be let out. He'd love a nighttime stroll over the cliffs, but, unlike me, he had the luxury of being able to curl up in a basket during the day to catch up on his beauty sleep.

I slapped my leg. 'Come on, Rufie. Back to bed. Come on, boy, come on.'

The sheets were still warm when I slid thankfully between them and Rufus settled himself at the bottom of the bed. But sleep wouldn't come. Chilled, I stayed in my cardigan. I twisted and turned, my body tired but my mind alive with everything that was happening to me.

When I finally dropped into a fitful doze, the cottage, the Gazette, Danny, George Thompson, Joe Keast, Mike Pedrick, Robert Melksham, John Harding, the message on my bed, the attack in the alleyway, the surf and the sea all swirled together in a thick soup of memories and fears. I was running hard, gasping for breath in a dark, damp lane interspersed by shards of moonlight. From what or to where? I had no idea.

CHAPTER TWENTY-THREE

I found the footprints, if they were footprints, when I dragged myself outside the following morning.

Twitching nose to the ground, Rufus trotted over to a weed-ridden square of earth set under a small window at the side of the cottage, which in happier times I'd set aside as a flower patch. The flower patch that never was. My calls to him were ignored. He snuffled and sniffed, and, eventually, I gave up and marched over to put on his lead.

The weeds had been pressed into the damp earth by something heavy. A man's boot? The imprint was big enough and about the right shape. There were any number of innocent explanations. A late-season hiker, following the coast path, might have stopped to admire my quaint, crooked little haven. A postman with a parcel needing to be signed-for might have peeked inside to see if anybody was home.

Were there other signs of a disturbance? The window and its sill appeared untouched. Nearby, another depression in the earth might or might not have been a boot mark. But there was nothing else.

The Gazette was calling. I checked that the front door was locked, gunned the Landy's noisy diesel engine and accelerated down damp Tregenna Lane with Rufus in the back. If only he could tell me what he had smelt in that square of damp earth. If only.

Should I report this to Dobbie? Report what? A barking dog and a few trampled flowers were hardly solid proof of a malicious late-night visitor. He'd decide I was at best a time waster or at worst becoming unhinged.

It was a bright, blustery day, full of life. People were out and about, going to work, dropping their children at school, opening shops or delivering milk or the post.

I drove past The Mermaid and thought of Danny. It didn't take much to make me think of Danny. He had big feet which would leave an impression among weeds and flowers. I imagined him still slouched in bed, sleeping off another dose of Wreckers Rebellion. But I was wrong.

He appeared on the street, having left the pub by a back door. A quick, purposeful walk. He was on a mission, headed somewhere. I dabbed the brakes of the Landy and wound down my window, keeping my voice cold and my face colder.

'Are you still calling in at the office today? The sooner you pick up your stuff the better.'

No smile this morning. Was he distracted or pissed off with me? 'I've got a number of appointments this morning. I'll stop by at lunchtime.'

I couldn't resist asking, 'What's so urgent?'

He stopped mid stride, his lips curved with the glimmer of a self-satisfied smirk. 'Oh, some leads on the Talan Bray. Important leads. It's a heck of a story.' A heck of a story that I was missing out on. Danny certainly knew his audience. The journalistic psyche is always fearful of being out-scooped by a rival.

I savagely pushed the Landy's gearstick into first but mistimed the clutch and a grinding noise emanated from somewhere down below. Another 'exclusive' in the Sunday newspapers would stir things up again. More anger. More recriminations. 'You've done enough damage with all that crap.'

A horn honked. Another joined in. Traffic was building up behind me. Commuting workers and school-bound mothers were becoming impatient. It didn't take much to set them off. More honks. A driver leant out of his window and shouted something abusive. I checked the rear view mirror. *Up yours, mister.*

'Catch you later,' Danny said as he turned a corner, moving quickly, his thick frame clad in his usual Burberry coat.

A woman in jeans and a hoodie was hurrying towards me as I parked the Landy in its usual parking space behind the Gazette offices. She had a pinched, bitter face which had forgotten how to smile. A vaguely familiar face. Angry. I stepped outside and locked the car.

'You bitch.' She spat at me. A fat globule of phlegm trickled down my cheek.

'What the—' I was cut short by a stinging slap, delivered by a hard hand toughened by domestic chores.

My knees buckled. I collapsed against the Landy, my hand on my burning cheek. 'I'm going to report you to the police,' I croaked.

Rufus snarled and pressed forward. He strained against the leash, his sinews tensed, no longer the cuddly, friendly animal I knew and loved. I struggled to hold on.

My attacker stepped back out of range of Rufus's teeth. 'Clear off, you bitch! Your press pals were all over us last night, asking questions they had no right to ask. I told them my sons were good boys. They were heroes. You should be strung up for what you've done. You all should.'

'Those people are nothing to do with me. The Gazette won't be running any of those accusations. We're running a feature paying tribute to the men who died. Nothing more.'

'They're lies, not accusations. All of them. That Irish guy you've been balling started all this and he's still sniffing around for any shit he can find. If I had my way, we'd run the lot of you out of town.'

I hauled myself up. 'You've got it all wrong. I've done nothing to harm you, your sons or anybody else.'

She pointed an accusing, bony finger. 'You'll be sorry, bloody sorry.'

And with that, apoplectic Mrs Ridley turned on her well-worn boots and stormed off down the street.

CHAPTER TWENTY-FOUR

After the nightmare encounter with Mrs Ridley, another demanding day at the office loomed like Everest – intimidating and gruelling. I wanted to scurry back to the cottage and tuck myself in bed for the day. Who the hell cared about the Gazette anyway? The truth is, I did. And so did Roy, Emily and the diminishing faithful who still bought it week in and week out.

I negotiated the usual front door, the usual narrow stairs and the usual door to editorial, which creaked and got stuck in the damp autumn and winter weather. The familiarity was comforting, reassuring.

I was soon at my desk, immersing myself in the routine day-to-day minutiae of office life. Hard work had always been my antidote to trauma. While I sipped a mug of tea – hot and strong like Danny's brews – I opened the post, sifted through stacks of papers and made the usual calls to the emergency services to see if there had been any incidents overnight.

The office came alive with a burble of voices and the tapping of keyboards as I was joined by Roy, Emily and Brenda. Striding here and there, typing up stories and speaking too loudly into the phone, my mood eased. This was my domain. I began to indulge in thoughts of a prawn sandwich from the delicatessen.

Brenda was leaning on the reception desk in a despondent, un-Brenda-like pose when I strode past intent on getting my hands on that prawn sandwich. Her head was in her hands.

I paused. 'I'm popping out for a sarnie. Everything okay?'

Her shoulders heaved. She stifled a sob. 'We've lost another two advertisers.'

I ground to a halt. 'Who? Why?'

'Darbyshires and Austins.' This time she was quick to add, 'I asked them why.'

'And?'

'They both said they were looking at other advertising opportunities. I offered them a discount, but it didn't make any difference.'

I, too, leaned on the reception desk, mainly to steady myself. Darbyshires was an auction house and Austins was a local builders merchants. Neither of them were big advertisers, but every Cornish penny counted. Melkshams and now Darbyshires and Austins. All in the space of twenty-four hours. Coincidence?

'Offer thirty per cent off,' I said. 'Tell them it's a reward for their long-standing support. Lay it on thick.' In my desperation to hang on to advertisers, my discounts were getting bigger. I took a deep breath and pushed away from the reception desk, heading for the door, intent on that sandwich.

The world could wait.

CHAPTER TWENTY-FIVE

I arrived back at the office half an hour later, having taken shelter from the world in a sunny spot overlooking the harbour. I'd done a Rufus, barely tasting the prawn sandwich as I gobbled it down in half a dozen bites.

Brenda was in a heavy conversation with somebody, probably Darbyshires or Austins. It didn't sound good. 'Can't we make you reconsider?' she implored. 'We'd be prepared to offer you a substantial discount.' In fairness to her, it sounded like she was throwing the kitchen sink at it.

She sighed windily when she put down the receiver. I was about to deliver consoling words about Darbyshires and Austins being minor advertisers when she said, 'Bromptons have cancelled their advertising. I offered them everything. Thirty per cent. Everything. They're not interested.' She gulped hard. Her eyes were bleary.

The ground moved under my feet and I reached for the support of the reception desk again. Bromptons was St Branok's largest car dealership and one of our biggest advertisers, taking full pages to promote the latest deals on trucks, cars, servicing, tyres and any number of other motoring products and services which kept St Branok's hordes of battered vehicles on the road. It was one of our mainstays and was owned by Mike Pedrick, of all people.

What was he up to? One minute he was offering to invest in the Gazette to give it a bright new future, and the next he was cancelling his advertising to sink it. Was this a ploy to force me to sell up?

'I'll give Mike a call,' I said.

'There's no point. It was him I was speaking to.'

'I'll still give him a call,' I insisted. If Pedrick was going to shaft the Gazette, he should have the decency of explaining it to me personally. Bastard. Bastard. Bastard.

I ascended the narrow stairs back to editorial, my legs shaky, wondering how best to approach the conversation. Anger, fear and righteous indignation…I felt all those in spades, but blustering fury wouldn't get me anywhere with a character like Pedrick.

As I was quelling frantic thoughts and scribbling a few notes at my desk, Emily came over. She was pale. 'Somebody called and threatened to burn down the Gazette.'

I couldn't believe it. The world – or at least the enclave occupied by St Branok – had become a hostile place. 'Who?'

'He didn't say. He made the threat, said all journalists were heartless, nosy bastards and ended the call.' She fished a tissue out of the back pocket of her jeans and blew her nose.

I hauled myself to my feet and put a protective arm around her drooping shoulders. Being strong for her helped me feel better. 'It's okay. It'll be a local blowing off steam. I'll report it to the police.'

Emily sniffed. 'He was furious. Really bitter. I didn't recognise the voice.'

When her tears dried, I called Dobbie and informed him of the latest incident. He spent a few minutes talking to me and Emily with an underlying tone of 'I told you so'. 'Feelings are running high in St Branok, Ms Tregillis. Until all this blows over, I'd advise you and your staff to take extra care.'

I didn't tell Dobbie about Mrs Ridley, concerned that levelling an accusation of assault at a well-known local person, especially one who'd suffered such a terrible personal loss, would stir things up further. The Gazette was unpopular enough already.

After I'd taken a deep breath, I gritted my teeth and dialled Pedrick's personal mobile, one of the most prized numbers in my contacts book.

'Mike? It's Kate from the Gazette.'

'I'm busy. What do you want?' Another cold voice. It was my conversation with Robert Melksham all over again. I forced myself to stay calm.

'I understand you've cancelled your advertising in our motoring section.'

'Yes, that's right.' No explanation. No clarification.

'Can I ask why?'

'We don't feel the Gazette is properly representing the local community anymore.'

Who exactly was 'we'? 'You've lost me completely, Mike. A few days ago, you were telling me you wanted to invest in the future of the Gazette, that it was the mainstay of the town. Now you're saying it doesn't represent the community. The Gazette has always championed the community. It's what we do.'

'Not when it comes to the Talan Bray. Your man Danny has set the whole goddamned press corps on St Branok like a pack of wolves, asking all the stupid questions they were asking ten years ago. We thought we'd put all that behind us, but no; you jokers had to drag it all up again. It's a blatant invasion of our privacy and grief.'

'That's nothing to do with the Gazette. Danny's a freelancer.' I was beginning to sound like a broken record. The trouble was nobody believed me. As far as most of them were concerned, the press were all the same and Danny and the Gazette were intertwined.

'He's working at the Gazette offices, Kate. You yourself told me he was working for you.'

'I told you he was helping us out,' I said, trying to remember how I had phrased it. 'And he's not involved with the Gazette any longer, even on a freelance basis.'

The conversation, terse and tense, went on a little longer but failed to achieve anything of value.

Another important advertiser, another drop of lifeblood, lost.

CHAPTER TWENTY-SIX

I was furious with Pedrick and all the other advertisers who'd ratted on the Gazette by pulling their advertising. But I was even more livid with Danny. The Irish Seventh Cavalry had delivered a potentially fatal blow to the Gazette. Thank God the bank was unaware of the latest developments. Thompson would have shut down the Gazette without a qualm.

Whatever my nagging fears, we had this week's newspaper to produce and get out on the streets. Slowly, we filled pages and met deadlines. The main story on the front page almost wrote itself. A tribute to the men who'd died on the Talan Bray. No wild accusations of conspiracies and paganism but a straightforward recounting of the tragedy and a recognition of the debt owed to the men who'd risked their lives for others.

No scoops. Nothing new. Just honest reporting, albeit predictable.

A memorial service at the St Mary Magdalene Church in St Branok was due to take place the next day, with a more formal service at Truro Cathedral the day after. We had enough time to include a picture and report of the St Mary Magdalene event in this week's newspaper and had set aside a space on the front page.

The man who had given me so much hope but was now

the cause of most of my problems trotted up the staircase as I was preparing to leave the office for a few minutes to stretch Rufus's legs on the town beach. He looked the same as when I'd first seen him. Same worn Burberry, same tousled hair and, astonishingly, even after everything, the same boyish grin. Danny clearly didn't understand the concept of lasting shame.

I said coldly, 'When you've got your stuff together, you can leave the keys with Roy or Emily.'

Danny filled the doorway, stopping me from leaving, by accident or design I couldn't tell. 'I was hoping we might have a bit of a chat.'

My blood pressure rose. 'Chat about what? We've nothing to discuss. You've caused us enormous problems. You might be interested to know that I was assaulted by Mrs Ridley this morning. She slapped and spat at me. And we're losing advertisers by the boat load, including Mike Pedrick, who's advertised in the Gazette for years.'

Danny's ruddy face creased. 'Jesus, why?'

'Mrs Ridley, Mike Pedrick and just about everybody else in St Branok blames the Gazette for all that rubbish you wrote in the Sundays.'

Danny held up his hands as if Irish butter wouldn't melt in them. 'Wait a minute, it wasn't rubbish. It was true. Most of it. Combined with reasonable supposition and a touch of journalistic licence.'

I faced him full on, fighting the urge to do a bit of slapping of my own. 'All that stuff about paganism? Oh, come on. That was bullshit and you know it.'

For the first time, something approaching shame flickered in those blue eyes. 'It helped to sell the story. They love all the stuff about Cornwall being a land of myth and magic.'

I ground my teeth. 'The truth is you made ridiculous allegations against men who died as heroes, all to make a quick buck.'

Emily and Roy had stopped typing, and Emily's eyes were even wider than usual at the latest fraught scene between myself and Danny.

'Most of that article was backed up by hard facts. There was something going on between the crew shortly before the disaster that has never been explained.'

I marched towards him, intending to shove him out of the way, if necessary. 'I need to give Rufus a walk. Please make sure you've taken all your gear by the time I get back. And don't ever...*ever*...come back.' I gulped down a lump in my throat.

Danny glanced at Emily and Roy and then looked back at me with pleading eyes. 'Wait, wait. I need to explain something to you. Can we talk, privately?'

'Don't you ever listen? I said we had nothing further to discuss. You've betrayed us all.'

He moved to one side, allowing barely enough space for me to pass. 'Hear me out. Please. One last time. You won't regret it.'

I pulled Rufus's lead and clattered down the stairs. Danny stomped along behind.

'At least hear me out,' he called again.

I didn't answer.

Brenda was at the reception desk, her mouth turned down. 'We've lost another two advertisers,' she blurted.

I didn't bother to ask who or why. I didn't have the strength. 'I'll pick it up with you when I get back from walking Rufus.'

I rushed out onto the main street and into the North

Atlantic breeze. At least that could be relied upon. I expected Danny to give up and wander off to The Mermaid to dream up his next work of fiction. But no. He stayed a pace behind. Still flannelling. Still asking for one last chance to explain. 'Kate…please…give me a couple of minutes. You owe me that at least.' His voice was raised. People stopped and looked.

'I owe you nothing. Leave me alone.' I kept my head down, gathering pace. We were like one of those warring couples who vented their anger against each other in the street, entertaining everybody except themselves.

The march down Crantock Street to the town beach proved torturous. The half glances I'd received the previous day were nothing compared to the stares we were both subjected to. Onlookers gave us a wide berth as Danny continued to follow, pleading.

He was still only a step behind when I reached the dried sand at the top of the beach, slipped Rufus's lead and walked straight towards the water's edge and the distant horizon. The rippled sand, interspersed with shallow pools of water, was firmer there, and my trainers only left a shallow imprint.

Danny's scuffed leather brogues were totally unsuitable for the salty, sandy, damp terrain, but that didn't put him off. At least he was no longer talking. The breeze caressed my face, easing my fury.

On we paced, me in front with Danny tagging along. I threw a ball for Rufus and he raced off in a blur of saltwater and sand. He brought the ball back and dropped it at Danny's feet, his eyes alive and his mouth open in a doggy laugh.

Traitor.

Danny hurled the ball twice as far as I was able to throw it. 'Well, at least Rufus still likes me,' he said with a sigh.

I turned to face him, having given up on the hope that he would wander off in defeat. 'Okay, what's so bloody important? Tell me now and make it quick.'

Danny's whole face glimmered triumphantly. His persistence had paid off. The man never knew when to take no for an answer. Typical reporter. 'I've been doing a lot more digging into the Talan Bray and I understand why there was a feud between the crew. I'm due to meet somebody later today. They should be able to confirm everything.'

I could have screamed. 'Haven't you done enough damage already? I've had enough of your brand of sensationalist journalism.'

He moved closer, placed his hands on my shoulders and held me gently. 'This time, it's not guesswork,' he said. 'It's hard facts. One more chance. That's all I'm asking. I'll see this person this afternoon, tie up a few loose ends and then call in at the office before you leave tonight and talk it all through in detail.'

'Ferchrissake, tell me now.' I'd had enough of the Danny doublespeak. This was another ruse to wheedle his way back into the Gazette.

'I can't. Not yet. But I know. Believe me, I know.'

'Know what?'

'The truth.'

'Stop playing with me, Danny. Tell me what you know or clear off.'

He hesitated, chewed his lower lip and then said, 'Look, give me a few hours and then I'll explain everything. If you don't like what you hear, you can tell me to take a hike.'

He pulled me closer and, stupidly, I succumbed, melting into him before shoving him away, furious with myself for the moment of weakness.

I was grateful when Rufus interrupted, racing back with the ball to, once again, place it at Danny's soggy feet. At last, I said, 'I must be going mad, but okay. Call in tonight and we'll talk about it. I want everything. The whole truth. No more half stories.'

Danny threw the ball, another long throw which sent Rufus on a mad scamper into the distance, before giving me a sheepish look. 'Absolutely. I'll tell you everything.'

We strolled back to the Gazette, struck by a surge of optimism. Rufus had had his beach walk, Danny had talked me round, for now at least, and I couldn't suppress a chuckle as he recounted, in his easy way, a story about an old man in Ballyshannon who rustled sheep. For a blissful few minutes, I didn't care that the denizens of St Branok saw me with the interloper who'd reawakened the Talan Bray nightmare.

Our laughter on the stairs announced our reconciliation to Roy and Emily who were sipping mugs of tea and chatting when we strolled into the office. On our arrival their talk stuttered to a stop and Emily's cheeks reddened.

Danny bathed editorial in a grin. 'I need to get off to meet my contact. See you later.' He disappeared with a wave, leaving all the usual paraphernalia on his desk. It was obvious his marching orders had been rescinded.

'I didn't think we'd be seeing any more of Danny,' said Roy matter of factly, doing a wonderful job of hiding astonishment.

I hesitated, unsure how to explain my change of heart after all that had happened, all that Danny had done. 'He says he has new information about the Talan Bray which is watertight and which we can use,' I said, struggling valiantly to make a sensible case. 'He's checking out a few details and I'll be meeting him later to decide whether he can continue at the Gazette. I'm prepared to give him one last chance to explain himself. He did good work for us before all this crap over the Talan Bray blew up in our faces.'

It was believable. Almost. I kept my voice as cool as possible, but deep down my heart was singing.

CHAPTER TWENTY-SEVEN

My mood had swung due south again by the end of the day. Danny hadn't reappeared by the time I was ready to go home. Roy and Emily had long since departed, but I hung on for an extra hour, dithering over a myriad of minor things which could have waited until the morning.

Still he didn't come. Yet again he'd let me down.

Angry, I called his mobile a few times but got the cheery recorded message: 'Hi, this is Danny Flanagan. Not available right now. You know what to do.'

I drove home quicker than I should have, stirring the gear stick and gripping the steering wheel. The Landy bounced through the potholes more violently than usual. It started to rain, the headlights picking out sparkling droplets. The windscreen wipers moved back and forth, smearing the screen with murky water, dead insects and Cornish mud.

A tingling surged through me as I reached the cottage, a sensation I was becoming used to. I couldn't get out of my head the threats and the cold, calculating person behind them. Who were they and why were they so determined to stop our investigations?

The external security light clicked on, its glare driving back the shadows. The front door was firmly locked but, accompanied by Rufus, I carried out the now familiar routine inspection established in the aftermath of the letter on the bed. Hallway, sitting room and kitchen first followed by the upstairs bedrooms and bathroom.

All normal. Undisturbed.

I gave Rufus his evening meal and a few treats and then settled in the cold sitting room with a tumblerful of whisky and a ham sandwich. It would do. It would have to. A black depression crowded in on me, deepened by the heady intoxication of my earlier happiness. Danny was a cheat, a liar and a general waste of space. I hated him more than anybody else on planet Earth. I didn't have the strength to take Rufus for a walk so I let him out the back door to do the necessary. He returned a few minutes later, wet and muddy, wagging his tail.

Bed was a blessed relief. With a sigh, Rufus stretched out in his usual spot to warm my feet and I drifted into a dazed stupor, half expecting the phone to ring. It would be an apologetic Danny calling to explain that the interview had taken much longer than expected. Or that his raucous car had broken down. Or that he'd tripped in a pothole and broken his leg. Any explanation would do. Any explanation which didn't involve him having broken his promise and let me down. Anything at all.

CHAPTER TWENTY-EIGHT

The phone stayed silent. By morning, the wind was gusting, rain was trickling down the windows and surf was thundering in the cove. Depleted, I climbed out of bed and tiptoed to the wardrobe, hugging myself against the morning chill. Jeans and trainers wouldn't do today, not for the Talan Bray memorial service at St Mary Magdalene Church.

I pulled out the black Mayfair dress I used for meetings with the bank. The material was cold and damp as I slipped it on with a thick, warming pair of black tights. One day I'd get Gwel Teg fitted with central heating – if the gas company ever found enough spare cash in its multi-billion-pound coffers to deliver mains gas to an achingly beautiful but remote cottage on the cliffs.

Danny was constantly in my thoughts. I'd surely see him at the memorial service, if not before. He'd need a bloody good reason why he hadn't kept his promise of returning to the Gazette last night. Most probably, I'd tell him he was a miserable bag of excrement who didn't keep his promises and we'd go our separate ways – or as separate as possible in a coastal Cornish town like St Branok.

It was going to be a long day. I was nervous of the reception I and any other press might receive at the memorial service. And then there was the job of getting everything ready for the Gazette's biggest edition of the year. There would be complications and late changes. There always were.

A leaden sky was lightening to pewter as I headed out the door with Rufus's dark, soulful eyes watching me go. With so much at stake, I'd arranged for Rufus to be collected by Suzie, my dog walker. She'd stretch his legs with a brisk walk along the cliffs or on the heathland where Kestrels hovered and Buzzards soared in high circles, screeching their cat-like 'kee-yaa' calls.

I'd chosen the most wind-proof coat I owned, which also, conveniently, was the newest. Many years of journalism and Remembrance Sundays had taught me that standing around at a memorial service with winter well on its way was a bone-jarringly cold experience.

Parking the Landy in its usual place at the Gazette offices, I kept an eye out for Mrs Ridley or anybody else who might be waiting to slap me, spit at me, kick me, punch me or cancel their advertising. There was nobody apart from Trevor Tangye, the milkman. He gave me a cheery, 'Morning, Kate.'

I fiddled with my jumble of keys, hunting for the one for the front door. As always, it was the last one which came to hand. I tutted to myself. Being stuck on the front doorstep with a cold and damp south-westerly howling up the street was a chastening experience even if you were in your warmest coat.

At last, I pushed the key into the lock, but it only turned a fraction and then stuck. I tried harder, with both hands this time, but still it wouldn't budge. I twisted. I pulled. I pushed.

The door swung inwards and I fell in after it. Another forced door or an old lock that had finally given up the ghost? The lock was unmarked. It didn't look forced. My anxious mind was more than ready to jump to all sorts of conclusions these days.

In editorial, everything was haphazardly normal – everything except Danny's desk. That was different somehow. Hadn't there been a laptop and a notebook there the previous evening? If he had returned to the office, why not ring me? The man was infuriating.

I slipped into my morning routine. A mug of scalding hot tea. The computer blinking awake. The morning check with the emergency services. The police reported that a man had been taken to Treliske Hospital the previous afternoon the victim of a road accident, a hit and run. He was in a 'serious condition' but wouldn't be named until relatives had been informed.

A sudden fear for Danny swept through me. I spat out a question. 'Where was it?'

'Near St Buryan.'

'Oh, right.' I couldn't disguise a hint of relief in my voice. St Buryan was twenty miles away at least and road accidents happened all the time.

I took as many details as possible. It would fill a space in this week's newspaper. I tapped out a few paragraphs for page two. The usual stuff: 'Police are appealing for witnesses…'

Roy, Emily and Brenda slipped into their usual positions and editorial was soon humming with phone calls, the tapping of keyboards and the brewing of morning cuppas.

CHAPTER TWENTY-NINE

Every living soul in St Branok turned up for the memorial service, or so it seemed. St Mary Magdalene Church, a towering, granite edifice set at one end of town on a blustery headland, was full to overflowing, with scores of people standing at the back, Roy and I included. Dressed in black, heads hung low, sharing an inadequate number of prayer books, we sang hymns and listened to speakers paying tribute to the eight men who'd died.

The names of the 'Talan Bray Eight' were read out slowly and sonorously. James Trelawney, Jedediah Ridley, Robert Ridley, Seth Maltby, Andrew McDaid, William Carpenter, John Ashby and Nigel Peters would be forever in our hearts and prayers, we were told. They were heroes and heroes deserved respect, not pettifogging, sensationalist articles in Sunday newspapers. Danny would realise how hurtful his article had been when he bothered to turn up.

The St Branok Choir sang Tennyson's valedictory poem 'Crossing the Bar' and, for a while at least, the incessant Atlantic wind and the crash of the surf was overpowered by human voices and our deep, private thoughts.

Afterwards, the crowd trudged along a windswept path to lay wreaths in a memorial garden for the lifeboat crew. The land had been donated anonymously and, with help from the local community, the garden had been completed in time for the tenth anniversary.

It was neat and tidy with a wonderful view of the surging Atlantic, and those responsible had done their best to give the garden colour – pale pinks and vivid yellows – even at this time of year. It was the sort of place for a long, thoughtful meander on a warm spring or summer evening as a south-westerly caressed your face and mussed your hair. Today, the Atlantic breezes were snatching and cold and far from friendly.

A message from the town council on a neat, square plaque set in granite paid tribute to the courage and self-sacrifice of the lost eight, the 'bravest of the brave'.

Camera crews from the regional television stations and a smattering of press photographers recorded the sad affair, careful to keep a respectful distance from slow moving, solemn crowds. Sullen faces turned away from them, and there was the occasional whispered profanity on the breeze.

Portly Mayor Eric Rowe stood to one side with a microphone thrust under his nose by a reporter from a local radio station. His resonant Cornish accent was audible, even from a distance. He was talking about the strength of the community, the power of the Atlantic and the enormous debt owed to the lifeboatmen. Stirring, emotional words which tugged at the heart strings but added nothing new.

Mrs Ridley walked slowly, eyes awash with tears, looking frail and vulnerable. A person more different from the swearing maniac who'd attacked me in the Gazette car park it was hard to imagine. She was wearing a black dress which might have fitted her once but was now a size too small; the material was taut and stretched on her waist and hips. I wondered if she had worn the same dress ten years earlier at the funeral of her two sons, Bobby and Jed. Her legs were thin and scrawny, almost bird-like. She hung on the arm of a much younger man.

Morgan Ridley. The third son. He worked on Mike Pedrick's trawlers as a deckhand and was a regular in The Mermaid. A hard, sour individual with fleshy bags already forming under his quick, cynical eyes. He was a troublemaker when he'd glugged half a dozen pints. There had been a few appearances in the local courts for minor offences. Might he have been the person who'd attacked me in the alleyway on the night of the Shout at the Devil event? No, that person was smaller. If you were punched by Morgan Ridley, you stayed punched.

I felt so sorry for Mrs Ridley then. I'd never had children, never had the desire to have them, but the loss of two sons – to whom she'd given birth, then suckled and raised to become men – had to be a crushing, never-ending burden to bear. She'd needed to take that grief and anger out on somebody, and that somebody had been me. I hadn't deserved it. I hadn't done anything wrong. But I understood it and, at that moment, I was profoundly sympathetic.

Joe, uncharacteristically downcast, was stood under an oak tree stripped of its leaves by the autumn winds. He was sucking hard on a cigarette, talking out of the corner of his mouth to a couple of harbour workers.

Pedrick was also present. As expected. He never missed an opportunity to be seen out and about in the local community. There was talk of him seeking election as a councillor the following year. He was with his usual entourage of trawler skippers and local businesspeople. Everybody, male and female, gravitated towards him, whether at the pub or at public events.

I kept a watch out for John Harding. Despite his

bitterness, he might have felt compelled to pay his respects to his former colleagues. But there was no sign of him.

Strangely, there was no sign of Danny either. His absence was inexplicable. Any journalist wanting to report on the tenth anniversary commemorations would be bound to attend in order to capture the mood of the community. A fresh bout of anxiety tingled through me.

Roy and I walked back to the Gazette together, thoughtful. It was impossible not to have been moved by the ceremony and the strength of feeling in the local community demonstrated by the silent hundreds dressed in black.

Emily was at her desk when we got back. But this wasn't the Emily we'd left three hours earlier. She was distraught, her eyes awash with tears. Trails of black mascara ran down her cheeks.

I put a protective arm around her shoulder. 'Emily, what's wrong?' Consoling her during the many minor crises in her young life was the closest I got to being a mum.

'It's Danny,' she said. 'He's been in an accident. It's serious.'

CHAPTER THIRTY

The walls closed in on me. 'Danny?' I blustered, desperate. 'No, that can't be right. There must have been a mistake.'

Emily gulped, suppressed a whimper and wiped away a smudged tear. 'I checked on that hit and run accident near St Buryan. One of my police contacts gave me the name of the victim even though it hasn't been officially released.' She took a deep breath. 'It was a Daniel Joseph Flanagan. He's in intensive care at Treliske.'

'Are you sure? Absolutely sure? St Buryan is miles away.'

Emily shook her head. 'No mistake. It's definitely him.'

It was true. In my heart, I knew it was true. His non-appearance at the office last night without any explanation, even a Danny explanation...his absence at the memorial service...his silence. It all added up.

I clutched the back of Emily's chair. 'I'm going down there.'

'What about the Gazette?' said Roy, ever the pragmatist, ever a loyal servant of the Gazette. 'There's still work to do if we're going to get it out onto the streets this week.'

Damn the Gazette. Damn the advertisers. Damn the world. 'There's no way I'm staying here re-writing reports from the Rotarians while Danny's fighting for his life in intensive care,' I blurted before muttering, 'I'm sorry, Roy. It's just such a shock.'

I saw empathy in Roy's wrinkled, friendly face. 'You go, Kate. I'll sort it out. Forget about the Gazette and go to Danny.'

'Are you sure you can manage?'

'Yes, it won't be the first time.'

'Thanks…thanks so much, Roy.' I looked at the floor, no longer able to hold his stare without revealing my inner agony.

'I'll come too,' said Emily. She hesitated. 'If you can spare me, Roy?'

Roy smiled, once again the omnipotent editor who'd ruled the Gazette for decades. 'Yes, of course. Let me know how Danny's getting on.'

I raced out to the Landy with Emily close behind and stabbed the key in the ignition, silently pleading with the metal lump under the bonnet. *Don't let me down, you bastard. Fail me now and you're history.* The old diesel clattered grumpily into life. I pressed the accelerator. Hard. The engine screamed.

'Will Roy be alright by himself?' Emily pressed a paper hankie to her watery eyes.

'He'll be fine,' I said. 'He's loving it. Just like old times.'

We careered along St Branok's narrow streets and then out into the country, the Landy's ancient suspension bumping and bouncing through the rough, sharp corners.

CHAPTER THIRTY-ONE

I'd only ever seen a vibrant Danny. Full of life. Laughing. Smiling. Winking cheekily. But he was none of those things when we arrived at his hospital bedside. Tubes kept him alive. Not that you could tell he was alive. He lay unmoving. In a coma, the doctors said.

Beneath bruised and grazed skin were multiple injuries. His condition deteriorated during the afternoon and a decision was taken that urgent abdominal surgery was needed.

We waited for the results. Anxious. Desperate.

Afternoon dragged into evening, and still we stayed. I gripped Emily's hand. 'Your family will be wondering what's happened to you. Shouldn't you let them know? You don't have to stay. It could be a long night. I can call a taxi. Put it on your expenses.'

Emily wiped away her latest tears. One trickled down to splash on the floor of the waiting room. 'I'll text my parents, but I'm staying here with you.'

We hugged each other. For all his brash behaviour, Danny had touched a chord in both of us.

'You've eaten nothing since lunch,' I said. There that mum inside me, usually so well concealed, coming out again.

'Neither have you.'

I nodded. Once again, I was trying to survive the day on a few snatched mouthfuls. Then I remembered Rufus. Heavens, Suzie would have returned him to the cottage after the walk and he would be waiting hungrily for me to return. 'I need to make a call,' I said, standing up.

'Roy?'

'Rufus,' I confessed. 'He's by himself at the cottage. I need to call Suzie and ask her to look after him tonight.' Plead, more like.

The conversation went better than expected. When she heard I was at the hospital, Suzie promised to go straight over to the cottage, pick up Rufus and take him back to her place for the night, which she shared with her husband, two dogs and a cat.

I returned to my vigil. Emily and I slouched on hard chairs, trying to pass the longest hours I could ever recall with snatches of conversation and leafing through well-thumbed copies of 'Hello' magazine strewn on a table. Seemingly, the world had nothing better to discuss than footballers cheating on their girlfriends, a celeb's lavish wedding in Antigua and the break-up of a Hollywood marriage. My world stood stock still, but it continued to turn for every other person on the planet.

Shortly before two in the morning, Emily and I were woken from a doze by a surgeon wearing blue theatre scrubs. He looked as pale and tired as I felt. 'Are you Mr Flanagan's wife and daughter?'

I stretched, my neck aching from having snoozed at an awkward angle. 'We're here for Danny, but we're work colleagues and friends, not family. His relatives are in Northern Ireland.'

'Do you know how to contact them?'

'Unfortunately, no. We've only known Danny for a short time, but we're good friends.'

The surgeon, a slim Scotsman in his fifties, sat down next to us, his demeanour sympathetic. 'The operation went well,' he said. 'Mr Flanagan is out of immediate danger and he's responding well to treatment.'

Emily wiped away a tear. 'Will he make a full recovery?'

The surgeon produced a reserved, professional smile perfected on thousands of anxious enquirers over the years. 'We hope so, but the injuries were extensive. There's nothing more that can be done tonight. I suggest you go home and rest. We can give you an update in the morning.'

He was right. There was nothing to be gained from hanging around in the brightly-lit corridors and rooms of the hospital. My lower back creaked as I got up, competing with a sore neck for the title of most stressed part of my tired body.

'Come on, Emily. I'll drop you home. You look exhausted.'

The usual breeze was whistling through the trees and clifftop grasses when I arrived back at the cottage. It snatched at my coat and my hair. I pulled my coat closed and suppressed a shiver.

The cottage was dark and cold. Of course. Without Rufus, I was more alone than ever, which was saying something. I was used to loneliness, had become inured to it. But Danny's accident, my tiredness and the strength-sapping chill of those early hours dragged me down to a new level of despondency.

I'd heard nothing from Roy and assumed he was well on his way to putting the latest edition of the Gazette to bed. Thank heavens for Roy. He'd probably got an ear-bashing from Marjorie, who was always telling him to take it easier. I'd buy him a bottle of his favourite whisky and get Marjorie a brooch I'd seen in a bric-a-brac shop off the high street. She loved trinkets.

Imagining the reserved pleasure in their faces that the gifts would evoke warmed me. The funeral and the shock of Danny's injuries had made it a very dark day indeed.

But I fell asleep easily enough when my head settled on the cold pillow. In every sense, I was done.

CHAPTER THIRTY-TWO

A thumping headache reverberated through my skull when I surfaced to the strident cry of seagulls. I trudged to the bathroom to splash cold Cornish water on sore eyes and dry, tired skin. The sun was high among fluffy clouds, chivvied by strong south westerlies. It was late, the day well advanced.

My conscience pricked me. I should have been at work long ago. For a few hours, I'd forgotten about the Gazette. I'd left it all to a frail septuagenarian and not even bothered to call him. My concern for Danny had been so all-consuming that, for once, the Gazette had been relegated to the minor league.

I was famished. I cooked one-minute porridge in the microwave and sank a large mug of hot, sweet tea. Three sugars, Marjorie style. I needed the energy. The tepid rays of an autumn sun slanted in through the kitchen window, warming me, while I rewound the events of the past few hours: the shock of Danny's accident, the frantic drive with Emily out to the hospital and then the long, long hours in anodyne corridors and rooms, waiting endlessly.

The phone rang and I stumbled into the hallway, still clutching my mug of sweet tea, the slate floor chilling my bare feet.

'Hello?'

THE ECHOING SHORE

'Kate, it's Roy.'

I gushed guiltily. 'Roy, I'm so sorry I haven't called you. I feel terrible about leaving you to pick up the pieces. Emily and I were at Treliske until two in the morning.' The nagging guilt held me back from asking whether the latest edition was ready to hit the streets or still languishing in the bowels of a computer at the printers.

'No problem. Anyway, we did it. The Talan Bray special edition is ready to go and I got home before Marjorie's lamb stew was totally ruined.'

'Who's 'we'? You did it all by yourself, didn't you?'

'Don't forget Brenda. She stayed almost as late as me last night to help with the layouts. She told Jeff that he'd have to sort out the evening meal for himself and the children.' Roy chuckled, adding, 'I don't think he liked it much.'

Brenda. Of all people. I'd always thought of her as work shy, a bit of a skiver when she got the chance. Perhaps the Gazette mattered to her more than I thought. Cometh the hour, cometh the woman, as Roy would say. I'd have to buy her something as a special thank you. A couple of bottles of Merlot should fit the bill. My list of peace offerings was growing.

'How's Danny?' said Roy.

'When we left last night the doctors said he was no longer in immediate danger but that he had extensive injuries and was in a coma. They're hoping for a full recovery but can't be sure.' My voice croaked to a halt as a lump grew in my throat. The possibility of Danny being anything other than the irrepressible individual who'd strolled into our offices on a wet and windy day was a nightmare I was determined not to think about, let alone discuss.

'Danny's as tough as old boots,' said Roy, equably. 'I

200

expect he'll bounce back. What do you want to do about the Talan Bray service at Truro Cathedral this afternoon? I could get down there. Larry Rowe will be taking pictures for the Western Morning News and the West Briton. I've asked him to get a few for the Gazette as well. He owes me a favour or two.'

'That's wonderful,' I said. 'Roy, you've been fantastic about all this. Incredible.'

'Oh, it was great fun. And the Gazette is looking good with its Talan Bray supplement. I don't think we'll have much difficulty selling those extra copies. By the way, I had difficulty locking up last night. There's something wrong with the front door.'

The broken lock. I'd forgotten about that. 'It was broken when I arrived yesterday morning. I was going to get Jerry to look at it, but it went out of my mind, what with the memorial service and Danny and everything.' Jerry Tallack was a local locksmith whose prices were about half of those demanded by companies in Truro.

'The sooner the better. I didn't like to leave the door unlocked last night, but there wasn't much I could do. In the end I jammed an old newspaper under the door to stop it blowing open. Anyway, everybody knows there's nothing much worth stealing here. I'll call Jerry and ask him to sort it.'

'Thanks. I'll get to the office as soon as I can, but please don't stay late again tonight. I'll be receiving angry calls from Marjorie if late nights become a habit.'

Straight after my call with Roy, I dialled the number of the Devon and Cornwall Police Press Office. Miranda Johnson, a press officer I knew well, answered.

'Kate, how are you?'

'Oh, bearing up,' was the best I could manage. 'I was

calling about that road accident near St Buryan on Tuesday afternoon. The person who was injured, Danny Flanagan, is a freelancer who's been working at our offices.'

'Very sorry to hear that, but we haven't yet released the name of the victim. Anyway, how can I help?'

'I want to confirm a few details – time, location, that sort of thing.'

'The victim was found lying near the A30 at about four o'clock by a local farmer. His car was parked in a lay-by. His injuries were consistent with him having been hit by a vehicle, but there was no sign of the other vehicle and no witnesses. We're treating it as a hit and run and, of course, are appealing for anybody with information to come forward.'

'Where exactly was he found? Is there any indication of why he got out of his car? Had it broken down?'

'The precise location was a lay-by at Changwens. The victim's car has been removed from the scene and is being held in storage. There was nothing to indicate it had broken down.'

'Why would anybody stop their car at such a remote place and then go for a walk?'

'There's an historical site nearby, a stone circle called Boscawen-un. People often stop there.'

I paced up and down the hallway, as far as the cord allowed, trying to make sense of it all. Danny didn't do ancient history and scenic walks weren't his thing. He'd said he was going to meet a contact who would reveal everything about the Talan Bray. Then he'd ended up three quarters dead in the middle of nowhere, near an historical site.

It was baffling, to say the least. Might there be something to all this paganism nonsense after all?

CHAPTER THIRTY-THREE

It was mid-afternoon and the autumn light was already beginning to fade. Striated clouds filtered a watery sun and, as ever, the wind was blowing from out of the cold heart of the North Atlantic.

The gorse and bracken, heavy with a recent downpour, dripped pearls of water as I brought the Landy to a crunching stop in a lay-by off the A30. A lay-by like any other. This remote spot was where it had happened. Danny had parked here, possibly in the same space now occupied by my Landy, stepped out of his rickety Volkswagen and, according to the police, been hit by a passing motorist. Who hadn't stopped. Had left him to die.

I zipped my ski jacket, pulled up the collar and trudged down an overgrown path. Somewhere behind me, a dog barked. I lengthened my stride, not wanting to encounter a protective farmyard canine. Not out here. Alone. I wished Rufus was with me, but he was still living the high life at Suzie's.

The barking stopped and the wind dropped, leaving only a hum from the main road traffic. I stepped around a large puddle swollen by the autumn rains, followed a fence and climbed over a stile. Then I stopped in wonder.

A shaft of sunlight pierced the gloom, illuminating the

curious stone feature which had stood for centuries in the Cornish wind, rain and sun.

Boscawen-un.

The air was heavy with humidity and cold as I ventured inside the circle of nineteen stones, which seemed to create their own light. One stood out. Made of an iridescent quartz rather than grey granite, it glittered in the dying daylight like a tarnished jewel.

Near the centre of the circle stood a taller, more pointed stone. It was set at a forty-five-degree angle, like an axe head hurled into the ground.

The breeze again gathered strength, blowing strands of hair into my face. I brushed them aside, irritated. I wanted to see everything, no matter how small and inconsequential it might seem, to better understand what had brought Danny to this lonely location.

A strange place, a solitary place, created for worship and rituals long ago by hard hands wielding ancient tools. I shivered, not only from the chill. Water seeped into my trainers from the mud and wet grass.

Beyond a hedgerow, near the lane leading back to the lay-by, a flock of crows rose into the air, cawing raucously, disturbed by something or somebody. I edged closer to the centre stone, wishing I could melt into its lengthening shadow.

Then I saw him. A single figure in a hooded jacket stood near the stile I'd climbed over to reach the circle. Tall and silent, he was facing me, though the hood shadowed his features.

I blinked. Twice. Three times. In the gathering dusk, my wary eyes and taut nerves had to be playing tricks. But no; he was still there. Still watching.

My breathing quickened. Was there another route back to the Landy? No, not unless I wanted to plunge through chest-high bracken and gorse and end up lost with a shattered ankle.

Long seconds passed. Still the silent, dark figure didn't move.

I was being silly. I began striding back the way I'd come, avoiding any appearance of haste, which would hint at weakness, at panic. The figure also began moving. Towards me.

The most prominent features of his face were visible now: angular cheekbones, thin lips, eyes set deep.

The gap between us closed. I looked ahead, into nothingness, giving him no reason to engage with me.

'Amazing,' he said as we passed within an arm's length of each other.

I shouldn't have answered, should have kept walking, but an automatic response caused me to slow and say, 'Pardon?'

'I was saying, this place, it's amazing. I often ride out here at dusk to feel the magic.' He was smiling. An open, honest smile on a young face. Barely a man, really. A freckly boy in his late teens.

My anxiety eased. 'Yes, it's wonderfully peaceful.' I went to move on, but his next words halted me.

'Do you know why the stone in the middle is set at an angle?'

'I thought it might be falling over,' I said. A lame answer, given without thought. I wanted to be out of here. Something – perhaps the dusky light, perhaps the remoteness, perhaps this being the place where Danny had been injured – set me on edge.

'Actually, it's been like that for hundreds of years. But

you might be right. Morons digging for treasure could have caused it to move. Or there might be a spiritual significance to it. I think it's spiritual.' He opened his gangly arms as if to bring the whole of the circle within his reach. 'This, all this, dates from the bronze age, you know.'

I edged closer to the stile. 'Thanks for the information. I can see why you come out here. It's a special place.'

'Yeah, it's cool, really cool. My friends don't get it, don't think it's special at all so I come out here by myself. To think. It's a great place to see the stars. My name's Tristan, by the way.'

'Kate,' I replied.

I was climbing over the stile, almost clear, when a thought struck me. 'Tristan, were you out here on Tuesday afternoon? A friend of mine was badly injured near the road. You might have seen something?'

'Wow, that sounds terrible, Kate. I hope he's okay. But, no, sorry. The last time I was here was Saturday evening.'

'Okay, thank you anyway.'

I strode away, glancing back a few times. The Landy was exactly as I'd left it. A moped was parked nearby – young Tristan's, no doubt. A nice lad. A bit of a dreamer, bit of a loner, but friendly and harmless enough.

I still breathed a sigh of relief as the Landy's engine burst into life. I'd been unnerved by that tall figure in the twilight, the very vision of the grim reaper, though the danger had turned out to be nothing more than an innocent young lad with myth and magic on his mind.

There was something ethereal, captivating and powerful at Boscawen-un. But no clue as to why Danny had gone to such a place.

CHAPTER THIRTY-FOUR

A grey day had slipped into night by the time I picked up Rufus and, as usual, received an effusive, waggy, licky welcome. Suzie waited at the door of her modern cardboard box of a house, with central heating and all the mod cons, to wave me on my way.

It was far too late to go to the Gazette. Roy, Brenda and Emily would be long gone. I had phone calls to make, though, and I'd eaten hardly anything, so I headed for the cottage as quickly as possible. I was going to grind to a halt if I didn't start looking after myself. Lack of sleep, little food, constant stress, too much booze and a growing nicotine addiction…I was on a downward path and it was steepening.

My first call was to Treliske Hospital to find that Danny's condition remained unchanged. The second was to Roy. I was pushing it with him, though. Marjorie, ever protective of her frail husband, would have something to say if I started to rely on him too heavily. I needed to get my act together.

'Kate, I thought you were going to call in at the office before we closed? I've been worried about you.' Roy was genuinely concerned, not accusatory. Workaholic Kate Tregillis disappearing with little explanation wasn't the Kate he knew.

'I'm sorry, Roy. Terribly sorry.' Most of my conversations

with Roy these days involved lots of apologising. 'I've been out to the place where Danny was found. It's close to an ancient stone circle called Boscawen-un.'

There was a pause and then, 'I know that area well enough, but why did you go out there?'

I shifted uneasily on the seat in the hallway. 'I'm not sure. I guess I was trying to understand the reason for Danny being there. It's a strange place, beautiful but also sort of creepy.'

'What do the police say?'

'They've put out an appeal for witnesses, but at the moment they're treating it as a hit and run. An accident.'

'What do you think?'

I stared out of the cottage window into the blackness of the night, trying to envisage what happened at Boscawen-un. 'I can see why they would think it was a hit and run. There have been a few accidents along that stretch of road, and the lay-by where Danny parked is only big enough for a few cars.'

'But?'

'It doesn't add up, doesn't feel right. He said he was going to see somebody who would finally help him solve what happened to the Talan Bray.'

'If that's the case, what happened to that person and why did he ask for a meeting in the middle of nowhere?'

I sighed. 'To get Danny in a remote place where he could be killed or seriously injured?'

Another pause, longer this time. 'That's a hell of a theory.'

'Is it? We know that somebody was trying to stop our investigations into the loss of the Talan Bray and that Danny wasn't prepared to listen. He said he was getting close to the truth.'

'Until Danny comes out of his coma, we're not going to

have the answer. By the way, Jerry popped round this afternoon and fixed the broken lock. His bill is on your desk.'

'What caused the breakage? Did he say?'

'No, he just replaced it and went on his way. You know Jerry, he doesn't waste time with chit-chat. Why do you ask?'

I rubbed an aching forehead. 'I'm wondering if it had been forced.'

'Who? Why?'

'Some of Danny's stuff in the office might have disappeared. I think a laptop and a notebook were on his desk when I left in the evening but not there the following morning.'

'Are you sure?'

I dragged my hand down my face. 'Not one hundred per cent, no.'

'What are you suggesting – that somebody broke into our offices to take Danny's laptop?'

Goosebumps broke out on my arm. 'It's possible if somebody wanted to remove any trace of what Danny had discovered. I'll call Jerry first thing in the morning and find out if there's anything more he can tell me about that broken lock.'

'Be careful, Kate. Be very careful. If half of what you're suggesting is true, then there's somebody out there who is prepared to go to any lengths to cover his tracks. You could be next in the firing line.'

'I'll be fine. I've always got Rufus.'

The call ended and, shivering, I went into the sitting room to start a fire. I needed its warmth. I needed to lose myself in those flickering, flaring flames and my thoughts.

About broken locks. About paganism. About Danny.

About murder.

CHAPTER THIRTY-FIVE

Jerry Tallack was a busy man who flitted from one job to the next. By the time I spoke to him, the fixing of the lock at our office was a distant memory.

'Did anything seem strange at all? As if the lock had been forced?' I said.

'Not that I noticed. To be honest, I didn't look that closely. I don't have the time to do an Inspector Morse on every broken lock. I replaced the mechanism and went on my way to the next job. It's been hectic lately.'

'Do you still have the old lock?'

'Sorry, it was disposed of. If I hung on to every broken lock I replaced…'

I called Dobbie to report a possible break-in, but by the end of the conversation I got the distinct impression he thought I was wasting his time. And perhaps he was right. 'So, we have a rusty old lock that could have broken and an office where a few items might – or might not – have been taken. It's not much to go on, Ms Tregillis,' he concluded.

Through the rest of Friday and into Saturday my downward spiral showed no sign of easing. Danny's condition remained stable but unchanged. More snatched drags on cigarettes ensued as I tried to pull the fractured bits of my life together. I got good at zoning out, incapable of doing anything that involved too much thought or effort. Even my investigations into the incident which left Danny bloodied and broken and what he had discovered were on pause. Fear and misery had conquered – for now.

I might easily be the next target. Why stop at Danny? Why not tie up all the loose ends, to be sure? His would-be murderer was out there somewhere, hiding in the shadows, and I had no idea who he or she was or where or when they would strike next. If they struck at all.

A woman living alone in a remote cottage on the cliffs – I could hardly make it easier for anyone who might be planning an unfortunate accident for me. It didn't need to be a road accident this time. There were any number of ways Kate Tregillis might die and nobody would be sure how it had happened. The surging sea. The loose, precipitous cliffs. The Atlantic storms. There was no shortage of possibilities. My body would be washed ashore, swollen and sodden, in the cove below my cottage.

I could save myself. Get out of St Branok. Go back to London. Find another job. I had the contacts, and I still had a vestige of my reputation, even after three years in the wilds of North Cornwall. There would be no disgrace in it. I'd worked my socks off at the Gazette, trying to turn it around. Nobody could say I hadn't tried. And where had it got me? A life of fear and debt in a freezing, clifftop cottage swept by the Atlantic winds.

There was one bright spark. The special Talan Bray edition of the Gazette had hit the streets and, by all accounts, was selling well. It was as good as Roy had promised.

I could have rung the hospital again to check on Danny's condition, but I wanted to go there in person – to see for myself, to show support and for all the other reasons why anxious friends, relatives and lovers gather in bleak, medical corridors waiting for news. Any news.

But first, I needed to look after one of the other significant males in my life. Rufus would be expecting a walk and I was determined not to disappoint him. A forty-minute hike through Nethercott Woods and then back along the cliffs to the cottage should be enough for now. I'd be back in time to take him for another stroll before it got dark. Rufus would forgive me for leaving him for a few hours. He'd forgive me for anything.

The path descended steeply to the valley floor and then followed a ribbon of muddy flowing water. The heavy rains had turned a tinkling trickle into a torrent, carrying dead leaves, broken branches and all the other detritus of late autumn. I wandered past gnarly oaks, Rufus cavorting ahead and stopping to sniff at a hole or the carcass of a dead squirrel.

On a bright spring morning, this was a place of dappled light, of bluebells, celandines and wild garlic. But on a dull autumn day such as this it was sombre and austere, the only colour coming from moss and ferns and rusty brown leaves.

Rufus disappeared on the scent of something. I called him but he didn't come so I strode deeper into the woods, away from the stream, intent on finishing the walk and getting to the hospital. Several minutes went by and still there was no sign of him.

I called louder, 'Rufus, Rufus, come here, boy. Rufus.'

The silence of this forested enclave struck me. So different from Gwel Teg, where the rush of the Atlantic and the whistling wind dominated. It was like walking in from a busy, thundering road to stand in the peace and quiet of an empty cathedral.

Off to my right, something moved among bushes.

Something large. But the fleeting shadow was gone by the time I'd turned my head.

I stopped, holding my breath.

Nothing.

My mind was playing tricks. I was being childish, inventing shapes and threats which didn't exist. Still, it would be comforting to have Rufus at my side. I walked on, shouting for him, but he didn't come.

The silence and the gloom deepened, became more sinister. The world was on pause. I sped up wanting this walk to be over. Where the hell was Rufus? I was annoyed with him for disappearing, for deserting me. Leaving me vulnerable.

Ahead, the path narrowed as it wound between two granite outcrops, tinged shades of green by moss and algae. The light was weakest here. I'd sauntered through a thousand times, barely giving it a thought, but this time it was different, forbidding.

A sixth sense or a renewed fit of paranoia? I eased my pace again, torn between pressing on and turning back. Retracing my route would take longer but would be lighter and less oppressive. It was the coward's way out. And I'd never thought of myself as a coward.

Out of the corner of my eye, I saw it again: a transient flicker of movement among the trees and the ferns. I edged backwards.

I could run. I could hide. But from what?

The ferns rustled. Something was coming closer. I turned to confront it, my whole body tingling—

Rufus. It was only Rufus.

He ran out from cover with his tail wagging, and I wrapped my arms around his neck, annoyed with myself, with my stretched nerves and with just about everything else in the world.

Annoyance eased into relief. I took a deep breath and hurled a stick for Rufus. I needed to get a grip.

CHAPTER THIRTY-SIX

The Mermaid was buzzing. A typical Saturday night hubbub of local voices punctuated by laughter and the clinking of glasses wafted through the bar as I traipsed in with Rufus, desperately in need of something. A new life, perhaps.

I licked my lips at the oily aroma of steak and chips. I'd eaten nothing all day. This wasn't good. I needed to get back onto an even keel, as the St Branok fishermen would say.

Easing my way through the crowd at the bar, I caught the attention of Angie, who was sharing a laugh with a bearded young fisherman still dressed in his yellow oilskins and boots. 'What can I get you, Kate?'

I delved in an inner pocket for some cash. 'Gin and tonic, please. Make it a double. I'll also have a rare sirloin steak with all the trimmings.'

'There's a forty-five minute wait for the steaks. We're very busy, as you can see.'

'No problem. I've got plenty of time.' Rufus and I had nothing else to do for the rest of the evening apart from slouch in a cold sitting room at the cottage. 'Is Joe around by the way? I was hoping to have a chat with him.'

Angie checked the clock behind the bar. 'He's been out for most of the day but he shouldn't be long – promised to be back by seven. I'll kill him if he's any later. We can barely cope.'

I picked up my gin and tonic and pointed at the snug, which still had a few spare seats and a table. 'Thanks. I'll be in there. Perhaps you could point him in my direction when he turns up.'

'Sure. I'll let him know.' Angie turned to deal with a gaggle of burly men leaning on the bar and waving ten-pound and five-pound notes at her.

I settled Rufus under the vacant table in the snug and took a long pull on the gin and tonic, relishing its bitter sweetness. It tasted damned good. Was I an alcoholic? These days, I wasn't able to get through the day without booze.

The gin and tonic disappeared in record time. The alcohol washed through my system, warming me and leaving me fuzzy at the edges. I felt almost human.

When Angie happened to glance over, I pointed at my empty glass. She held up a hand in acknowledgement. Another one. Another double. And there might be another one after that. Who cared what I did to myself? Nobody. Nobody at all. Well, maybe Roy and Marjorie. And Rufus.

Rufus was stretched out with his eyes half closed. I reached down and patted him. He sighed contentedly.

As the initial hit of the alcohol passed, a seeping sadness took over. It'd been an appalling day. There'd been the silly scare in Nethercott Woods, which had metamorphosed from friendly, familiar woodland into a shadowy, sombre place embodying all my fears and vulnerabilities. And then there'd been another visit to the hospital with a drama of its own.

Danny was still being kept alive by tubes and wires. I'd been allowed to sit next to him for a while and even hold his hand. The interaction might help, they'd said. The search for his family in Northern Ireland was still under way.

My presence had had no noticeable effect. The hand had been lifeless, though warm and dry. A vision of when we'd first met had flashed into my mind – of his firm grip, damp from the Cornish rain. That had been a couple of lifetimes ago. So much had happened since then. Danny had given me a hope I hadn't felt for a very long time. A hope which probably misplaced.

I'd felt helpless as I'd sat by his hospital bed, his face uncharacteristically immobile with none of his usual sparkle of life and humour.

Would I ever again see that boyish cheekiness or hear his jokes and clumsy compliments?

Joe slipped out of the crowd to appear at my table, holding my second gin and tonic. He produced a sympathetic smile, revealing that either he knew about Danny or else my emotions were so bloody obvious they could be detected a mile away. 'Evening, Kate. I think this is yours.' He placed it carefully on a mat on my table and sat opposite me. 'Angie said you were hoping to see me.' He looked into my eyes more deeply than usual. 'Roy told me about Danny. It's terrible. How is he?'

I gripped the glass hard and took a sip. The same bitter sweetness as the first drink, but nowhere near as good. 'He's still in a coma. All we can do is wait.' My voice became hoarse as a surge of grief swept through me.

Joe placed a comforting hand on my shoulder. 'What happened?'

'The police are treating it as an accident, a hit and run, but...' My voice faded away.

'Go on. But what?' prompted Joe.

After a long silence, I risked raising my gaze from the table. 'Frankly, I've got my doubts. The circumstances are strange. He appears to have been hit by a passing vehicle close to the A30, near St Buryan.'

'That's a nasty stretch of road. There are often accidents. The youngsters tear up and down there like it's the Monaco Grand Prix.'

'So I've heard. But why did Danny go up there? It makes no sense. There's nothing there apart from an ancient stone circle.'

Joe shrugged. 'There's your reason. Those stone circles have a massive history. Danny told me he was investigating Cornwall's pagan past.'

I focused on two ice cubes jostling for position with a slice of lemon. 'I think there's something more to it than an accident,' I said. 'Both Danny and I have been threatened and attacked over the past few weeks, but Dobbie's not getting anywhere with his investigations.'

Joe leant forward. 'There's still a deep hurt running through St Branok about the Talan Bray. Danny's upset a lot of people with his stories and his investigations, but this accident is an unfortunate coincidence. The tenth anniversary has now passed, the memorial services have been held and the pathetic press have had their little drama and told their lies. St Branok needs to move on, get back to normal.'

'I'm a member of that *pathetic press* you're talking about,' I pointed out.

Joe held out his hands in a gesture of placation. 'I meant no offence to you, Kate. I never think of you as one of those bastards.'

'I don't know whether to take that as a compliment or

an insult.' There was irritation in my voice. 'The Gazette is a bona fide member of the press, like any other.'

Joe ran a hand over his chin. 'Sure, I know, but the Gazette has acted responsibly and given the crewmen the respect they deserve. That's more than can be said for most of the others. Anyway, it's all over now. The national press have run back to their rat holes for another ten years.'

A burst of laughter at the bar interrupted him. The crowd there was three-deep. Angie and the rest of the bar staff were struggling to keep up with the drinks orders.

Joe stood. 'Duty calls. I need to get back to the bar. What was it you wanted to talk about?'

'I'm determined to discover what Danny found out. You knew him as well as anybody around here. Did he say anything to you, mention any names?'

Joe blew a long sigh. 'Kate, can't you let it rest? Whatever you find out now isn't going to help Danny. It's just going to draw out all the hurt.'

His plea ignited the obstinate side of my nature. 'I'm not going to give up. Not now. Tell me anything you know. Please. Anything at all.'

For long seconds, Joe's eyes glittered with indecision and concern. Then he whispered, 'I'm not sure how much I should say.'

'Joe, anything you say to me will be treated in absolute confidence. And Danny was working with me. I have a right to know. Was he looking into anybody in particular?'

Joe glanced over his shoulder at the milling crowd of drinkers as if fearful of being overheard. 'Well, he was interested, very interested, in Mike Pedrick and his business dealings. He asked the trawlermen and some of the guys who work down at the harbour a lot of questions.'

'Questions about what?'

'About how Mike had made so much money in a town where most people are struggling. About who he did business with.' Joe blinked a couple of times and chewed his lower lip. 'Look, Kate, Mike is a reasonable guy. Most of the time. But he can also be a real shitty bastard to anybody standing in his way. I wouldn't mess with him. I'd have thought that you, of all people, would appreciate when to move on.'

'I'm tougher than you think. I can look after myself. And Rufus will take a chunk out of anybody who turns up uninvited at Gwel Teg. I'm never scared when I'm with Rufus.'

'The ultimate bodyguard, eh?'

'The ultimate companion,' I said. 'I don't know where I'd be without him.'

Joe bent to stroke Rufus's wiry fur before turning towards the bar. 'You're the journalist. You know best. Be careful, that's all.' And then he was lost in a throng of giggling, happy people.

The steak and chips arrived at last, and I tucked in. It was a good sirloin, tender and full of reddish-brown juices. I cut off a few slices for Rufus and quietly fed them to him while he waited under the table, his hungry brown eyes boring into me.

As I chewed, I thought of Mike Pedrick, a rare example of home-grown success in cash-starved Cornwall. A man who'd hauled himself above lowly beginnings on the slippery pole of Cornish life. Who'd started from nothing and now had a finger in every Cornish pie. Trawling, fish processing, gastropubs, shops, a car dealership…you name it. A pillar of the local community. But ruthless.

A man who would do anything to succeed.

CHAPTER THIRTY-SEVEN

By Monday morning I had a plan. It started with an interrogation of the fount of all St Branok knowledge, Roy, as soon as he turned up for work. A lifetime of journalism in St Branok had ensured that Roy knew everybody and everything. He had heard all the rumours and the tittle tattle, the half-truths and the lies.

Wheezing lightly, he slipped through the editorial door at his usual time, in his familiar tweed jacket and moleskin trousers with the Calabash pipe in his top pocket.

I surprised him by pulling up a chair and sitting next to him as he was firing up his computer.

I flicked open my notebook and held a pen over an empty page, the classic pose of the roving reporter. 'Roy, what can you tell me about Mike Pedrick?'

He did his usual 'thinking' thing of taking off his glasses and rubbing them with a small cloth. 'You know about as much as I do. He's a self-made millionaire. Started from nothing, an only child. His family scratched a living working for local farms and on boats – anything that paid the bills. He worked on the trawlers for a few years, became a skipper and then bought his own boat in partnership with a local businessman, Kevin McCreary. McCreary provided most of the funding and Pedrick the fishing expertise. They did well together. Very well. Bought more trawlers, took over the fish processing plant when it fell on hard times and then diversified into a few other businesses.'

'I remember McCreary,' I said. 'I met him when I was a trainee before I went to London. He always seemed an astute guy. I'm not surprised they did well together.'

Roy murmured agreement. 'They built quite an empire. But then something happened and they went their separate ways. Pedrick did what Pedrick excels at. He put the squeeze on and bought out McCreary for a fraction of the true value, if the rumours are to be believed.'

I imagined the scene. Ruthless. Brutal. Very Pedrick. 'What was the reason for the falling out?' I said at last.

Roy sat back in his chair, head tilted to one side. 'Why are you so interested in Mike Pedrick, Kate?'

I waved a hand as if batting away a fly. 'Oh, Joe mentioned that Danny was asking a lot of questions about him before he was found at Boscawen-un.'

A spasm of concern flashed across Roy's lined face. 'Pedrick's only ever been interested in two things: influence and money, though probably not in that order. If you want to investigate him, I'd recommend you do it mighty carefully.'

I nodded. 'Joe said something similar. He tried to warn me off. But if Pedrick is in any way responsible for Danny's injuries and the recent attacks, then I'll do my best to nail him. I've faced people before who think they're untouchable because of their wealth and their contacts. And usually I've come off best.' I sounded way more confident than I felt. 'Do we know why they split up?' I persisted.

Roy emitted a barely audible groan, but he knew his protégé wasn't going to give up. 'Most people assumed it was simply the case that Pedrick wanted to be the one and only boss. He didn't need a partner, and he found a way of getting rid of McCreary.'

'It was bitter then?'

'Goodness me, yes.'

'Where's McCreary now?'

'Having Pedrick as your enemy in a town like St Branok is a nightmare. He moved down the coast to Perranporth.'

'How long ago?'

'About ten years, I think.'

Excitement shivered through me. 'About the time when the Talan Bray was lost?'

Roy squinted and then said, 'Yes, I guess it was. Nobody's heard anything from him for years, as far as I know. I'm not even sure he's still alive.'

I sucked on my pen. If he was still living in Perranporth, a man like McCreary should be easy to find. Like St Branok, it was a small town where everybody knew everybody out of season. But when could I carve out the time to find him? It was always all hands to the pumps at the start of the week with stories to be written and edited, cavernous pages to be filled and looming deadlines to be met.

The phone on my desk buzzed. 'I'd better get this, but thanks, Roy. That's really helpful.'

It was Brenda, sounding breathless 'Mr Thompson is on the line, demanding to speak to you.'

I hesitated. George Thompson, the bank manager, was at the bottom of my wish list of callers, but I couldn't avoid him forever. Brenda added, 'You know, Mr Thompson from the bank?'

'Yes, yes, I know who you're talking about. Please tell him I'm out and that you'll ask me to call him later.'

I plunked down the handset, wondering what new stumbling block the bank was going to put in my way this time.

At my desk, a myriad of jobs was piling up. My hands were shaking. Slightly. Not noticeable to anybody else, thank God. But disconcerting for me.

I slunk out the back door and, in the alleyway, took a few long drags on a cigarette. I'd sworn not to become a regular smoker again, but everything was contriving to set me on the slippery slope of a fresh addiction.

An easterly was blowing, gentler than some of the recent south westerlies but still finding its way into this narrow space between buildings. The blue smoke from my cigarette was spun into a spiral before being swept upwards into a Cornish sky of light, wispy clouds.

The nicotine did its work. By the time I ground the poisonous stub beneath my heel, I was able, once again, to play the role of confident Kate Tregillis. I'd made a decision. To hell with the Gazette. To hell with the looming deadlines. To hell with Thompson and the bank.

I was going to find Kevin McCreary.

CHAPTER THIRTY-EIGHT

Kevin McCreary's home was a big, bay-fronted Victorian property, set high on a hill. Its appearance typified the man – neat, orderly and well maintained by no shortage of money.

Far below, the town of Perranporth and its four-mile beach lazed in the midday sun, epitomising the Cornwall dream. A green Atlantic, tranquil for a change, had retreated to expose vast swathes of golden sand. Dogs were being walked, horses were being ridden and a few distant wetsuit-clad figures were surfing the surging waves rolling shoreward.

I adjusted the rearview mirror of the Landy to stare at a tired, haunted face which had aged years in a few weeks. Wrinkles had deepened, blemishes had become darker and gravity had taken its toll. A touch of lip gloss was the best I could manage to mask the damage. I'd rushed out of editorial spouting assurances to be back by early afternoon, come hell or high water. Emily's mouth had opened and closed as though struggling to form the right question, Roy had frowned but his hard look had quickly morphed into gentle permission. He understood.

A stab of McCreary's doorbell prompted melodious chimes from deep within. There was the patter of swift, light footsteps and then the door swung open to reveal a trim figure. He was much the same man I remembered from my fledgeling journalist days. Equally dapper, just greyer with a few more wrinkles. The dark polo neck jumper and stylish chinos went well together. He still looked after himself.

I forced my most engaging grin. I needed to get off the doorstep if I was to have a conversation that might yield useful information.

A reserved smile played on his lips. 'Yes?'

'Kevin, it's Kate Tregillis from the North Cornwall Gazette. You might remember me from your time in St Branok. How are you?'

His mouth opened and his hand flew to his chin. 'Little Kate? My goodness. Yes, I remember you well. You were a real livewire in those days, always dashing here and there to ask questions. I don't think I ever saw you without a notebook in your hand. How the devil did you find me?' It was the same question raised by Harding, but in an infinitely less guarded manner.

'I asked around in Perranporth.' My simple explanation didn't do justice to the intensity of my enquiries, my determination to find him.

'Well, I'm honoured you took the trouble. How can I help?' Friendly, perceptive eyes studied me.

I edged closer. I needed to get off that doorstep. 'It's complicated. Can I come in and explain it to you?'

'Sure. I have plenty of time these days. Cup of tea?'

'That would be lovely, thank you.'

McCreary led me into a lounge decorated with smart, clean furniture. A large bay window provided a stunning sea view that rivalled Gwel Teg. In an adjoining room, there was an elegant dining table with a mirror-like surface and a silver candelabra.

Photographs of smiling people and places I didn't

recognise were dotted around the lounge. I studied each of them while McCreary brewed tea and clinked cups in a nearby kitchen. None of the pictures were of his old life in St Branok. I stopped at a photo of a stone circle taken on a sunny day on high, open ground. It wasn't Boscawen-un, but it was certainly Cornwall.

McCreary reappeared with a bamboo tray carrying cups, a tea pot, a milk jug and a plateful of digestive biscuits. 'Ah, I see you're admiring my picture of the Merry Maidens of Boleigh.'

'I've heard of them, but never visited.'

He put down the tray on a glass coffee table and we settled on the sofa. 'Yes, a fascinating site. Nineteen stones in an almost perfect circle, all carefully chosen. They get gradually smaller from the south west to the north east to mirror the cycle of the moon. Legend has it that a group of girls were turned to stone as punishment for dancing on the Sabbath.'

McCreary pointed at another photo, this time of a granite standing stone. 'Now, this one's also interesting. It shows one of the two menhirs nearby, which are the tallest in Cornwall. They're known as the Pipers of Boleigh. Their story is similar to the Maidens; they were the pipers turned to stone for having the audacity to play on the Sabbath.'

'Sounds like you've a real passion for the subject.'

McCreary grinned. 'Cornish folklore has always been a great fascination of mine and I have plenty of time these days to indulge myself. Many of the old Cornish beliefs are still very much alive. Our history is full of stories of rituals, witches, giants, changelings and fairies.'

'Those beliefs seem especially strong in St Branok,' I said.

'Why do you say that?'

'The Shout at the Devil festival seems more popular than ever.'

'Yes, it's quite an event these days, so I hear. It's important that these harmless traditions aren't lost.'

'They sometimes seem more secretive than harmless.' I watched McCreary closely. Could there be anything in all this superstitious nonsense about paganism Danny had touted?

He chuckled. 'Oh, there are always rumours flying around in a place like St Branok. I wouldn't take too much notice of the local banter. It's a hobby for a few and nothing more than a passing interest for most people.'

We continued chatting with enthusiasm about all the things that make Cornwall so unique. It was soon obvious that McCreary lived alone and welcomed company, any company. Of all people, I was well qualified to diagnose loneliness.

He poured the tea into fine, delicate china cups. There was something motherly about the precise way he did so. 'So, what have you come all this way to discuss? Not ancient history, I'm sure.'

'History, yes, but not quite so ancient. You might know that we've just had the tenth anniversary of the loss of the Talan Bray.'

McCreary sipped his tea, still relaxed. 'Yes, I saw a piece on telly. Terrible accident.'

'The Gazette last week produced a special anniversary supplement about the Talan Bray, which was popular. We're running further publicity this week, paying tribute to the crew, that kind of thing. We're keen to speak to more St Branok citizens who remember the heroes who died. You were a prominent figure in the local fishing community. You must have strong memories.'

He sat back, watchful. 'There must be loads of people in St Branok who have much better memories of the crew than me.'

'You were suggested as somebody who…' I licked dry lips, floundering, and McCreary interrupted.

'Well, whoever suggested me hasn't got their facts straight. I knew a few of them, but only in passing. Anyway, I moved out of St Branok before the sinking of the Talan Bray.'

I paused halfway through a sip of my tea. 'You left before the Talan Bray was lost?'

'Yes, several months, in fact.'

'And you moved straight to Perranporth?'

McCreary nodded but said nothing.

'Why did you leave, if you don't mind my asking?'

'It's no great secret. I parted ways with my business partner, Mike Pedrick. Pedrick bought out my share. There was nothing left for me in St Branok, so I decided to make a new start here.'

'What can you tell me about Pedrick?'

'What do you want to know? He's an astute businessman with powerful connections.'

'Is he trustworthy and reliable?'

A flicker of wariness swept his face. 'What's this all about, Kate? Really all about?'

My cup rattled a touch as I put it down on an ornate coaster. 'Pedrick has proposed going into business with me, a sort of partnership to run the Gazette, so I wanted to better understand the person I might be dealing with – and there's no better person to ask than his old partner.'

McCreary's mouth twitched. 'My advice to you would

be to stay well clear. Pedrick's a money-grabbing, despicable blackguard.'

'How so?'

'He forced me out of the business we'd built together. We were friends, good friends, but he threw away all that. He wanted it all and did everything to make life intolerable for me, spreading lies and rumours about my private life. I hate the man. There's no denying it. In the end, I couldn't take any more. That's why I upped sticks.'

'Was Pedrick involved in anything underhand while you knew him?'

McCreary brushed a hand across his chin. 'Not illegal, if that's what you're suggesting. He pushed the boundaries and was certainly ruthless, but he did it with the help of an army of grubby lawyers and accountants.'

'A colleague of mine, Danny Flanagan, has also been making enquiries. Did he contact you at all?'

He shook his head. 'No, I've never heard of a Danny Flanagan. Sorry.'

I walked out of McCreary's house having gained little more than a lesson on Cornish folklore, a good cup of tea and half a plateful of digestive biscuits. I'd munched too many of them and felt bloated, but they would be my lunch. My watch told me it was nearly two o'clock. I quickened my steps to the car. I needed to get back to the Gazette if this week's newspaper was to see the light of day.

McCreary had been a dead end. The Mike Pedrick he'd described was nothing more than a hard-nosed businessman. Hard-hearted and ambitious, yes, but not a murderer. And whatever Danny had discovered hadn't come via this genial, elderly man.

What now? I was getting more desperate by the day.

CHAPTER THIRTY-NINE

The Gazette was in a state of high anxiety which exceeded even the usual Monday mayhem when I returned, guilty and a little breathless. Brenda, Emily and Roy were all flustered or excited in their own way.

Brenda waved a scrap of paper at me as I walked through reception. 'Thompson's called twice more since you were out. He's insisting he speaks to you as soon as you return. I have his phone number here.'

'Thanks. I've got it already.' I kept walking. Oh yes, I had his number alright.

'And two more advertisers have suspended their advertising,' she called after me in a plaintive tone as I climbed the stairs.

I didn't ask who or why. I knew why, and whoever it was could go take a running jump off Tregloss Point.

In editorial, Roy was speaking earnestly into the phone while Emily cleaned up the remains of an overturned mug of coffee. She had become nervous and clumsy since our late-night vigil at the hospital.

I couldn't tell from Roy's expression whether he was relieved to see me or peeved that I'd deserted him for the morning. I started sifting through the growing pile of paper on my desk. None of it was surprising: the usual reports from local clubs, a few letters, mostly for the letters page – and plenty of bills.

I was still mulling over the McCreary interview as I knuckled down to the task of getting the next edition sorted. What to do next? Where to go?

Roy put down his phone, obviously pleased. 'I've got a good story for a front-page lead. A London hotel group is proposing to build a hotel on the site of the old paint works. It'll create a hundred jobs.'

I jumped up, my thirst for a good news story always insatiable. 'Wow, great story. How did you hear about it?'

'Joe Keast tipped me off. I've just got off the phone from the hotel group's press office and they've confirmed the details.'

'Wonderful. Good old Joe. We can also run a feature on an inside page about the hotel group itself, who owns it, how long it's been in existence, which hotels it owns, that kind of thing.' An experienced hack like Roy would have worked that out for himself, but he played along politely enough.

I found myself ringing Mike Pedrick's personal mobile number, almost without thinking. I couldn't help myself. He answered on the first ring.

'Mike, it's Kate Tregillis. I was wondering when I might come over for a chat.'

He cut in brusquely. Typical Pedrick. 'If it's about the advertising, I've nothing more to say—'

'Mike, hear me out. It's about that business proposition you put to me a while back. I was hoping we might discuss it further.'

I waited for an answer. Pedrick didn't do silence even for a millisecond, so I must have surprised him. Surely, the prospect of the Gazette being up for sale would hook even a cynical character like him. At last, he said slowly and with an infuriating smugness, 'Giving my offer a second thought, eh? I was hoping you'd see sense. I'm stacked up with appointments for the rest of today, but I'll be in the boardroom at the factory early tomorrow. How about nine o'clock?'

'Great. I'll see you at nine. Thanks Mike.' I tried to sound grateful. A humble approach was more likely to put him at ease.

I replaced the handset and stared sightlessly at the top of my desk.

CHAPTER FORTY

A clinging fog had drifted in from the Atlantic overnight, shrouding the harbour as I stepped along the St Branok quayside. The salty dampness was permeated by the tang of slaughtered fish.

I'd made an attempt with my appearance today – a touch more make-up, a blouse I hadn't worn for ages and trousers rather than jeans. Pedrick had an eye for the ladies, Joe had once told me.

The rusting, barnacle-encrusted St Branok fishing fleet, much of which was owned or part-owned by Pedrick, loomed out of the mist. He ruled this place. His name was everywhere. The Mr Big of St Branok. His rise had been rapid and astonishing. He had to be hiding something. Had to be.

A group of white-coated men stood chatting and smoking on the quay, having taken part in the hustle and bustle of the early morning fish auction. One or two flicked glances in my direction. I upped my pace, intent on getting to my meeting, stifling a yawn as I did so. Another restless night was taking its toll.

Pedrick's fish processing factory was alive with movement and noise. A line of St Branok women with the knife-wielding skills of a company of Gurkhas filleted the fish before dumping it on a conveyor belt to be frozen or smoked. I slipped past it all to reach the well-worn stairs at the far end.

On the first floor were the company offices, full of desks, computers and finance and admin staff. This was the heart of the operation which sold Cornish fish to companies across the UK and the Continent. It was big business. And all this had started with a young and endlessly ambitious Mike Pedrick taking shared ownership of a single trawler with Kevin McCreary.

Neon overhead lights illuminated a corridor with a door at the far end marked 'BOARDROOM'. It was solid and heavy and made of a dark wood. Expensive mahogany. Pedrick liked quality. There were muffled voices on the other side, and Pedrick's stood out – demanding and commanding, as always.

I knocked firmly and, when I didn't get an answer, put my head round the door. Pedrick was conferring with a couple of company minions, in full corporate flow, pointing with an accusing finger at figures on papers spread on the boardroom table. 'I'm not going to accept—' he was saying, but he stopped abruptly when he saw me. Irritation flickered across his face. 'Kate, you're earlier than I was expecting.'

I sniffed. The boardroom was hot and stuffy with a smell of beeswax and linseed oil, tainted by the reek of dead fish, which was inescapable even here.

'Would you like me to wait outside until you've finished?'

He waved his hand in a dismissive gesture. 'No, no, I'm tired of talking about the ups and downs of the monkfish and hake markets, anyway.'

He gathered up the papers in front of him and put them

to one side before turning to the minions. 'Kate and I have important things to discuss. We'll pick this up later.'

I exchanged polite expressions with his employees as they slipped from the boardroom, and then Pedrick walked towards me. He was wearing an open necked shirt and jeans – casual but expensive items. Pedrick had serious money and he liked people to know it.

A broad smile transformed his face for the better and reminded me that his rise hadn't been achieved without a degree of charm. 'Coffee? Tea?'

'Tea, please. Thank you.'

He led me out of the boardroom to a small kitchen area. He might be a zillionaire, but Pedrick was still a hands-on sort of guy, as happy unloading a trawler as chairing a boardroom meeting. 'So, Kate, you've been thinking again about my proposal,' he prompted while clattering around in a cupboard for two mugs.

'I'm interested, yes, depending on how much you're prepared to offer and what you want in return.'

He laughed, as if I'd made a joke, while pouring boiling water onto tea bags in two mugs. 'Well, that will very much depend on what sort of financial shape the Gazette is in. Since we last spoke, I've heard more rumours about things being a bit shaky.' He glanced at me, gauging my reaction.

I ran a hand over my forehead, wondering who'd been talking. Probably nobody. Most likely, Pedrick was putting two and two together, based on Brenda's unguarded comments and the fact that a raft of local businesses, including his own, had withdrawn advertising.

'We're not shaky,' I said, indignation rising in my voice. 'We're rock solid, actually.' I spouted figures which bore no resemblance to reality. It didn't matter. Pedrick would never get his hands on the Gazette while I was in charge.

He handed me a steaming mug and then stepped aside to allow me to walk back into the boardroom first. 'Those figures sound good. Frankly, better than I expected,' he said. 'I'd have to get my accountants to look over your books, due diligence and all that, but if the figures are correct then I think an offer in the region of three hundred thousand pounds for a controlling share in the business might be possible.'

I gripped my mug tighter. That was far more than I'd expected. It would solve all my money problems. Tempting, so very tempting.

'If I was to go into partnership with you, I'd need to know more about you and your business,' I said as I sat at the boardroom table.

Pedrick steepled his fingers, his eyes flinty. 'All you need to know is that I'm prepared to inject hundreds of thousands of pounds of hard cash into the Gazette.'

'But, as a partner, whatever you do in your other businesses could affect us.'

His eyes softened. 'What do you want to know?'

I took a deep breath. 'Your business has grown massively over the past twenty years. How can I be sure it's not all financed with a mountain of debt?'

Pedrick sipped his tea and leaned back easily in his chair, his lips twitching in amusement. 'I've nothing to hide. In fact, there's a huge amount to be proud of. Everything is above board, our profits are growing and our debt is minimal. I'll tell our accountants to share with you the headline figures for the past three years – on a strictly confidential basis, of course. I'm a good businessman, Kate. Our partnership could be a great success. You'd be able to focus on writing stories and I'd look after the business side. It would give the Gazette a new lease of life.'

I leaned forward, determined to prick his self-satisfied bubble. 'Kevin McCreary doesn't think you're a good partner. He says you forced him out of the business.'

Pedrick shifted in his seat, his expression more guarded. 'McCreary. That's a name I haven't heard in a long time. When did you talk to him?'

'Yesterday. He called you a money-grabbing blackguard.'

He spread his hands. 'All that was ages ago. Why waste your time speaking to a person who's had no contact with me for years?'

'When the future of the Gazette is at stake, I'd like to know who I might be doing business with. I doubt you're on his Christmas card list.'

'I understand why he might be angry. But he lacked ambition. He was holding the business back. We made a lot of money together – all above board – but in the end the business outgrew him. He was well looked after in the final settlement.'

I sucked a breath and took a wild shot into the unknown. 'What about your dealings with John Harding? Why did he leave St Branok ten years ago?'

He frowned. 'What's all this crap now about Harding? He carried out the odd repair job on a couple of my trawlers and we chatted occasionally when we came across each other at The Mermaid – and that was it. We weren't anything like close. He walked away from St Branok and I don't know why he left or where he went. I haven't seen him for years.'

'You say you want to help the Gazette and yet you've stopped all your advertising. Is that another of your schemes to get a better deal?'

He banged his mug on the desk. I'd riled him. But he did his best to hold himself in check. The prize of the Gazette was on his horizon and he was determined to get it. Truly, a man who loved the chase and the deal. 'Of course not. What kind of businessman do you think I am? Your guy, Danny frigging Flanagan, was hurting a lot of people with his accusations and investigations about the Talan Bray. It was irresponsible journalism.'

'And now he's fighting for his life in Tre…Treliske. I stuttered to a halt, my voice thick. Several gulps helped me recover my poise. 'Somebody nearly killed him on the A30 near St Buryan. It was deliberate.'

Pedrick's mouth hung slackly open. When he got it moving again, he said, 'I was told it was an accident.'

I stood up. The boardroom with its fishy, waxy tang was claustrophobic, and I'd had enough of 'Mr Big' Mike Pedrick to last me a couple of lifetimes. There was no way I would ever go into partnership with him, no matter how much he offered, no matter how desperate the financial situation became.

'I'm needed back in the office. There's a newspaper to get out. Thanks for your valuable time. I'll give your offer consideration.' I turned and snatched open the heavy, dark boardroom door. It swung wide on well-oiled hinges. Not the most diplomatic of exits. I hadn't even offered to shake Pedrick's hand by way of goodbye.

Pedrick was unfazed, perhaps because in the fishing trade he was used to blunt business encounters. 'It's a generous offer. The extra money would go a long way,' he called after me as I hastened down the corridor. 'I'll get my accountants to send over those figures.'

Outside, I leant against a brick wall, looking out over the

harbour, and tugged a crumpled packet of cigarettes out of my handbag. It was half empty already and I'd only bought it yesterday. As I lit one, I realised my trembling was getting worse.

The familiar warmth of nicotine flooded my body as I sucked hard. Pedrick had been his usual cocky, intransigent self, switching on the charm when he'd wanted to and stretching a smile but unable to conceal his desire to dominate, to control everything and everybody around him.

Yet he had seemed genuinely shocked when I'd insisted that Danny's injuries were no accident.

But, if not Pedrick, then who?

CHAPTER FORTY-ONE

Roy pointed the mouthpiece of his empty pipe at me. 'Mike Pedrick having an involvement in the loss of the Talan Bray is hard to believe. Why would a successful businessman risk everything to murder eight lifeboat heroes and nearly kill Danny?'

I nodded reluctant agreement. There was a ruthless streak in Pedrick for sure but no evidence that it extended beyond the boardroom. Emily was out and about, interviewing local residents protesting against a proposed housing development on the edge of town, so Roy and I were able to talk together in private.

'The one person we know must have been involved is John Harding,' I said. 'He found a reason not to go on the rescue that night – either because he knew something was going to happen or because he committed sabotage.' I held my head in my hands. I had a nauseating feeling that I was heading down a blind alley.

'We need to check out that filing cabinet Danny always keeps locked,' said Roy after a long pause. 'There might be something in there.'

'Danny didn't use it much. It was mainly a place to keep his old files.'

Still…

I strolled over and pulled on the cabinet's handle. The drawer was locked, as Roy had said. And there were no keys.

'Try the keys from one of the other cabinets; they might open it,' said Roy.

I tested all of the cabinet keys. None of them worked.

'We're going to need to lever it open,' I said. I scanned the office for something heavy duty but found nothing useful. Crowbars aren't standard equipment in a newsroom.

'Jerry would have it open in no time,' said Roy. 'I'll give him a call?'

'Yes please. Thanks.'

The phone rang. It was Brenda. 'Thompson's back on the line again, demanding to speak to you.'

'Put him through,' I said. I couldn't dodge him forever.

I forced a cheery voice and said, 'George, thanks for the call. I'm sorry I didn't get back to you yesterday. It's been so busy.'

His reply was the polar opposite of cheery. 'We need to have a meeting, Ms Tregillis. An urgent meeting.' Ms Tregillis – that was ominous. He was going all officious on me. 'It can't wait,' he said. 'Head office is getting increasingly worried about the Gazette's finances.'

'What's the problem?' Head office? Like hell. With bureaucrats like Thompson it was never them that delivered the final killing blows. They were always acting as a messenger for a supreme being in 'Head Office'.

'You've exceeded your overdraft again. This really can't go on.'

'Oh, that'll be sorted out very soon,' I said airily. 'We're waiting for additional advertising revenue to come through.'

'When…when will it come through? I need to report

back to the regional director.' He wasn't going to be put off easily this time.

'Imminently.'

'Please be more precise, Ms Tregillis. Precision is vital in business. Are we talking a few days?'

He continued pressing. In no time, I was cornered. 'By the end of the next week at the latest,' I blustered at last.

'We need that overspend to be cleared within two weeks. Otherwise, head office will have no alternative, no alternative at all.' He lapsed into silence, leaving the obvious unsaid. Closure of the Gazette. Redundancies. The loss of my beloved cottage.

Maybe I could live with a partnership with Pedrick, after all. He'd managed to stay married to the same woman for the last twenty-five years; perhaps he was easier to get along with than I thought.

Desperation gnawed inside me as I hung up.

Roy, the master of understatement, nodded at the phone. 'More problems?'

CHAPTER FORTY-TWO

I parked the Landy in a dilapidated street in Plymouth, full of worn-out cars. I was back to see John Harding again. This time, alone. Harding remained the one link to the Talan Bray mystery I could be sure of and, in desperation, I'd decided to visit him again. To get something out of him. Anything. I was clutching at the thinnest of straws.

I knocked on the front door, remembering that the doorbell didn't work. There was the rustle of movement from within and then the door squeaked open. Harding's unshaven face twisted in annoyance.

'Jesus Christ, what are you doing here again? Haven't we made ourselves crystal fucking clear?' His eyes swept the street behind me, but he didn't ask about Danny.

I inched forward. 'I was hoping you might spare me a couple more minutes, Mr Harding. Just a couple of minutes. That's all I'm asking.'

My feigned affability calmed him a little. 'If it will get rid of you once and for all, then okay. But don't ever come back. Not ever. And if I find out you've given my home address to anybody else in St Branok, I'll…' He blocked the doorway, making it clear that any conversation would take place on the doorstep or not at all.

'Look, I understand that there was a disagreement

between the crew members before the Talan Bray was lost,' I said. 'What was all that about?'

His eyes rolled upwards. 'What has that got to do with anything? There are always going to be a few stresses and strains between a close-knit team. It didn't have anything to do with the loss of the Talan Bray. The weather that night was appalling. When can you idiots get into your dull skulls that it was all a terrible accident?'

'What were these stresses and strains?'

'Nothing much, nothing at all.'

'Bad enough for you to end up in a fight with Jed Ridley outside The Mermaid, though eh?'

His face turned crimson. 'Look, you've had your couple of minutes. Goodbye.' He swung the door closed.

'I'm not going to give up,' I shouted at the door, which had been slammed in my face. 'If these disagreements were minor, why won't you talk about them?'

I was rewarded with silence. And so another meeting with Harding had ended abruptly. Another brick wall. Where next?

CHAPTER FORTY-THREE

The Gazette offices still blazed with light after my tedious return journey from Plymouth, during which my mood had plumbed new depths. The truth was plain to see: my investigation was going nowhere and the Gazette was heading towards oblivion, dragged down by debts and falling income.

In editorial, Roy was at his computer, doing his best to fill the remaining spaces in that week's edition. A fresh pang of guilt swept through me; I was asking too much of him.

'Any luck with Harding?' he said as I unzipped my coat and hung it on a hook.

'A bit. He was a little more talkative this time but then got angry and aggressive and slammed the door in my face.'

'Sounds like he could be violent. You should have gone with somebody.'

'Who? It wouldn't be fair to put anybody else at risk. Anyway, he seemed scared more than dangerous. I think the reason he answered the door this time was because I was alone.'

'Did he say anything helpful?'

'Yes, it wasn't a complete waste of time. He admitted that there had been disagreements between the crew of the Talan Bray, though he claimed they were minor. Then he made a curious comment. He said, "Haven't *we* made ourselves clear?" Not "*I*" but "*we*". I got the impression he wasn't expecting to see Danny again, either. He knows more – a lot more. I'm sure of it.'

'So, what now?'

I sighed deeply, trying to bleed the tension and frustration from my body. 'I don't know. Did you manage to get Jerry to open Danny's filing cabinet? There might be something in there.'

Roy shook his head. 'Not yet. He's out of town for a few days. Won't be back until next week.'

'We'll have to force the lock ourselves.' I pursed my lips and willed the locked filing cabinet to miraculously slide open. 'Billy Couch might have a tool at his workshop we could use. I'm also going to try to get into Danny's room at The Mermaid. I'll pop in there when I finish tonight.'

'I know Joe and you are old mates, but won't he wonder why in heaven's name you're wanting to root around in Danny's room?'

'I can offer to pack up Danny's stuff so that it can be stored until he returns. It's not as if Danny is going to be back any time soon or there's anybody else to do it.'

'It's worth a try, I suppose, though Danny's working notes and equipment appeared to be kept here, at the Gazette.' Roy tapped a few keys. 'This week's edition is looking good, by the way. We should be able to easily fill the remaining pages. And Emily's developing into an excellent journalist. She'll be producing more copy than me soon.'

I opened a white envelope on my desk to find a handwritten report about the proceeds achieved from a fundraising lunch. 'Thanks, Roy.'

'For what?'

'For everything. For being positive when I'm down in

the dumps. For getting the Gazette out. For helping Emily. Everything. Bloody everything.' That hard lump in my throat, which made itself felt during moments of tension, was growing again.

Radiating pleasure, he continued tapping away on his keyboard. 'Always happy to help.'

Progress on the next edition hadn't been quite as good as Roy had indicated, and I spent the next three hours filling a few gaping holes to keep the following day's workload manageable. But he was right about Emily; she was developing into a determined, accurate journalist. I tightened up a few of her longer stories, but her work overall was excellent.

At last, duty done, I plodded over to The Mermaid. The pub was busy even mid-week in late autumn. Wednesday night was quiz night and more than a dozen teams had turned up to battle for the weekly prize – usually a hamper, fifty pounds worth of steak or a side of smoked salmon.

The questions hadn't yet started when I strode in, but most of the teams were sipping drinks at their tables and there was a buzz of expectation. Their frivolity was enticing. A part of me wanted to lose myself in that careless, happy atmosphere. Perhaps the Gazette should enter a team in future. Roy's extensive knowledge would almost guarantee victory.

Joe was behind the bar, pulling on a tap handle to deliver another dose of Wreckers Rebellion. 'Ah, Kate, how are things? Anything exciting in the Gazette this week?'

'There's always something exciting in the Gazette.' My tone was a touch brittle. I was tired.

A sceptical grin creased his face, but he confined himself to, 'What can I get you?'

'Double gin and tonic please.' I took a deep breath. 'Joe,

Danny's going to be in hospital for weeks, maybe months. I'm going to arrange for his stuff to be put in store until he's well again.'

Joe placed my drink on the bar. As ever, it was a generous double. 'Aren't there any relatives who can look after that?'

I sucked on it gratefully, relishing the release it offered, fleeting though it might be. 'None that we've been able to contact so far. The police are still making enquiries.'

He hmmed agreement. 'If Danny's not going to be back for some time, I could do with having the room available. He's already stayed longer than expected. When are you thinking of getting his stuff together?'

'I can pack it up this evening and collect it in the morning. We'll keep it at the Gazette until Danny's able to pick it up.' We were all playing this little game of saying *when* Danny would be back, not *if.*

'Okay. I can let you in now if you like.' At a grateful nod from me, he disappeared into a back room and emerged with a bunch of keys.

I swigged the dregs of the gin and tonic and followed Joe up to Danny's room. He unlocked the door and stood to one side, allowing me to enter. 'Ladies first.'

The room was less tidy than I remembered it being. A couple of pairs of jeans and a sweatshirt were draped over the room's only armchair, and the open wardrobe revealed a dozen items on hangers. A few pieces of paper that looked to be receipts were spread over a table.

On an impulse, I said, 'Has anybody been to Danny's room since he was injured – the police or anybody?'

Joe shrugged his shoulders as he stood with a hand on the doorframe. 'I haven't seen any sign of the police. The cleaner was in here yesterday. Why?'

'It looks different somehow. Messier.'

He stepped into the room with hands on hips. 'It was always messy when I looked in.'

I hauled down two large suitcases from the top of the wardrobe and began filling them. If this was the extent of Danny's life, there wasn't much of it.

Joe hovered near the doorway, which wasn't helpful. I wanted to search the room alone. For what, I had no idea. There didn't seem to be any notebooks. Just clothes and a few other bits and pieces.

'Don't let me hold you up,' I said. 'I'll put everything in the suitcases and then the room will be clear.'

Joe retreated into the corridor. 'Great. Anyway, I better get back downstairs to start the quiz. Can't keep the punters waiting. Give the room key to Angie when you've finished.' His footsteps faded as he retreated along the passageway and down the stairs.

I took a creased shirt off a hanger, intending to place it in a suitcase, but on a whim held it to my face. It smelt of Danny. It also muffled a sob. A dreadful premonition washed through me that he might never wear this shirt again. *For god's sake, get a grip.*

I folded a tan jacket almost reverentially and, as I did so, a small metal item slipped out of an inside pocket to land softly on the cheap carpet. I held it up to the light, a tremor running through me.

Two tarnished keys on a ring gleamed in the light – the keys to Danny's four-drawer filing cabinet in the Gazette's offices.

CHAPTER FORTY-FOUR

The quiz night was in full swing by the time I trotted downstairs. I found Angie at one end of the bar, giggling as usual, this time with a couple of girlfriends, and handed her the room key.

'I've packed up Danny's stuff and will be back in the morning with the Landy to collect the suitcases,' I said. 'Joe knows all about it.'

Angie slipped the key under the counter. 'Thanks. That didn't take long.'

'No, there wasn't much to pack up.' I turned, eager to be on my way. 'See you tomorrow.'

A smiling Joe was speaking into a microphone saying, 'What is the capital of Ecuador?' as I headed out into the cold, damp night air.

The Gazette offices were in pitch darkness. I flicked on the lights and climbed the stairs two at a time, energised by my discovery. In editorial, I strode past the empty desks and headed straight for the row of four-drawer filing cabinets.

My hands were shaking again as I slotted the keys into the cabinet. They fitted. The lock turned and the drawer opened with a clunk and a grating sound to reveal a mound of files. I pulled out the top few and scanned the contents.

They were as Danny had described: papers about old cases he had investigated.

I delved deeper. Two notebooks seemed promising. I flipped through them. One had been used about six months ago, every page filled with Danny's hieroglyphics, jottings and doodles. The second was also full but much newer. Deciphering Danny's sweeping, sloping writing was a challenge worthy of a Bletchley codebreaker, but I soon realised that some of the notes were about the Talan Bray disaster. The Ridley brothers and John Harding were named. Now I was getting somewhere. Amid the familiar names was one I didn't recognise.

Sean Capper. It was underlined three times.

Sean Capper…Sean Capper…I racked my weary brain. Who in heaven's name was Sean Capper? I'd never heard of him. But he was clearly an important part of Danny's investigations. There was a date next to his name: August 28, 1991. About three months before the loss of the Talan Bray.

I went back to the filing cabinet to clear out the remaining items. A few pens and a few pictures of a more youthful Danny with a middle-aged woman and a younger man in his teens or early twenties. All had the same broad, open faces. Family.

There was also a shoe box, sealed shut with several strips of duct tape. My curiosity was piqued. I raced around the office and eventually found a pair of scissors under one of the piles of paper on my desk. They were old and blunt, and it took several attempts to hack through the thick tape.

At last, the final strip was broken. I tugged open the lid – and gasped.

The box held a handgun.

CHAPTER FORTY-FIVE

The gun's blue steel glinted dully in the white neon office lighting. A shuddering sensation ripped through my stomach. The weapon scared me – not only because of the death and destruction it could inflict but also because of what it said about Danny and the vein of darkness which must pulse through him. Beneath the affability, beneath the carefree nature, beneath the jokes, something disturbing was carefully hidden.

There were also two boxes of bullets.

I'd trained to use a handgun during a brief reporting spell for The Enquirer in the Middle East, but that was a long time ago. I hadn't held anything more deadly than a kitchen or filleting knife since returning to Cornwall. I picked up the gun with the tips of my fingers, turned it over and took a firmer grip, reacquainting myself with its heavy, cold lethality. It was solidly reassuring – and terrifying. How wrong I'd been when I thought I was putting the darker side of life behind me as I packed up my few belongings and came home to St Branok.

Gingerly, I placed it back in its innocent shoe box as if it was made of porcelain, closed the box, put the files back on top and locked the drawer again. Getting it out of my sight brought relief. Thank heavens, I'd had the presence of mind to pocket the two interesting notebooks. I would study them in more detail later.

I drove to the cottage, my mind so awash with thoughts of the gun and Danny that I nearly forgot to pick up Rufus from Suzie's. Barely a mile from Gwel Teg, I remembered him, cursed and did a rapid U-turn – as rapid as possible in a narrow Cornish lane – to head back the way I'd come at breakneck speed.

Suzie's home shone with lights from downstairs rooms. Dogs barked as I pressed the bell. Her modern house, on a new estate of identical homes on the outskirts of St Branok, was its usual warm and dry and friendly self. She appeared with an excited Rufus on a lead.

'You're late. I've fed Rufus.' She was a little exasperated.

I got a slurpy lick from Rufus's long tongue as I took his lead. 'Sorry. Things have piled up today. You're a marvel, Suzie, you really are. Thanks.'

She stepped closer and placed a hand on my arm. 'Is everything okay, Kate? You look tired. Would you like to stop for a cuppa?'

I swept away a long strand of hair from my face. I was a wreck. 'You're too kind, but I must get back to the cottage.'

I mumbled about needing to do the washing, but she persisted with a smile: 'We've got plenty of spag bol left if you're feeling peckish.'

I turned to go, not wanting her to read anything more in my haunted face. I reeked of desperation. 'No, I'm fine. Really. I've got a meal waiting for me.' It wasn't a complete lie. I did have Cheddar, tomatoes, a sachet of boil-in-the-bag rice and, more importantly, a reasonable stash of whisky. It would do. It would have to do. I wasn't going to drive back into town at this time of night. Why did my psyche place feeding myself at the bottom of every list?

Suzie wrapped her cardigan around herself tightly. It was a cold, breezy night. 'Do you need me to have Rufus tomorrow?'

I paused my retreat. 'Just take him for a walk, please. I'll leave him at the cottage. Thank you, thank you so much.'

Gwel Teg was its usual unwelcoming self. Dark. Cold as a fridge. There were more than the usual draughts coming from somewhere. My now familiar 'welcome home' investigation with Rufus revealed a ground floor window in a back storeroom ajar. The paranoia kicked in again. Had it been forced? Had the clifftop breeze eased it open? There was a dent in the wooden frame which might mean something – or nothing at all. It could have been there for months.

And yet…and yet…hadn't I closed every window?

I stood in the hallway, uncertain. The only noises were the odd creak and groan – part of the character of every old building – and the ocean breezes. They gusted from almost nothing to forceful as they do so often on the Atlantic coast.

At last, having triple checked every corner, window and door, I sloshed three fat fingers of Jameson into a glass and settled in the sitting room with a carelessly concocted evening meal on my lap. Rufus curled up on the hearth nearby and watched me lovingly with a half-closed eye.

I flipped through the newest of Danny's notebooks, the one with the name Sean Capper, as I sipped the whisky and shovelled into my mouth the rice and cheese and tomatoes without tasting them. Except for the names of places and people and dates, everything was in a form of shorthand. It looked like Pitman's, the same shorthand I'd learnt as a trainee, which over many years had turned into a form unique to Danny, only legible to him. On the same page as Capper's name, I thought I recognised a few words, such as 'beach', but I couldn't be sure. At least the name and the date were clear.

With the electric fire pulled up close, exuding a musty smell and some welcome heat, my head slipped forward and my eyes closed. The surges of adrenaline which had washed through my body earlier in the evening had long since dissipated, leaving me exhausted.

With the aid of a heavy blanket, it would have been easy to have stayed the night in the old armchair. But I hauled myself out of its lumpy embrace, switched off the heater, stretched an aching back and lumbered up the stairs.

'Come on, Rufie. Time for bed.'

I had no appetite or energy for the creams and indulgences many people slathered themselves with at bedtime. But I did brush my teeth and slip into a nightgown before descending into oblivion with Rufus warming my feet at the end of the bed.

Tomorrow, I'd discover the truth about Sean Capper.

CHAPTER FORTY-SIX

I slept better than I had for a long time. Having a good night's sleep then, of all times, made no sense. It had to be pure exhaustion.

Another mist had rolled in from the Atlantic and the wind had died. An unnerving stillness prevailed. The ocean swelled languidly, seemingly as thick as treacle, exuding a quiet menace. Fat drops of condensation hung from branches and sills, and the air was salty and damp, its chill seeping into my cardigan as I went outside to examine the ground below the storeroom window – the one I'd found ajar the previous night. I needed to satisfy myself that it was nothing more than my own carelessness.

But a closer inspection left me far from satisfied. The mass of dripping weeds and flowers below the windowsill looked as if they might have been trodden on. The possibility of another unwanted visitor loomed like a lengthening shadow in the background.

Rufus had followed me outside and he, too, spent time nosing around in the undergrowth. He smelt something, certainly, but he could always smell something. And ninety-nine per cent of the time it was a harmless fox or badger.

I glugged down a cup of the necessary sweet tea and headed off into the dense sea mist with the Landy's headlights on full beam. Rufus, stretched out in the hallway, had given me a final reproachful look as I locked the front door.

The mist was as dense as any I could remember, and it took me twice as long as usual to reach the Gazette offices. In fact, Roy arrived before me. He was typing steadily at his desk, ever the calm professional.

'Thought I'd make an early start,' he said as I walked in.

I put my coat on its usual hook. 'I managed to get into Danny's filing cabinet last night. Have you ever heard of a Sean Capper?'

Roy squinted. 'It rings a bell, but I can't quite place it. Why do you ask?'

'The name was in one of Danny's notebooks, next to John Harding and the Ridley brothers. It was underlined three times. And there was a date: August 28, 1991. I thought you might remember something.'

'Sean Capper…Sean Capper…well, he's not a local. If it was August, he might have been a tourist. We get enough of them.'

'Once we've sorted out this week's edition, I'm going to have a good look through our August 1991 back copies,' I said, firing up my computer.

The day went surprisingly smoothly. The final spaces were filled. The next edition was in good shape. Roy's story about the new hotel dominated the front page. Alongside it was a picture of a local primary school's pupils dressed for their upcoming nativity play. All fun and festive and positive. It might help to encourage some of the advertisers who'd deserted us to get back on board.

I needed every penny. The upcoming showdown with the bank hovered like a threatening cloud, drawing ever closer.

Late afternoon, I found time to open the Gazette's old records, scrolling through the rolls of microfiche straight to the week which included August 28, 1991, and found…

Nothing.

There were the usual stories about fundraising for worthy causes, car parking issues (as ever), local hotels and restaurants commenting on the last big week of the summer season being busy – but nothing about Sean Capper.

August 28 had been a Wednesday. The Gazette might not have had time to cover the story until the following week. I scanned every page of the next paper, even the sport section.

Still nothing.

I studied the pages a second time. And then I saw it – a small article on page two, easily missed. '*An inquest has been opened and adjourned into the death of a man found last week on Waterlock Beach. The body of Sean Capper, aged 42, of Tregloss Street, St Branok, was discovered at the water's edge on the morning of Wednesday August 28. Mr Capper is believed to have moved from London to Cornwall earlier in the year.*'

That was it. Why had a drowning more than ten years ago interested Danny? On the North Cornwall coast in the summer, the deaths of visitors caught in vicious sea currents and rip tides were tragic but not unusual occurrences.

I trawled through the records for the following months and eventually came across a report of the full inquest. It was revealing, but it also raised questions.

Sean Capper had been living alone in Cornwall for several months without a job. The reason for his stay was unclear. He'd been found wearing swimming trunks at the water's edge. Death was by drowning and there were no unusual marks on the body, but a Detective Chief Inspector Nigel Somers told the hearing that the death hadn't fitted the usual circumstances of a swimming tragedy. One of Capper's relatives described him as a poor swimmer who disliked water. The coroner had recorded an open verdict.

Roy was still at his desk patiently waiting for our customary Thursday evening celebratory drink when I emerged square eyed, having been peering at the microfiche for several hours.

He stared at me. 'Anything?'

'Yes, quite a lot. Sean Capper died in questionable circumstances on Waterlock Beach. Do you know a senior detective called Nigel Somers? He gave evidence at the inquest.'

'Nigel? Yes, I know him well. Nice chap. Helpful. He retired a few years ago but now works locally as a security consultant. We were in the same cricket team together for a few years.'

'Do you think he'd be willing to give us a bit of background on the Capper case, off the record?'

'He might. Worth a try, certainly. I'll call him from home this evening.'

I switched off the lights and locked up, and we strolled over to The Mermaid, talking eagerly. 'I was thinking that we might perhaps pay him a visit tomorrow. Emily can hold the fort for a few hours while we're gone.'

As we walked, Roy tamped down the tobacco in his Calabash pipe and then held a flame to it, looking for all the world like an elderly Sherlock Holmes. The fire took hold and he was soon puffing away contentedly. 'Sorry, I still don't understand. How is a dead man on a beach connected with the Talan Bray?'

'I don't know, but Danny made a link.'

'Danny's jumped to a few other conclusions, some of

which were sensationalist, to put it mildly,' Roy pointed out. 'What about all that pagan nonsense?'

We arrived at the bar to order a couple of pints of 'local' from Joe. I was thirsty and I needed something more substantial than a gin and tonic. 'Danny was on the track of something,' I said. 'That was why he was nearly killed. And the death of Sean Capper might hold the key.'

Joe placed the frothy pints on the bar in front of us. 'You journalists, don't you ever stop talking shop? Where's that shaggy dog of yours, Kate?'

I glanced at my watch. Rufus would be lying in the hallway with his eye on the front door, willing me to return. 'Guarding the cottage,' I said. 'I need to get home as soon as possible.' I sucked on the beer from Joe's microbrewery, savouring the earthy bitterness.

Joe's expression turned serious. 'Guarding it from what? A lost hiker?'

'We've had a few disturbances recently.' Uncomfortable, I raised my glass to bring an end to the conversation. 'Cheers!'

Typical Thursday evening. Typical celebratory drink with Roy. Typical Joe, leaning with both hands on the bar, laughing with customers. Typical happy buzz in The Mermaid. Its conviviality was reassuring after the trauma of recent weeks.

CHAPTER FORTY-SEVEN

Rufus was barking down in the hallway and the security light had flicked on, bathing the front of the cottage in a white, intense glare. I lay in the darkness, muzzy from sleep, reluctant to give up my warm bed. Another fox or badger sloping past the cottage? At last, the light clicked off and the barking stopped. Rufus's paws pattered on the hallway flagstones. Then sleep reclaimed me.

When I woke again, it was daylight – not sunny, but bright and clear. I had overslept. A gentle breeze had come up again, sweeping away the mist and murmuring in the eaves of the cottage. I stretched and yawned. Had Roy been able to fix an interview with Nigel Somers and, if so, what would the retired policeman be willing and able to tell us?

Rufus was absent from his usual place at the bottom of my bed.

I called him.

He didn't come.

I called him again, louder this time, and waited.

Still no sign.

A raging thirst swept through me. I needed a mug of tea, maybe not so sweet this time. Pulling on a sweater, I trotted downstairs to find Rufus asleep on the floor in the hallway.

'Silly dog, Rufie, what are you doing down here?'

He always gazed at me lovingly with his head on one side when I called his name.

But not this time.

'Rufie…' I bent down and stroked his lean, wiry body.

He was stone cold.

My dog was dead.

CHAPTER FORTY-EIGHT

I found a fertile, sunny patch under an elm tree in the back garden, one of Rufus's favourite haunts, and channelled all my anger and distress into attacking the ground with a spade. The bottoms of my pyjamas were soon soiled with slate-grey Cornish mud. My breathing was harsh and fast, tears flowed full and unchecked and my arms and back ached – but I didn't stop digging. Not for a second. Doing something hard and physical helped somehow.

When the hole was long enough and deep enough, I gently laid Rufus in his final resting place, cocooned in his favourite blanket. Then, with a lingering kiss of his head, I said the most heartfelt of goodbyes. Beside him, I left a few of his favourite toys: the ragged rabbit with one ear, the teddy with a bitten-off nose and the spongy ball. If there was a doggy heaven, then he'd need all of those.

And when it was done and the only sign of the tragedy was a mound of freshly tilled earth, I said a tearful prayer for Rufus. My Rufus. His trusting, simple nature had touched me more than almost any human.

The phone was ringing as I dragged myself back inside. It was Roy.

'Kate, is everything okay? It's nearly midday.'

I sucked an agonised breath. 'Rufus died last night.'

There was a stunned silence and then, 'How?'

'I don't know. I…I still can't believe that he's gone.'

'Oh, my goodness, Kate. That's terrible.'

'He must have had a heart attack or stroke of some kind,' I said.

'These things can happen with little warning. Our neighbour's Great Dane dropped dead last year while out on a walk. She was devastated.'

I clutched the handset, remembering the disturbance. 'Something woke Rufus in the middle of the night. It triggered the security light. But I didn't see or hear anything. It seemed a false alarm – the wind or an animal.'

'I'll come over straightaway.'

'Thank you so much. See you soon.'

My gaze swept around the hallway as I replaced the handset. There was a scrap of folded white paper in a corner near the front door. I snatched it up.

The handwriting was in blue biro. In capitals. YOUR DOG IS DEAD COS YOU WOULDN'T STOP. THIS IS YOUR LAST CHANCE.

CHAPTER FORTY-NINE

Roy arrived within half an hour to find me slumped at the bottom of the stairs in the hallway with the piece of paper clutched in trembling fingers. He was wheezing as he knelt and put a loving arm on my shoulder.

The note wasn't my only discovery. I'd also found a small red blood stain on the flagstones near the front door.

I dropped the hateful note on a side table. 'Rufus was killed, poisoned. The bastards must have posted meat through the letterbox.'

He took my hand and looked into my burning eyes. 'Kate, I'm so sorry. We all loved Rufus.'

The sympathy caused me to well up again. Usually, I couldn't cry. Now I couldn't stop. I sobbed, holding my hands to my face, sucking air, unable to speak.

Roy studied the note, his expression grim. 'We need to show this to the police. It should convince even Dobbie that you're in real danger. The fewer fingerprints on it the better. Do you have a pair of gloves?'

'Yes, in the kitchen. I'll get them.' Fingerprints, of course. I should have been more careful.

In the kitchen, in a renewed convulsion of distress, I clung to a table. For once, I was blind to the changing beauty of the Atlantic outside the window. All I was able to think of was Rufus and Danny and the hidden person or people behind all this.

I wiped my wet cheeks with the heel of my hand. 'Did you manage to contact Nigel Somers and fix an appointment?'

Roy gaped at my more assertive tone. 'I did. Half past three this afternoon, but it might be best to cancel. Or I could go alone while you rest.'

'No, it's okay. Let's keep the appointment, and I want to be there. If those murderers think I'm going to give up now…'

Roy made me a cup of super sweet tea and toasted stale bread he'd found in the bread bin. 'Here, have this. It'll make you feel better. Are you sure you're up to interviewing Nigel Somers today?'

I gulped down tea and chewed endlessly on the toast. 'Absolutely sure. I want to hear what he has to say.' Rufus's biscuit treats were still on the side in the kitchen. I held down another explosion of emotion. Barely. Roy wouldn't want to be accompanied by a blubbering wreck when we met the retired policeman.

Roy sipped his own mug of tea. 'You can't come back here tonight, Kate. Not alone. Stay with us. Marjorie and I always love your company.'

He was right. I couldn't face tonight at Gwel Teg by myself. 'Thanks,' I muttered. 'Yes, that would be nice. You're very kind.'

Roy gathered the remainder of Rufus's things, strewn in various rooms of the cottage, and placed them in a black bag to avoid them being a constant reminder.

Without Rufus, Gwel Teg could never be the same. He had been my constant companion since I'd bought the place.

His life had been snuffed out by an unimaginable evil. I would find it and destroy it, no matter what it took, no matter the risk involved.

CHAPTER FIFTY

Nigel Somers, retired chief inspector and now security consultant, lived alone in a modest house in the sticks, about ten miles from St Branok. Another loner. Another person who'd given up his personal life for his career, like me and McCreary. The world was full of career loners.

He and Roy greeted each other with the back-slapping and smiles of old friends. Then he showed us into a modestly-furnished front room that looked out over the rolling Cornish countryside. He was a little overweight and bald apart from a few wispy hairs above his ears, and he had restless, intelligent eyes, which flicked from one place to the next as he talked.

The two men spent a couple of minutes on the obligatory chat about cricket and the lack of local spin bowlers, a subject on which my knowledge was nil. I did my best to look interested until Somers turned to me. 'Are you a cricket fan, Kate?'

'Not really, I'm afraid. The only time I pick up a ball is when I throw one for my dog, Ruf…' A lump grew in my throat, making speech impossible. I couldn't believe he was gone. I gulped down fresh tears.

Roy intervened, his voice steady, calm. 'Kate's dog died today. It's still raw.'

There was an embarrassed silence, broken by Somers saying, 'So, how can I help you?'

I pulled myself together for the umpteenth time that day. 'We noticed you were the investigating officer for the Sean Capper case.'

Somers's face was blank, so Roy added, 'He was found dead on Waterlock Beach about ten years ago. You spoke at the inquest.'

The retired policeman's features came alive with understanding. 'Oh, yes, I remember that one. An interesting case. Most of the details came out at the inquest.'

Roy said, 'We were hoping you might be able to give us a bit more background, Nigel. Off the record. As you say, the story is already in the public domain.'

Somers nodded. 'Well, the whole thing was a long time ago so I doubt it can do any harm, and as it's you, Roy…'

'We read the press reports of the inquest,' said Roy. 'The death was suspicious. Sean Capper drowned, but he didn't sound the sort to go anywhere near the sea.'

The ex-policeman sat forward, his gaze flicking from Roy to me and back again. 'Sean Capper was a nasty piece of work – a hardened criminal with a string of offences longer than your leg, ranging from robbery and grievous bodily harm to trafficking and smuggling. Yes, cause of death was drowning, but it was suspicious to put it mildly. It wasn't revealed publicly that he was the subject of a police surveillance operation at the time. We had reliable information that a major drug smuggling operation was taking place in Cornwall. A lot of heroin was being brought in by boat and then transported to London and other major UK cities. Capper got pally with some of the locals. He came down from London and lived in St Branok for many months with no reason to be there and no obvious form of income. Unfortunately, he died before he could lead us to the people behind the operation. It was a shame because we were getting close.'

I'd liked to have taken notes, but a notebook and pen might have discouraged Somers from talking. My memory would have to do. 'You think he was killed by other people involved in smuggling?' I said.

'That's my theory, yes.'

'Turf wars by rival gangs?' I said.

Somers shook his head. 'No, not in an out-of-the-way place like Cornwall. It's more likely he was killed by the criminals he was working with. My theory is that, for some reason, he'd become a problem. The gang behind the smuggling might have realised he was under police surveillance.'

'What happened to the police operation after his death?' I said.

'We focused on the local people Capper associated with in St Branok. It looked like we were getting somewhere. Two brothers, fishermen, caught our eye. They'd spent a lot of time with Capper. They weren't criminals, but they had a bit of a chequered past. They also had a lot of money and weren't subtle about concealing it.'

I leaned forward. 'What happened to them? Were they arrested?'

Somers shook his head. 'They also died, but in an accident. It knocked back our investigations. We didn't have any other strong leads. We continued monitoring a few other people, but it never led to anything. And the smuggling operation seemed to have been brought to a halt or, at least, moved out of the area.'

'What was the accident that resulted in their deaths?' I said, then held my breath. I already knew the answer.

'The loss of the Talan Bray lifeboat. They were crewmen.'

CHAPTER FIFTY-ONE

We headed back to St Branok, Roy driving his little red Volkswagen Polo as sedately as if we'd come from a flower show. After a few miles of silence, he said, 'Sean Capper dies in suspicious circumstances while being investigated by the police. Then, police attention falls on the Ridley brothers and, hey presto, they too die. That's more than a coincidence.'

I gazed out the window at the bleak Cornish landscape, stripped of colour by the onset of winter. 'Yes, the Ridleys had become a liability – just like Capper. They needed to be disposed of quickly in a way that would be seen as nothing more than a terrible accident.'

Roy licked his lips in thought. 'Nobody would link the tragic loss of a lifeboat to smuggling or murder, but there must have been an easier way to silence them?'

'Maybe there wasn't. The Ridleys were well known in St Branok with lots of friends and relatives. If they'd disappeared without an explanation, they'd have been missed big time. It would have sparked a major police investigation.' I chewed a fingernail before adding, 'We're dealing with a multiple murderer who will stop at nothing, but they've only tried to frighten me off. Why?'

'They might not see you as a serious threat. At least, not yet. But the more you dig and the more you find out, Kate, the more you're likely to become the next victim. It's not worth the risk. Perhaps we should step aside, hand over everything we know to the police and let them get on with it. I don't want to hear of your body being washed up on a beach.'

I thumped my fist against the dashboard. 'I can't sit back and do nothing. Not after everything that's happened.'

The catch in my voice drew a brief, worried look from Roy. 'Might all this be John Harding and nobody else – the attacks, the warning notes, the poisoning? As the second mechanic, he was in an ideal position to sabotage the Talan Bray.'

I shook my head. 'It can't be him alone. He's living seventy miles away in Plymouth and has no interest in returning to St Branok. It's somebody closer, somebody with influence, somebody who is aware of what's happening in St Branok from day to day. But I think Harding is in contact with them. When I last visited him, he seemed to know that Danny wouldn't be turning up on his doorstep again. And each time we've rattled Harding's cage, something big and terrifying has happened. That's also not a coincidence. I'm beginning to wonder who we can really trust.'

'We should look again at Mike Pedrick. He's become very wealthy in a short space of time, knows everybody and already has a big network of hangers-on and contacts. And Danny was asking lots of questions about him before he was run down.'

I scribbled in my notebook while thoughts were still fresh in my mind. 'Yes, Pedrick's ruthless. Yes, he's brash. Yes, he's ambitious. But I haven't found any evidence of him making money illegally – at least not yet. I compared the financial figures he gave me with accounts at Companies

House and they checked out. Why would a man risk running drugs and killing when he's on his way to becoming a multi-millionaire?'

'People do strange things. He might not have been so secure ten years ago, and a shrewd high roller like Pedrick would know how to cover his tracks.'

I sighed and nodded. 'You could be right. Paying off McCreary wouldn't have been cheap.'

Roy changed gear and we reached the heady speed of fifty miles per hour. 'If not Pedrick, then who?'

'I don't know. And I don't feel much closer to finding out now than a month ago.'

We lapsed into silence again as the little hatchback bounced through the Cornish potholes. Then I said, 'Harding, Harding, Harding. It all comes back to him. He's the one connection we can be sure of.'

We pulled into Roy's driveway. Marjorie stood outside the front door, biting her lip and fidgeting with her wedding ring. Diminutive but strong, she opened her arms and hugged me. 'Kate, I was terribly sorry to hear about Rufus. You must be devastated. He was a wonderful, adorable dog.'

I hugged her back, drawing strength from her warmth and her empathy. 'Marjorie, you're so kind. Thanks for having me tonight.'

'Stay as long as you like, m'dear. You're like a daughter to us, you know.'

That night I lay in bed in Roy and Marjorie's spare room staring at wallpaper full of cute jungle animals. A child's room for a child who never came though the wallpaper remained. I'd never asked what happened, didn't feel I had the right to. Roy and Marjorie would have made wonderful parents, caring and fiercely proud of their son or daughter. I sighed. Life seemed full of unfulfilled hopes and missed chances.

The bed was warm and the house was cosy – a thousand times more welcoming than my damp and draughty clifftop cottage – and I had a substantial meal inside me for a change. Somebody was taking care of me, and I felt more safe and secure than I had for a long time.

I wriggled my toes. Lovely Rufus. This time yesterday he'd still been bursting with life, had taken up his customary position at the bottom of my bed with his head resting on my feet. And now he was gone.

How could such a bright, burning light be snuffed out so completely?

Harding was my only hope.

CHAPTER FIFTY-TWO

I arrived at the hospital during an afternoon lull. A clinical calmness pervaded the corridors under an unforgiving white light, which left few shadows. Staff moved purposefully back and forth, while behind screens and in nearby rooms patients fought for their lives. When visitors shared a few words, they talked in hushed tones as if they were in a church or a library. The walls were adorned with posters promoting the latest fundraising efforts of the hospital's League of Friends, sharing tips for dealing with dementia, advising how to recognise the first signs of a stroke and what to do in the event of a heart attack.

I strode towards the Intensive Care Unit a few steps behind an older woman in her early sixties. She was slim but strongly built, about my height with wiry grey hair tied back into a bun. Her pace was urgent, and there was something familiar about her stance. 'I'm here to see Daniel Flanagan. I'm his mother,' she said to a nurse at the reception desk. Her Northern Ireland accent was unmistakable. Just like Danny's.

I joined her at the desk. 'I'm here for Mr Flanagan as well.'

Before his mother could speak, I said with a weak smile, 'I'm a work colleague and a friend.'

Her returning smile was bleak. 'I'm Sarah McDaid. I

only learnt yesterday that Danny had been involved in a serious accident. I flew straight over.'

I racked my brains as I held out my hand. She had a different surname to Danny, but there was a familiarity about the name McDaid which I couldn't place. 'Kate Tregillis,' I said. 'I'm the editor of the newspaper where Danny's been working.'

She swallowed, working hard to contain deep emotions before turning back to the nurse. 'When can we see my son?'

'The doctor's completing an examination. He won't be long.'

Sarah and I sat on seats with blue coverings.

'Do you know what happened?' she said after a pause.

I wondered how much to tell her and then decided to tell her everything. A mother deserved that, at least. 'The police believe it was an accident, but I'm not so sure. Danny was involved in investigations which caused a lot of upset in the local community. The police have had difficulty tracking you down.'

'I expect my different surname confused things. I remarried but Danny kept the Flanagan surname out of respect for his father. He was a fine man, but headstrong. Danny's just like him. Every time I look at Danny, I think of Ryan.' She rubbed her forehead with bony and calloused fingers. 'I tried to stop him coming here. How I tried! But, no, he wouldn't listen. He's been talking about it for years and, as we got close to the tenth anniversary, he became more determined than ever.'

My mouth was dry. 'Sorry, I don't understand. What was his reason for coming to Cornwall?'

'My other son – Andy McDaid, his half-brother – moved here. He worked as a trawlerman. Andy was a crewman aboard the Talan Bray, the lifeboat which was lost at sea. Danny was never satisfied that it was an accident, said there were too many unanswered questions. Andy told him in a telephone call that something was happening, some sort of trouble, but he was vague about what it was. Danny said he'd find out the truth. He's a wonderful son, but when he gets an idea in his head there's no turning him. Just like his father.'

'He risked his life,' I said.

'Oh, he's used to that. He spent many years reporting on the Troubles in Northern Ireland. He's a good, loving boy, but he knows how to look after himself when he needs to.'

The description of brawny Danny as 'a boy' was incongruous. Clearly, mothers never stopped being mothers to their children, no matter how big and boisterous they became. I made sure we couldn't be overheard and then whispered, 'Looking after himself includes having a gun. I found one in a locked cabinet in our offices.'

Her eyes became wary. 'Have you told anybody?'

'No, but he had no right keeping a deadly weapon at my newspaper offices.'

She sighed in obvious relief. 'You're right, of course. It was a stupid thing to do. Don't read too much into it. Danny's not a violent man, but he knew investigating his brother's death might be dangerous. It was an insurance policy. It's easy to get a gun in Fermanagh if you know where to look.'

'I had no idea that Danny was personally involved in the loss of the Talan Bray,' I said. 'He told us all that he was here as a freelance journalist to write a few Cornish stories for the national press.'

She patted my arm. 'Don't take it to heart. He knew it would be safer if people didn't realise he was the brother of one of the lost men. He said he was going to stir things up and see where the pieces landed. Felt it was the only way he was going to get to the truth. I told him to give it up, to get on with his own life. Begged him, I did. But he wouldn't listen.' She looked at the ceiling, her eyes ablaze but not tearful. 'This place is cursed. I've lost one son here and nearly lost another. You'd think it would be safe in a backwater like this.'

'I lost my parents when I was young, but I can only imagine what you've gone through.'

Sarah flushed. 'I won't deny it. Life's been hard at times. When Ryan died, I was still quite young. He went out one night for a drink with friends and was killed in a drive-by shooting as he walked out of a pub.' Her voice dropped to little more than a whisper. 'He said he'd be back late and that I shouldn't wait up. But I did stay up. I always did. By the time the police came to the house the following day, I knew something awful had happened. It was a terrible, terrible time. Danny only had a few years to get to know him. He and Andy were very close.'

At last, we were ushered through to see Danny. He was as lifeless as the last time I'd visited, though there were fewer tubes and wires. We were told that he was making progress but that the outcome was still uncertain.

Sarah rushed to him, her control finally broken. She sobbed, her shoulders heaving. 'Oh no, Danny. My boy.'

Her deep grief brought me to tears and we clung together, taking strength from each other.

Afterwards, we walked side by side down long corridors, speaking softly. Danny's mother appeared tough and self-sufficient but also genuine. I liked her. 'Can I buy you a coffee?' I said.

'I could do with something strong for sure. Thank you.'

We took seats in a corner near a drinks machine, out of earshot of the nearest occupants, a solemn elderly couple sitting close together with heads bowed. 'I'm going to find out who is responsible for all this,' I said. 'Nothing's going to stop me.'

She frowned. 'Be careful, Kate. I've seen too many well-meaning people die in the Troubles. They were brave. They were confident. They were determined. And, before you knew it, they were dead.'

I tried a frothy coffee produced by the drinks machine but gave it up after one swallow. It was insipid swill. 'How long are you here for?'

She pulled a bleak expression. 'I'll stay until Danny's better. I found a nice little bed and breakfast place nearby. Out of season, they're pleased to have guests. If it looks like I'll need to be here for a while, then I'll rent a small flat.'

'I have a spare room in my cottage you're welcome to use,' I said. 'The heating's non-existent, but it has wonderful views. And to be honest, I'd welcome the company.'

The thought of my cottage with its clifftop position and its nearness to the great Atlantic raised my spirits, despite its draughts and the cold and everything that had happened there.

'That's a generous and kind offer. If it's not an inconvenience, then I'll take you up on it.'

We held each other's gaze for several seconds as I turned over in my mind a massive, terrifying idea. Should I share it with this woman I had only just met? Yes. It had to be her. It could only be her. I took a deep gulp and said, 'How far would you go to find the person who's done all this to Andy and Danny?'

Sarah's face was as still as stone, but her eyes shone with a dark intensity. 'As far as it takes and more. I'd love to see the bastard responsible get his comeuppance.'

'I have a plan, well, more of an idea really,' I said. 'It will involve risk.'

She pursed thin lips and then said, 'I'd do anything for my boys.'

I gave Sarah a lift in the Landy back to her bed and breakfast, a semi-detached house with pebble-dash walls. Its winter rates for customers would be modest. We agreed to meet again the following afternoon, by which time she would have her suitcases packed and be ready to move to Gwel Teg.

We hugged and held hands when we parted and I felt no embarrassment. In a few hours, we'd grown from complete strangers to partners in an endeavour which might see both of us killed.

CHAPTER FIFTY-THREE

I was grateful for Roy and Marjorie's easy hospitality that night, looking forward to good company, warmth and a hot meal. I parked the Landy as they were returning from a stroll on the sea front. They were invigorated by exercise and conversation, happy in each other's company. I envied them. I couldn't imagine getting to know somebody as well as Marjorie knew Roy and Roy knew Marjorie, to have the lifelong intimacies and shared secrets of a loving couple.

Marjorie unlocked the front door. 'It's been a beautiful afternoon, but I doubt you saw much of it at the hospital, Kate. How is Danny?'

I stuck my hands in my coat pockets and contemplated the ground. 'He's showing progress, but it's a long haul.' My voice quavered and I cleared my throat. 'I met his mother today at the hospital. She's come over from Northern Ireland, having only just heard what happened. She's lovely. Danny means the world to her. Of course, she's devastated.' I hesitated, unsure how to share the revelation of Danny's brother. 'She dropped a bombshell. Danny's younger brother died on board the Talan Bray. He was a member of the crew.'

Roy's eyebrows rose half an inch. 'There wasn't anybody on board the Talan Bray called Flanagan. But wait a minute, Andy McDaid was Irish. Half-brother?'

I nodded. Roy was as quick as ever. 'Correct. Danny came here to stir things up and find out what happened to his brother. He was convinced that the loss of the Talan Bray was more than an accident before he even got here.'

We gathered in the kitchen. Roy brewed tea, I chopped carrots and Marjorie peeled potatoes. A happy, homely scene – but it couldn't last. I couldn't stay at Roy and Marjorie's forever.

'You've both been wonderful to me,' I said. 'Being able to stay here with you for a few days has meant the world to me. But I'm ready to go back to Gwel Teg.'

'There's no need to rush it,' said Roy. 'Stay with us for a few more days at least.'

'Thank you, but no. I'm heading back tomorrow. Danny's mum is going to stay with me while he's in hospital.'

'The company will do you good, Kate,' said Marjorie as she tipped the potato peelings in a bin.

'What are you going to do about the Talan Bray investigation?' said Roy.

'I have a plan,' I said and then wished I hadn't.

Roy paused from pouring the tea. 'This plan – might I ask what it is?'

'I can't tell you the details right now, but I've been thinking it over and this is the only way we're going to prevent the snake behind all this from slipping back into the shadows. If it works, it'll settle the whole issue once and for all.'

Roy scratched his head, then waved his hand in the air. 'Why keep going with this, Kate? Why put yourself in such danger?'

'It's personal,' I said. 'I owe it to Danny and I owe it to Rufus. And I owe it to myself.'

CHAPTER FIFTY-FOUR

Sunday morning. Heavy rain had passed through overnight, saturating the already sodden ground, and ushered in a bright, blustery day of towering white, fluffy clouds in a bright, boundless Cornish sky. Beyond the surfline, the Atlantic was the colour of the vibrant bluebells which carpeted Nethercott Woods in spring.

I drove through the narrow St Branok streets to the Gazette offices with a nervous stomach, steadied by one of Marjorie's formidable bacon and egg breakfasts. If I'd stayed at their house much longer, I'd have put on some serious weight. My body usually survived on hasty nibbles and snacks, not three hearty meals a day.

At the Gazette, I went straight to Danny's locked cabinet in the corner. The contents were exactly as I'd left them. A tingle pulsed through my fingers as I picked up the box containing the gun and the ammunition and slipped it in a carrier bag. Back outside, the street was empty and there was no sign of any prying eyes at windows. I breathed a sigh of relief as I slipped the bag under the driver's seat of the Landy.

That was part one of my plan, the easy part, completed. Now for part two. After that, there could be no going back.

CHAPTER FIFTY-FIVE

I eased the Landy into a downtrodden street in Devonport. A familiar street, full of grey walls, dirty vehicles and deprivation. John Harding's street.

Outside his grubby house, I repeated in my mind the sentence that had brought me there. 'Whenever we rattle Harding's cage, something big and terrifying happens,' I'd said to Roy. And now I was going to rattle his cage again, bang it really hard and do my best to make sure *everything* happened.

I rapped smartly, steeling myself for another angry doorstep encounter. The front door opened six inches and there was Harding, even more unkempt and haggard. His stubbled chin hadn't seen a razor for days. My visits had prised open old, festering wounds.

He exploded. 'What the fuck are you doing here again?'

The door started to close, but I got a trainer in the way, *a la* Danny, and it juddered to a stop. 'I know everything. I'm running a newspaper story this week about how you and the Ridley brothers were involved in a smuggling operation. You sabotaged the Talan Bray, didn't you? Eight men, six of them innocent – completely innocent – died because the Ridleys had become a liability and needed to be eliminated. I'm giving you an opportunity to comment. Nothing will stop me. And then I'll be handing everything over to the police.'

Something new swept across his face – a dark guilt, a vulnerability – and I knew that my mixture of fact and guesswork contained at least some truth. He knew. Oh yes, he knew. Harding had harboured this secret for the past ten years and it had eaten away at him, hollowed him out.

He screamed another profanity and heaved against the door again. I snatched my foot away and it slammed closed.

I hastened back to the Landy, my innards churning.

It was done.

CHAPTER FIFTY-SIX

The gun bucked in my white-knuckled grip and my first bullet went way too high. It sent a flock of black crows flapping into a mackerel sky. The sharp crack echoed off the walls of the steep valley before it was lost in the rushing sounds of a rising wind and distant surf. The risk of being overheard was slight. There was no sign of anybody nearby and, even if the gunfire did attract attention, a local farmer out on a shoot would be assumed to be the cause.

Sarah stood beside me, giving encouragement. 'You look tense. Try to relax. Hold the gun firmly but not too hard. Easy now. Keep breathing. Steady.'

I pulled the trigger a second time and again the bullet went skyward, albeit marginally closer to its target. 'It's been years since I held a gun.' I passed her the weapon. 'Here, you have a go.'

Sarah grasped the revolver and took careful aim at the coke cans we'd lined up on an old wall of Cornish slate. The gun barked twice in quick succession, and as the second shot rang out, a tin was sent spinning out of sight.

'Wow, you hit it.'

'More luck than judgement, I expect,' she said. 'But we're getting there. We'll be ready.'

She slipped the gun back into my sweaty grip. 'Have another go.'

I settled into my old familiar stance and tried again. This time the bullet clipped the corner of a tin. I jumped up and down, like an excited child who'd won a toy at a fairground hoopla stall.

Sarah clapped me on the shoulder. 'That's better, much better. See, it's all coming back. You're not a bad shot, not bad at all.'

We egged each other on, our shooting becoming more accurate and our confidence growing.

Sarah picked up the first box of bullets which was now more than half empty. 'A couple more shots should do the trick. Let's save most of the ammo for our real target.'

'One bullet could be enough,' I said. 'Or we might be able to hold the person at gunpoint until the police arrive.'

Sarah nodded. 'Let's hope so. There's been enough blood spilled. But the sort of merciless snake we're dealing with doesn't sound like the kind who will go quietly.'

My stomach clenched. She was right. Our vigil would likely end with injury or death. Did I have what it took to point a gun, pull the trigger and blast a person's life away? It was easy to aim at a line of coke cans, much harder to shoot a living, breathing human being no matter what crime they had committed.

By the time we trudged back to Gwel Teg in the fading light, we were as ready as we were ever going to be for what was coming.

I'd turned myself into bait to catch a killer: a lonely woman in a remote cottage on cliffs high above the Atlantic – a persistent fool who refused to stop despite being warned.

From the killer's point of view, who would be an easier, more deserving target?

But I wasn't alone. I had an accomplice. And we were armed and ready. We agreed on three-hour watches like the deep sea trawlermen roaming the Atlantic, hunting the perfect catch.

The gathering darkness became blackness. We switched on the radio for a broadcast I'd listened to countless times but never more intently. 'And now the Shipping Forecast, issued by the Met Office on behalf of the Maritime and Coastguard Agency at 17.54 today…warnings of gales…in Sole, Lundy and Fastnet.'

'It's going to be a rough night,' said Sarah matter of factly. It wasn't what we'd wanted to hear. Windy, wet conditions brought extra uncertainty.

We talked little over a hasty dinner, and then Sarah settled in a chair on the first-floor landing, overlooking the approach to the cottage. The gun was on a small table beside her. 'Kate, you should rest. I'll take the first shift until midnight. Then you cover from midnight until three, when I'll take over again. We mustn't switch on any house lights.'

Wrapped in my warmest cardigan, licking my lips, my stomach unsettled, I imagined who or what might be outside. Sarah had assumed control and seemed the better prepared.

It would happen in the dead of night, I was sure. Maybe tonight.

CHAPTER FIFTY-SEVEN

Midnight. The alarm on my bedside table beeped and I groggily sat up. The wind had strengthened and the surf in the cove was louder, the booming echoing off the cliffs as each great surge of water crashed against the land. My head was groggy and my arms and legs sluggish. When we had agreed the plan in the warmth and light, it had been brilliant. Now, in the depths of a wild night, it seemed insanity itself.

But there was no going back. Not now.

Sarah was the same as when I'd left her, stretched out on the chair in the darkness, alert.

'Anything?' I said.

There was enough light to reveal her grim expression. 'No, nothing important. Are you sure you're up to taking over?' She continued to exude confidence. I wondered how many sleepless nights she'd endured, protecting her family or wondering when loved ones would return.

'Yes, absolutely.' I forced myself to sound far happier than I felt. There was no way I was going to allow Sarah to take on all the guarding duties. I had my pride, after all.

She stood up, stretched and handed me the gun. 'Okay, see you at three o'clock. If you find yourself dropping off, have a swig of strong coffee.'

'Thanks. I'll be fine. Really.' A chill dread shivered

through me as I weighed the gun in my hand. I heard Sarah settle on the bed in her room and contemplated the enormity of my task. Responsibility for our safety now sat squarely on my shoulders. Oh my God, could I go through with this?

Get a grip. Focus. I strained my eyes to see anything outside, anything at all. At last, I picked out the skeletal outline of a few trees, stunted and shaped by the Atlantic winds. Further away, lines of white surf striated the black ocean.

The minutes dragged. I was restless, dividing my time between standing up and perching on the chair.

An edgy expectation kept me alert for the first hour. The second was tougher, seeming much longer. As the initial anxiety wore off and tiredness seeped back into my body, I spent more time sitting in the chair. I stood up for the umpteenth time, breathing deeply, clenching my fists. Anything to stay awake.

Coffee. I needed it. Now. I tiptoed downstairs with the gun clasped in one hand. The third stair from the top creaked as it always did. In the hallway, I paused. Water spilled from a leaky drainpipe outside, splashing on a flagstone near the front door. Drip. Drip. Drip. Trees creaked in the wind. A tawny owl hooted. Nothing unexpected. Nothing untoward. Nothing to worry about.

Fumbling in the dark kitchen, I flicked on the kettle. Its red light illuminated a small part of a wall as it hissed away. I poured steaming water into a mug and clumsily splashed some of it onto the work surface. Spots of boiling water landed on my jeans, and the pin pricks of pain jarred me awake.

I shivered. Despite a smouldering fire in the sitting room, the cottage was cold and, in the early hours, my body was at its lowest ebb. I put the gun on the kitchen worktop next to me and wrapped my hands around the mug to warm frozen fingers. Sips of coffee soothed me.

The security light burst into life. Raindrops sparkled like diamonds in its glare. I stepped forward, nearly dropping my mug. The remains of my coffee spilled on the slate floor. Where was the bloody gun? I swung round to find it still on the worktop. Relief surged through me as I grabbed it.

Crouching, clinging to the gun with both hands, I slunk over to the kitchen window. There was movement outside, but it was only the sway of leafless branches and the driving rain.

My first-floor vantage point offered a better view. I tiptoed upstairs, careful to avoid the creaky stair.

At the upstairs window, I settled into a kneeling position with one hand on the gun and the other on the windowsill – holding my breath as I peered outside. A pulse throbbed behind my eyes. The hand holding the gun was clammy. I switched the gun to my left hand and rubbed my damp palm on my jeans.

The security light highlighted every detail of every object in its glare. But its brilliance blinded me to anything beyond. My dread deepened. The murderer was out there in the dark, watching and waiting for the right moment to slip inside the cottage, intent on clearing up one last loose end, achieving one last kill.

He was coming.

He was coming for me.

I tiptoed to Sarah's room to find her face down on the bed. I touched her shoulder. 'Sarah. Sarah.'

She sat bolt upright, instantly awake. 'What is it?'

'I think there might be somebody outside.'

'Where? What did you see?'

'The security light has just come on.'

She stood. 'Yes, it came on for me as well. The sensor seems a bit sensitive. Did you see or hear anybody?'

'Not…not exactly. I had this feeling that we were being watched.' I chewed my lip and then forced my voice to a lower, more reasoned tone. 'I'm sorry. I probably shouldn't have bothered you. The light could have been tripped by a fox or just some swirling leaves. With all this wind and rain, it's difficult to hear or see anything.'

'I know. The conditions couldn't be much worse.' Sarah squeezed my arm. 'You did the right thing to wake me. It was a sensible precaution. Let's go and have a look.'

She strode to the window on the landing. I followed and for long minutes we waited in silence, all our senses on high alert. The wind rose and fell, the rain pattered and then died away, and dead leaves rustled.

The light flicked off, leaving my dazzled eyes unable to glimpse anything outside at all. Slowly, too slowly, my vision adjusted to the dark. Shapes and shadows swayed and twitched in the breeze. In daylight, they were trees and bushes. On a night such as this, it was all too easy to allow them to become a waiting man crouching or standing in the shadows.

At last, Sarah said, 'Looks like it was a false alarm. I'm going to try to grab a bit more sleep.'

My guilt at waking her grew. The night was proving tiring enough without needless interruptions. 'I'm so sorry for waking you.'

'Don't worry about it. Best to be on the safe side. How are you feeling?'

'I'm fine.' In truth, I sounded anything but fine.

'You're doing well. The early hours are always the hardest. We just need to hang in there, see it through.'

She returned to her bedroom, I took my place at the upstairs window and this most stretching and nerve-racking of nights continued.

Sarah took over at the three o'clock prompt. The springs on her bed creaked and there was a whisper of stealthy movement before her hand fell on my shoulder. 'Anything else?'

I passed her the gun. 'All clear,' I said.

'Did the light come on again?'

'No. There was nothing.'

'Good. Get some rest. You look exhausted.'

I pulled myself upright, like a soldier passing an inspection. 'I'm okay. I...' My voice faded as more words of wellbeing deserted me.

'We're through the worst of it. It'll be light in less than five hours.'

I managed a tepid smile. 'Yes, nearly there. See you at six. Don't hesitate to wake me if anything happens.'

Sarah settled at the seat by the window. 'Yes, of course.'

I shuffled back to my room and curled into a foetal ball on my bed, willing blessed sleep to take me. It wouldn't come. I yawned, stretched out my legs and, without thought, wriggled my toes, searching for the warm comfort of Rufus.

But he was gone. Forever. A bleak loneliness washed through me.

Slowly, too slowly, my mind closed in on itself, shutting out the wind, the surf and the rain.

CHAPTER FIFTY-EIGHT

I jerked awake, disturbed by a sound or a movement. Violent. Penetrating. Shocking. But gone by the time I struggled into consciousness. My bedside clock said it was just past four o'clock.

I fumbled for the switch on my side lamp, then remembered: no lights. I stayed in darkness. What had happened? Had anything happened?

The wind was whistling harder, the surf bellowing louder. The rainfall had progressed from a tap on the window to a heavy drumbeat. But none of this would have cut short my sleep. It had become little more than a lullaby.

I swung my legs over the side of the bed, gathered my thoughts and my strength, and then tiptoed onto the landing to find Sarah.

But there was no Sarah.

And no gun.

The chair by the window was empty.

'Sarah,' I whispered. 'What's happened?'

No response. Nothing.

I crept over to the half open door of her bedroom and peeked inside. In the darkness, I was able to make out the outline of the bed, the wardrobe and the dressing table.

'Sarah, are you there?'

She was not there.

I was alone.

The shadows closed in on me. What'd happened? Where was she?

In the kitchen perhaps, making a cup of hot, strong coffee to keep her awake, help her make it through the rest of the night.

I padded softly downstairs. A whispering draught of cold air halted me in the hallway. The front door was ajar, moving in the breeze.

She was outside. Had to be. Must have heard or seen something.

Or somebody.

An explosion rang out. A gunshot. Outside. Not far. Instinctively, I knew that this was the sound which had woken me a few minutes earlier. Piercing and brutal but gone in a second.

This time it was followed by a shriek. High pitched. Female.

My blood curdled.

We needed help. I picked up the phone, punched out 999 and was rewarded with silence. No dial tone.

What now? Panic gathered momentum, scrambling my reasoning. Where were the keys to the Landy? A frantic search in the hallway failed to find them.

I pulled on my trainers and then, without bothering to find a coat, slipped outside into the breeze and downpour. Where was Sarah?

The wind tugged at my hair and my clothing. In seconds, I was drenched. The gravel crunched under my feet. I wanted to run. As fast as possible. Away from here. Anywhere. To escape. To hide.

But what about Sarah? I couldn't leave her to deal alone with whatever or whoever might be out there. *Calm down! Think!*

The gunshot and cry had come from near the cliff edge.

I edged forward, crouching low, staying close to a line of bushes and stunted trees, stopping every few seconds to listen and catch my breath. Why hadn't the security light flicked on when I stepped outside? It should have been triggered by my movement.

The howl of wind, surf and rain hammered my senses. Then the downpour eased and a beam of moonlight broke through silver-edged clouds, illuminating the shiny wet ground.

I took shelter in the shadow of a scraggy ash tree, which had miraculously managed to grow in this most exposed of locations. Sudden movement in a branch above sent me into a fresh panic. Something flashed past. Instinctively, I ducked, as beating wings brushed my face.

Gulping, clenching my fists, I sagged against the tree, fighting to restore my composure. At last, some measure of rationality returned. It was an owl, nothing more than an owl. But where was Sarah? Where? Where?

Could she have blundered over the cliff? A few hundred metres away a hillock of craggy granite concealed a precipice which sucked the unwary into its depths. On a clear day it was all too easy for the unwary to stride over the top and find themselves staring at jagged rocks and a seething sea far below. On a godforsaken night such as this the risks were far greater.

I worked my way up its slope, fearful of what I might find. Close to its summit, I dropped to my knees and then wriggled forward on my belly. An updraft caught me full in the face as I peered over the edge to stare down.

I stretched out to get a better look. Could Sarah – or what might be left of her - be down there? In the blackness it was impossible to tell. I imagined her body broken and bleeding below, washed this way and that by the swirling currents. Death would have been almost instantaneous, the only crumb of comfort. She would have had a sickening moment as she realised her mistake before oblivion.

I pulled myself back from the precipice. *Please God, let her still be alive. Let me find her safe and well.*

A scream made me freeze. It came from further along the cliff. Not far.

Then, another sound - more of a whimper - was carried on the breeze. I sprinted towards it.

An arm's length from a deep crevice, a figure lay twisted, face down. A familiar, slim outline.

Sarah.

I tried to turn her over but barely moved her. I heaved again and she rolled onto her back, her head lolling to one side. Her eyes were closed, but a gasp escaped her lips.

I shook her shoulder. 'Sarah, Sarah, what happened?'

Her eyes flickered. 'I was in the kitchen. Saw somebody moving outside...went out. He came up behind.'

'Why didn't you wake me?'

'No time...there was no time.'

'Where's the gun?'

'Gone...over the edge...knocked out of my hands.' She fell silent.

The silvery moonlight faded. Out of the corner of my eye, a shadow moved. As I twisted, something hit me on the back of the head and I crashed down onto broken rocks, splitting my lip. A coppery tang filled my mouth. Blood trickled down my throat.

I needed to move, to run, but I'd lost control of my arms and legs. Steely hands squeezed my neck. Tighter. Tighter. I coughed. I spluttered. I was dying.

My grasping fingers found a jagged rock, the size of a fist. I swung it with all my strength and it crunched against soft flesh and bone. There was an exclamation of agony and the pressure on my neck eased.

Scrambling to my feet, light-headed, I faced my attacker. He was bent over, holding his head. I'd hurt him. Payback time.

'You stupid fucking bitch,' he spat. The voice was familiar. Who? I had no time to place it.

He hurled himself towards me with outstretched hands. I ducked and then sprinted away, arms and legs pumping, breathing ragged.

A hand tugged at my cardigan, but I wrenched hard and was free. I stumbled back towards the cottage. My home. My refuge. I could lock the front door and sit it out until daylight. But no. That wouldn't work. I'd be trapped. And Sarah needed help.

His pounding feet, his grunts and his snorts told me I was only just ahead, only just clear.

I raced onwards, fortified by the raw instinct of survival.

He was faster than me. A grasping hand touched my right shoulder. I swerved left and it was gone. His breathing was rapid and harsh now, roaring like mine.

The ground became loose and slippery as I slithered downhill, my body twisting, my arms flailing in a desperate attempt to keep my balance.

Too late, the terrifying realisation of having made a fatal

mistake hit me. I'd blundered onto the path leading down to the cove. I shouldn't have gone that way. It was a dead end, only one way in or out. But it was too late to go back. I had to keep going.

A rock tripped me and I pitched forward, rolling head-first down the slope. Over and over. My mouth filled with mud and scum. I spat it out as I jumped up and continued a frantic slipping, sliding descent.

Down.

Down.

The thunder of the surf grew with every panic-stricken stride. The moon slipped from behind clouds again to reveal an apocalyptic scene of dark mountains of water, topped with froth and spume, hurling themselves against the beach. They surged up the shingle before pulling back in a sucking, fizzing retreat, each wave a little higher than the last. The cove was disappearing on a rising tide, the advancing sea compressing the cove into a sliver of land below the cliffs.

No way out.

My tumbling descent had given me a few precious extra metres of a head start on my attacker.

I sprinted across uneven stones. My left foot slipped on a slimy rock, my knee twisted and a bolt of pain shot up my leg. I staggered on, half running, half hopping.

This was the end.

I turned to face him and, in the moonlight, saw my attacker properly for the first time. He was wearing a balaclava and dark clothing. 'Who are you? Tell me. I know you…'

He grunted. And kept coming.

I held up a hand. 'Please. For God's sake.'

A wave washed over my feet. The ice-cold seawater oozed into my trainers and socks.

'You crazy bitch. You wouldn't give up, would you?' There was that twang in his voice again. Oh, so familiar.

Who?

He flung out a fist. It floored me. A wave washed over my legs and arms while I crouched on all fours trying to recover my shattered senses. I staggered into a standing position but was kicked hard in the ribs and went down again. My bruised and bleeding face hit the cold wet shingle as another wave washed up the beach and over me.

Salty sea water flowed through my hair, into my mouth. I gasped and took in a lungful of ocean. I coughed. I spluttered.

An iron grip held me down in the water. I couldn't see. I couldn't breathe. I was going to die. Like all the others. *The last loose end.* The wave pulled back and I gasped for air, hissing, wheezing.

My attacker was screaming at me. 'Stupid, stupid bitch. I did everything I could to warn you to stay away. I didn't want to kill you. It's your fault. You've forced me to do this with your endless bloody snooping.'

Recognition hit me like a hammer. I could scarcely believe it. Even muffled by the balaclava, the timbre and accent were now unmistakable. I'd heard that voice so many times – in very different circumstances. Always affable. In The Mermaid Inn.

The voice of Joe Keast.

'Joe, please, no,' was all I could manage.

Another wave battered me. I was pushed under again. I writhed. I wriggled. I twisted. But this time I was ready and held my breath until the wave receded.

'Bitch.'

'Get off me.'

He dragged me deeper into the numbingly cold water by the collar of my cardigan. I scrabbled, hit out, tried to dig in my heels. To no avail. There was no stopping him.

A bigger, heavier wave crashed against us and knocked us both down. His grasp still tugged at me, pushing me down into a churning turmoil. I grabbed both his arms and tried to prise them away, but his grip held, unbreakable. The freezing water crushed my chest like a vice.

I bit down on his wrist, chewing, gnawing, slashing his skin with my teeth until he screamed in fury and agony and let go. A lungful of precious air gave me strength as my head bobbed clear.

Another mountain of water rushed towards us. It threw us both off our feet again. I kicked out against his flailing arms and squirmed free, holding my breath in the pounding breakers.

By the time I surfaced again I was out of my depth and further out to sea. Thrashing, I searched in vain for hard sand. The current held me in its almighty grip, dragging me further from the shoreline. A rush of panic swept through me.

Got to get back to land. Got to. I struck out for the cove, swimming hard, desperate to fight it. In no time, my limbs were burning from frantic exertion. It was hopeless, the current too strong. I'd escaped one malevolent force to be taken by another.

I bobbed up and down, my chin just clear of the sea, sucking air and trying to think while the gripping cold of the North Atlantic seeped into me.

Now I was beyond the surf line, riding over the great

mounds of water rather than having them crash into me. The dark outline of the cliffs was more distant, the thundering of the waves in the cove fainter.

From far away came an anguished cry: 'Help!'

I might have been wrong. It might have been the shriek of a seagull, distorted by the wind.

I started to swim again – not against the current this time, but with it, trying to stay parallel with the shoreline. I was being dragged not only out to sea but also down the coast.

Time passed at a snail's pace. My face and hands lost feeling, my arms became heavy, my shoulders ached. My swim stroke faltered and then stopped. In the distance, a line of orange streetlights marked the seafront road at St Branok. Hanging from them, like the jewel of a necklace, was the brighter cluster of white lighting at the harbour.

As I drifted, so did my mind. An acceptance of my fate grew inside me. The Atlantic swirled and flowed, taking me where it wanted. I accepted it, no longer battled against it. I was the lightest of straw in a breeze, pushed this way and that, thrown here and there by a power far greater than me. The ocean swell cosseted me, rocked me back and forth like a child in a cradle, while its chill fingers bored their way deep into my body. Delirium took hold.

I saw Mum and Dad on a beach on a sunny day. They were laughing, holding hands. So very happy. Wherever I was going, I knew they would be there, waiting for me. After all these years of pain, so carefully concealed, we would be together again. And Rufus would be there too, of course, with his doggy laugh and his question mark of a tail and patient, soulful eyes.

A wave washed over my face, dragging me out of my

trance. I gasped. I was among crashing, crushing waves again. They pummelled, pushed and pulled.

I kicked out. My feet touched sand.

I was on a beach. Not the cove below my cottage, but another. The Atlantic had carried me there.

I staggered out of the surf in heavy, sopping clothes and collapsed at the water's edge, the remnants of powerful waves washing gently around me. I lay there. For how long I have no idea. It could have been seconds. It could have been minutes. It could have been tens of minutes.

At last, I lifted my head. Before me was an expanse of rippled beach, bordered by dark cliffs and a few coastal lights. The gale tugged at my clothes as it swept over the sands to whistle up the sheer rockface, through the coarse grass and between rocks.

I crawled forward, frozen to the core by the sea and the wind. I had no energy, no strength. Blood had retreated from my extremities. I could have chopped off a finger without pain.

But still I felt one thing – fear. Where was my attacker? Where was Joe? Was he dragging himself from the sea to deliver the final killing blows? I glanced behind, my breath shallow, fast. There was only the heaving blackness of the Atlantic, broken by surf, and clouds edged with moonlight. Not a living soul.

The sand became softer and dryer until the cliff face towered above me like a great wall. I hauled myself into a standing position and began climbing a narrow path, concentrating on one step at a time, too drained to think further ahead than the next torturous step.

At last, I stood at the top, swaying giddily, the beach and the sea far below. My stomach clenched, expelling salt water and bitter bile. As I bent over, puking, the world around me went into a dead spin. I lurched away from the edge before I could fall.

Blood crept back into my fingertips, bringing warmth – and agony. I flexed my fingers and rubbed and blew on my hands. My suffering grew as life and movement returned. I whimpered.

Ahead, a tall, angular shadow loomed out of the dark. A building. Modern, two-storey. I tottered forward and stumbled up steps to find a door and, beside it, a lighted doorbell. With whatever strength I had left, I rang it over and over again.

Lights flicked on upstairs and then downstairs. There were urgent, puzzled voices and footsteps. The door eased open a few inches to reveal a short, dumpy man and woman in night clothes peering out into the night. Their jaws dropped with shock when they saw me – a dishevelled, wet female figure – shaking on their doorstep.

The man pulled the door wide, exposing himself to the full blast of the wind and rain. 'What's happened?'

I got my frozen lips working. 'Call the police. My friend needs help. She's hurt.'

'What in heaven's name are you doing out here on a night like this?'

'We've been attacked. At Gwel Teg, my cottage, along the coast.'

The woman pushed past him and put a shoulder under my left arm. 'Don't just stand there, George. Help me! She's exhausted.'

Together, they carried me inside as my knees finally gave way.

Warmth. Light. Safety.

I'd survived.

EPILOGUE

Danny returned to us on a day when the Atlantic was the brightest of blues and in the most placid of moods. Sarah and I were sat by his hospital bed when his blue eyes flickered and then squinted against the strong lighting.

I took his hand in both of mine. 'Danny? Can you hear me?'

He moved his head slightly towards me, groaned and then murmured, 'Mary, Mother of Christ, where the fuck am I?'

Sarah's eyes glittered with tears. 'Daniel Joseph Flanagan, I'll let you off from blaspheming just this once.'

'Mum? What are you doing here?'

'I'm here to see you get better, as is Kate.' She nodded in my direction. 'Kate's been picking up all the rubbish you left behind. And, might I say, doing a fantastic job of it.'

Danny swallowed and took in the room. 'How long have I been like this?'

'Quite a few weeks,' I said. I, too, was tearful. It was easier to cry these days. Something inside me, long held in stasis, had been freed.

His grip on my hand tightened. 'Did I miss the deadline for the Gazette?'

'You missed every deadline,' I said.

Sarah chuckled. 'Typical man, leaves a hell of a mess and then expects the women to sort it all out.'

'And we did sort it all out in the end,' I said. 'Everything is fine now. Absolutely fine.'

Later, when Danny was stronger, I told him everything.

The Gazette's finances were healthier. I'd sold my exclusive story to a national tabloid and suddenly everybody wanted to read my little newspaper. John Harding was dead. Suicide, said the police.

Danny frowned and clenched a fist. 'What about the bastard who was behind it all and nearly killed you and me? What happened to him?'

I managed a wry smile, having held the most important piece of the jigsaw until last. 'He's dead. He was dragged out to sea by the current, like I was. His body was washed ashore the following day.'

'Who? Mike Pedrick?'

I shook my head. 'It was Joe Keast. The Mermaid was a neat cover for a smuggling operation and money laundering. When I told you that Joe knew everybody and everything in St Branok, I never dreamt how close to the truth I came.'

'Friendly old Joe. Of course, I should've seen it. I'm losing my touch.' Danny settled his head back on the pillow and whispered, 'You've been amazing, Kate.'

It was still light as Sarah and I drove back to Gwel Teg that evening. The days were growing longer and warmer, and with a new year came a new optimism.

We crested the last rise before the cottage and the Atlantic lay before me, serene. Wavelets wrinkled an iodine ocean.

I'd played in those waters since I was a child. They were

a part of me. And, in the end, they'd saved me, drowning my attacker while carrying me to safety.

The Atlantic looked after its own.

THE END

COMMENTS

'A gripping story full of twists and turns. J.H.Mann writes compelling fiction set in Cornwall. He transports his readers to rugged coasts and moorlands and introduces us to a range of complex, fascinating characters living in a beautiful but sometimes forbidding part of the world, where even the land itself can be both hostile and benign.'

- Margaret James, Writing Magazine

'An enthralling read that keeps you guessing to the end. I absolutely loved this.'

- Victoria Howard, author and judge for the international 2023 Yeovil Literary Prize in which The Echoing Shore was an award winner.

MESSAGE FROM THE AUTHOR

Thank you so much for reading *The Echoing Shore*. I hope you enjoyed reading about Kate Tregillis's adventures as much as I loved writing about them.

Cornwall and its wild Atlantic coastline will always be a special place for me. I have swum and surfed there much of my life and, in fact, my father was one of the county's early lifeguards. I have huge respect for the lifeboat crews who risk their lives to rescue people at sea. Many hundreds have died in the UK and Ireland alone. I have played a small role as a shore-based volunteer and have seen for myself the great dedication which is needed.

St Branok and all the characters in this story are, of course, fictitious though some of the other locations mentioned do exist, such as the curious stone circle of Boscawen-un and the wonderful seaside town of Perranporth with its vast beach.

My previous Cornish thriller *Hidden Depths* is also on sale and I am now working on an historical novel called *The Silver Tide* which returns to the Cornish community of St Branok more than a century earlier. If you wish to make contact or get updates, please go to my website www.jhmannauthor.com

HIDDEN DEPTHS

On a wild Cornish headland, Catherine Carlyon takes a decision that will change her life forever.

She is facing the bleak prospect of years in prison after being sucked into a fraud by a man she thought loved her.

Catherine has found a possible way – to disappear. But disappearing comes at a price. She must abandon her family and everything she holds dear.

The greatest challenge of her life is looming, an epic adventure in the North Atlantic which will take her to her limits and beyond.

Printed in Great Britain
by Amazon

47848618R00182